FELLOWSHIP OF IRON

Rick was in his late twenties, a tall blond biker, his hair hanging down well past his shoulders. Under his leather waistcoat he was bare-chested: his spare, pale flesh covered with tattoos of skulls, burning angels and other motifs; the twining reds, blues and blacks extending along both arms as well. He was wearing black gloves and impenetrable black shades. Mike stared straight ahead, catching Rick's eyes only as he passed in front of him; he was determined to remain calm. The room was warm and close, the heavy scent of leather filling it like musky perfume. The only sound was the creaking of the leatherman's gear and, in Mike's ears, the pounding of his own heart.

1991

FELLOWSHIP OF IRON

Jack Stevens

First published in Great Britain in 2000 by
Idol
Thames Wharf Studios,
Rainville Road, London W6 9HA

ISBN 0 352 33512 2

Cover artwork by Gavin Harrison Photography

Typeset by SetSystems Ltd, Saffron Walden, Essex
Printed and bound in Great Britain by
Mackays of Chatham PLC

The Terrence Higgins Trust

SAFER SEX GUIDELINES

We include safer sex guidelines in every Idol book. However, while our policy is always to show safer sex in contemporary stories, we don't insist on safer sex practices in stories with historical settings – as this would be anachronistic. These books are sexual fantasies – in real life, everyone needs to think about safe sex.

While there have been major advances in the drug treatments for people with HIV and AIDS, there is still no cure for AIDS or a vaccine against HIV. Safe sex is still the only way of being sure of avoiding HIV sexually.

HIV can only be transmitted through blood, come and vaginal fluids (but no other body fluids) passing from one person (with HIV) into another person's bloodstream. It cannot get through healthy, undamaged skin. The only real risk of HIV is through anal sex without a condom – this accounts for almost all HIV transmissions between men.

Being safe
Even if you don't come inside someone, there is still a risk to both partners from blood (tiny cuts in the arse) and pre-come. Using strong condoms and water-based lubricant greatly reduces the risk of HIV. However, condoms can break or slip off, so:
* Make sure that condoms are stored away from hot or damp places.
* Check the expiry date – condoms have a limited life.
* Gently squeeze the air out of the tip.
* Check the condom is put on the right way up and unroll it down the erect cock.
* Use plenty of water-based lubricant (lube), up the arse and on the condom.
* While fucking, check occasionally to see the condom is still in one piece (you could also add more lube).

* When you withdraw, hold the condom tight to your cock as you pull out.
* Never re-use a condom or use the same condom with more than one person.
* If you're not used to condoms you might practise putting them on.
* Sex toys like dildos and plugs are safe. But if you're sharing them use a new condom each time or wash the toys well.

For the safest sex, make sure you use the strongest condoms, such as Durex Ultra Strong, Mates Super Strong, HT Specials and Rubberstuffers packs. Condoms are free in many STD (Sexually Transmitted Disease) clinics (sometimes called GUM clinics) and from many gay bars. It's also essential to use lots of water-based lube such as KY, Wet Stuff, Slik or Liquid Silk. Never use come as a lubricant.

Oral sex
Compared with fucking, sucking someone's cock is far safer. Swallowing come does not necessarily mean that HIV gets absorbed into the bloodstream. While a tiny fraction of cases of HIV infection have been linked to sucking, we know the risk is minimal. But certain factors increase the risk:
* Letting someone come in your mouth
* Throat infections such as gonorrhoea
* If you have cuts, sores or infections in your mouth and throat

So what is safe?
There are so many things you can do which are absolutely safe: wanking each other; rubbing your cocks against one another; kissing, sucking and licking all over the body; rimming – to name but a few.

If you're finding safe sex difficult, call a helpline or speak to someone you feel you can trust for support. The Terrence Higgins Trust Helpline, which is open from noon to 10pm every day, can be reached on 020 7242 1010.

Or, if you're in the United States, you can ring the Center for Disease Control toll free on 1 800 458 5231.

One

———

Mike fell back on to the tangled sheets of the bed and stared up at the muscular body straddling him. He reached out and smoothed his hands over the curves of Dave's heavy pecs, kneading the nipples with his thumbs the way he knew the other guy liked it. Dave moaned with pleasure, closing his eyes and throwing his head back. Mike let his hands slide down the broad chest, over the valleys and troughs of the six-pack of abdominals, moving them outwards, either side of the heroic cock standing proud against Dave's belly, along the swelling muscles of his thighs.

Dave opened his eyes and looked down at the younger man underneath him. 'Yeah,' he said simply.

Mike smiled back lazily. 'Yeah,' he agreed.

Very slowly Dave leaned forwards and down until his lips were brushing Mike's. Gently he kissed him. Mike went to circle his waist with his own powerful arms, to pull Dave's body back down on to him. Shaking his head, but with a grin, Dave reached back and grasped both Mike's wrists, brought them up above his head and pinned them there. Then he leaned forward to kiss his bedfellow again. His tongue drove deep into Mike's mouth.

Without releasing his lover's wrists or mouth, Dave lowered his body down on to Mike's, resting his chest on the younger man's chest, his belly on Mike's, until finally his meaty member was stiff against Mike's straining cock. Slowly and powerfully he ground his cock into Mike's; Mike's gasps muffled in his hungry mouth. The man pinned underneath arched in ecstasy, his well-developed muscles driving his body up against the greater weight of the man on top and the relentless pressure of his grinding love-making. For long minutes the two bodybuilders writhed on the top of the bed, their bodies locked into a desperate and quickening rhythm, until finally Mike tore his mouth away and gasped out, 'Stop! For Christ's sake, stop!'

Dave let go of Mike's wrists and pushed himself back up and away. Flushed and breathing heavily, he looked down at Mike's swollen cock. The head was a wine purple, shiny with pre-come and visibly spasming. Mike was close – very, very close. Dave grinned again. 'I think we're ready now, don't you?'

Mike laughed shakily, still riding the waves of sensation pulsing through him, fighting the primitive urge to let this orgasm that had been building for the last hour or more explode out of him. He swallowed hard a couple of times, and only when he thought he was back in control again looked up at Dave. 'Yeah,' he said.

Dave reached over to the bedside cabinet for the pack of condoms that had been waiting there all evening. Just the sight of Dave breaking the thing out of its foil, bringing it to the tip of his dick and slowly rolling it down the impressive length and awe-inspiring girth of his shaft, was enough to set Mike's heart pounding again in his chest and his dick pulsing dangerously. Dave squeezed lube on to his finger tips and went to smooth it along his cock.

'Wait. Let me,' said Mike. He scooped the lube from Dave's fingers and gently rubbed it over the fully-stretched latex. It was like a rock under his fingers. The feel of it made him want to grab his own throbbing tool and pump hard, but he knew that if he did that he'd come in an instant and that pleasure just had to wait until this incredible man was inside him.

'Over,' Dave growled.

Mike immediately rolled over on the bed, drawing himself up on his knees. His hands clenched at the rumpled sheets as he waited for Dave's approach. He could feel Dave looking at him, drinking in the sight of his smooth skin, his broad shoulders, flaring lats and narrow waist. He felt Dave's hand come to rest on the small of his neck and shivered uncontrollably at the touch. The hand moved down his spine with delicious slowness until it reached the base, just above the beginning of the crack between the firm cheeks of his buttocks where it paused. With a small shock, Dave felt the coldness of more lube being squeezed on to Mike's fingers before they continued their journey, down and round and up, deep into his arse.

There was no hesitation. Dave didn't pause at the involuntary tightening of Mike's ring, confident after all these years of the almost immediate relaxation that would follow. He worked at the young man, preparing him for the full pleasure that was to follow so very soon after. Mike closed his eyes and hung on. This was the merest foretaste of what was to come and yet after all that they had already done that night it was almost too much. When Mike withdrew, he couldn't help himself.

'Now, man! Now!' he gasped.

Dave thrust into him hard.

The power of Dave's entry, driving the unforgiving ramrod of his dick through Mike's muscle ring, pushed Mike down flat to the mattress. For a second his body was shot through with conflicting white-hot impulses of pleasure and pain. The cry that was forced out of him could have been of either. But Dave held himself tight against Mike's arse, thrusting with his hips and pulling with his arms wrapped round Mike's waist, and the moment of keen uncertainty passed as it always did and the almost unbearably sweet sensation of taking and holding a man deep inside him ignited like fire through Mike's loins, and blasted away any last scraps of control he'd been holding on to.

'Oh, fuck, man! Do it! Do it!'

Dave drew back then thrust in again, drew back and thrust in. Again. And again. Oblivious to everything else, Mike closed his eyes tight and clenched and unclenched his arse-muscles to the rhythm of his partner's fucking, working that iron cock inside him with all the strength he could muster. Someone was shouting out loud, wordless noises. Dimly he was aware it was him.

When Dave's animal-like bellow of release came it was the sweetest sound Mike had ever heard. It triggered his own orgasm, sending hot gouts of come into the mattress, the climactic rush like a series of hammer blows along the muscles at the base of his dick. 'Oh, man,' he gasped. 'Oh, man.'

The last thing he heard before slipping into blessed sleep was Dave's breathless voice from somewhere on top of him. 'Yeah.'

It was the absence of the weight of Dave's body on top of his that brought Mike back into the land of the waking. When he opened his eyes and turned over he found Dave standing at the foot of the bed, his back to him. It took him a second to realise that Dave was staring into the full-length mirror. 'I'll fit one over the bed, if you like. You won't have to wait until after then to admire yourself.'

Dave jumped slightly at the sound of Mike's voice. 'The way you do DIY? Thanks, but no thanks.'

Mike was surprised to see that Dave still looked flushed and that his skin still had a sheen of sweat on it. Mind you, he thought, it had been a pretty strenuous evening.

'So, what do you think?' Dave asked.

Mike placed his hands behind his head and grinned broadly. 'I thought I'd made that pretty obvious.'

Dave bent down, picked up one of the pillows that had been kicked from the bed very early on in the proceedings and threw it at Mike. 'I meant me. The body. What do you think?' Smoothly he moved into one of his favourite competition poses: torso twisted to emphasise the narrowness of the waist, both arms raised with biceps flexed. He held the pose for a moment, then turned into another, clasping his wrists behind his back to bring out the triceps development and opening out his pecs. 'Well?'

Mike raised one eyebrow. He picked up the pillow from where it had landed in his lap, threw it to one side and pointed to where it had been. In its nest of jet black hair, his heroically-worked cock was already beginning to stir again and show itself ready for yet more action at the sight of Dave's impromptu display. 'Need I say more?'

Dave turned back to the mirror. 'Great. So as long as the next competition I go to is judged by a bunch of sex-starved size queens with their brains in their pants, I'll do fine.'

Mike leaned forward. Something about this conversation was beginning to work its way through the rosiness of afterglow and make him a little uneasy. 'I didn't know you were going in for competitions again. I thought you'd given all that up.'

Dave dropped his pose and turned back to him. 'Should I?'

'No. Of course not. Not if you don't want to.' The abruptness of Dave's words made it plain. Something was wrong. 'Dave. What's up?'

Dave sighed and came and sat back down on the bed. 'What's up is I'm forty-five years old, Mike.'

'So? I know that.'

'No, you don't. You're twenty-five. Look at you.' Dave slapped Mike's naked thigh. 'Area champ two years running now. National potential, if you'd just shift your arse. Bodybuilding mags crying out for your pictures. And you're still nowhere near your peak. You've got years yet of getting bigger, stronger. Better.' He let his hand fall back to the mattress. 'That doesn't go on for ever, Mike. It can't. And when you get to the point where you're not getting better . . .' His voice trailed away.

Mike looked across at this man who had been so much to him: teacher, training partner, benefactor, lover and friend. He'd never heard Dave talking like this before. It made him uncomfortable. Something was called for; there was something he had to say. He just didn't know what. He was intelligent, compassionate – all of those things. He just didn't have the way with words you needed in situations like this. Richard would have known what to say. But Richard, of course, was the very last person he could have around right now. In the end, he had to go for the only thing he could come up with. 'Dave. You're fucking ace!'

Dave stood up from the bed again. 'Am I? Am I really? Come on, Mike, take another look. A proper look – with your head, not your dick. Tell me what you really think. Am I really as "fucking ace" as I was five years ago?'

Right there in the bedroom, Dave went through his whole competition routine, the entire series of moves designed to show off each of the muscle groups: legs, stomach, arms, chest, shoulders, the lot. He moved from one to another with the deceptively easy grace that only came after long years of development and practice.

His skin gleamed, the sweat acting like a natural oil. His face was a mask of concentration. This wasn't some casual routine to turn on a one-night stand. This was the real thing.

Mike sat up in the bed and watched him silently, making himself concentrate on the technicalities of movement, size and condition that Dave wanted him to, refusing to allow his thoughts to wander to thoughts of just what he'd like to do with those solid buttocks, those tree-trunks of thighs and the heavy ball sac hanging so temptingly above them. He forced himself to mentally work through the familiar marking schemes of bodybuilding competitions, and surreptitiously reached for the discarded pillow and laid it across his lap again.

When Dave had finished, he was visibly breathing more heavily, and the sweat was gathering in tiny rivulets that trickled down the tanned sculpture of his body. 'Well?' he said.

It was some time since Mike had looked at Dave critically like that, putting aside the sexual attraction and, yes, love that was between them. In fact, he probably hadn't since that very first meeting five years previously between the seasoned and successful pro bodybuilder and the young kid just starting out. But now he had looked, and Dave was asking him for his opinion. Mike himself was surprised at the answer, but the truth was undeniable. 'No,' he said. 'You're not as good as you were five years ago.' He rose, crossed the small floor space between them and wrapped his arms tight around the other man's waist. 'You're better.' And it was true.

They kissed. Mike let one hand fall down and slip, accidentally, between Dave's legs. He whispered something in Dave's ear.

'Yeah,' said Dave, and he laughed.

It was eight o'clock the following evening that they came to tell Mike that Dave was dead.

Two

———

Mike sat in the small living room of his flat and struggled to take in what he'd just been told. Richard sat across from him, arms folded across his chest, regarding him but making no move towards him. The other two men in the room remained standing. One, the inspector, was talking; the other – a sergeant, Mike thought he'd said he was: young, only about the same age as him and Richard – was silent. He looked occasionally at Richard, but mostly kept his attention fixed on his boss. He didn't seem able to look Mike in the eye. Mike didn't care.

The inspector droned on, but Mike wasn't listening. From downstairs came the faint chinks of metal on metal as guys slapped weights on dumbbells, barbells and squat racks and worked out in Mike's gym. Mike didn't hear them either. Dave was dead. That's what they'd told him. Heart attack. But that wasn't possible. Only last night . . .

'Mike. Mike!' Mike looked up. It was Richard calling his name, leaning forwards in his chair. 'The inspector's asked you a question.'

Mike cleared his throat and tried hard to focus. 'Sorry. What did you say?'

'I was asking, sir, if it was correct that you and Mr Ross had spent the night together.'

'Yes. Yes, we did.'

'And how did you spend the time?'

Mike hesitated. 'We talked, had a meal, that sort of thing.'

' "That sort of thing." '

'Yes.'

'Anything else?'

The sergeant taking notes paused, his pen held above his small pad. Mike glanced across at Richard. Richard sat, arms still folded, expression still unreadable. He was very good at that. 'Not really.'

The inspector nodded, as if the answer was much as he expected, but not what he wanted. 'And how did Mr Ross seem to you, last night?'

'Dave.'

'I'm sorry?'

'His name was Dave.'

'Quite. How did he seem?'

'The same as ever, I suppose.'

'Nothing at all unusual? In his appearance? His manner?'

'No.' The answer had come automatically but almost immediately afterwards came the nagging memory of Dave's uncharacteristic moodiness, that posing display and that question. *So, what do you think?* Too late to mention that now. The moment had passed. What did it matter anyway? Mike didn't see why he should share those last memories with this man standing in his flat like he owned it. There was something about him Mike found himself instinctively reacting against. Then the inspector spoke again, and Mike realised exactly what that something was.

'Was Mr Ross your boyfriend, sir?'

It was faint, almost undetectable, but it was there. The slight inflection on the word 'boyfriend'. The subtle taint of contempt. Mike gritted his teeth and looked down at the floor. He didn't want to catch Richard's eye. 'No,' he said softly.

'I am.' It was Richard. He had shifted his regard from Mike to the inspector, fixing him with a steady gaze. It was clear to Mike, who knew how to read all the signs, that Richard too had picked up on the inspector's tone. 'In case you were wondering,' Richard added, turning now to the sergeant who hurriedly looked down at his pad and scribbled something there. Richard transferred his attention back to Mike.

'Ah. So you're in an "open" relationship.' There it was again: that inflection. Mike continued to look at the floor. Richard remained silent. 'I see,' said the inspector. 'But he had been your boyfriend, some five years ago?'

How to sum up for this man just what Dave had been to him? Mike knew from experience that it wasn't worth the effort. 'Yes.'

'And he helped set you up with your gym business just over two years ago?'

'Yes.'

'And then you split up?'

'No.'

The inspector adopted an exaggerated expression of surprise. 'No? But I thought you said . . .'

'We'd . . . grown apart before then. It happens, you know?' No, Mike thought, looking directly at the inspector for practically the first time since he had broken the news. No, you probably don't know.

'So you remained friends even after you'd "grown apart", and he lent you money, a substantial amount of money, to set up your business.'

'He was a good man.'

'Obviously. And you continued to see him regularly for sex?'

Mike stormed to his feet. 'It wasn't just sex!'

In the face of this blazingly angry, powerfully built man, the inspector didn't retreat by so much as a centimetre. 'I see,' he said calmly.

His calmness just infuriated Mike even more. 'Look, just what the hell is going on? You come here telling me that Dave is dead; then, next thing I know, you're asking me all sorts of questions as if I –' Abruptly Mike stopped. His face drained of colour. 'You don't think –' He could hardly get the words out. The idea was so preposterous. 'You don't think that I had something to do with it, do you?' The inspector remained silent, just looking at him. 'But you said it was a heart attack.'

'You're a very well built man, sir. You obviously work out. Well, who wouldn't, with all that equipment downstairs?' Mike blinked, confused by this apparent change of direction. The inspector gave a small, very cold smile. 'Do you use steroids, sir?'

9

At last, understanding dawned. Mike barked out a harsh, humourless laugh. 'Steroids? You're saying Dave took steroids?' He shook his head vigorously from side to side. 'Oh, you are so wrong.'

'Actually, I was asking you, sir, whether *you* took steroids. Professional muscleman like yourself, always in competition – some pretty big prizes these days, so they tell me – and all these drugs floating around for the taking, with everyone on them if we're to believe the papers. Who'd be surprised if you were on them, Mr Kilby? But, since you raise the matter,' he went on, not giving Mike a chance to interject, 'yes, we do have reason to believe Mr Ross had been taking steroids.'

'You can't possibly have done a blood analysis by now, inspector,' said Richard calmly from his chair.

The inspector looked down at him. If he wondered at the contrast between the heavily muscular, fiery Mike and the slim, outwardly calm but intense Richard, he gave no sign of it. 'In forensics are we, sir?' Richard met his gaze but said nothing. 'You are, of course, correct. What I was in fact referring to was the sizeable amount of illegal steroids we found in Mr Ross's home.' He turned back to Mike. 'When the autopsy results come through, I'm pretty sure we'll find your boyfriend – sorry, *ex* boyfriend – was a user. It's just a matter of time.' He nodded to his sergeant, who closed his writing pad and tucked the pen into his top pocket. 'Right now, though, I think we've outstayed our welcome. We'll be on our way. I'm sure you have a lot to talk about. We'll be in touch again soon. Don't bother showing us out.' With a short nod to Mike and Richard, the inspector left the room. The sergeant hesitated, looked as if he was about to say something, then just nodded too and followed his boss out of the room and down the stairs.

Mike stood. Richard remained seated. They heard the door open and then close behind the two policemen. Neither of them moved. Muffled by distance and floorboards, the sounds of the gym beneath them carried on. Finally it was Richard who spoke. 'Now, would you like to tell me just what the hell you've been up to?'

'Not now, Rich. Please. This isn't the time.' Mike ran his

fingers through his hair, still struggling to take in what he'd been told.

'I think this is exactly the time, Mike,' Richard insisted. 'When the police come round and tell you that your boyfriend's still screwing around with someone he said he'd finished with years ago, that is precisely the time to start talking about what has been going on.'

Mike rounded on him. 'We weren't screwing around!'

'Could have fooled me! But then, you did, didn't you?'

Mike took a deep breath. He hated arguing with Richard. When Mike argued, he liked to shout, rave, make a big fuss and carry his points that way. And whenever he tried, Richard would stay quiet and outwardly calm and pick every one of those points apart with icy logic. But this wasn't just one of those arguments over politics, football or what television programmes they were going to watch that night, was it? This was a betrayal of trust and he'd been found out in the worst possible way. He took another deep breath. 'Dave had lent me money. I was paying him back. I had to see him every now and again. You knew that.'

'My bank lends me money,' Richard replied coldly. 'That doesn't mean I end up fucking my bank manager every time I go to discuss my overdraft!'

Mike threw himself back on to the sofa and closed his eyes. 'Maybe. But you have to admit you've said you'd like to.' His ploy didn't work, as he'd known really it wouldn't.

'Don't try to joke your way out of this one, Mike. You've been screwing around and you've been caught with your pants down, big time.'

'It wasn't . . .' Mike began again, and then wisely decided to drop it. 'C'mon, Rich. The inspector was a prick but he was right. We do have an open relationship –'

'Which works because we tell each other exactly what we're up to.'

'Yes, and –'

'And you didn't tell me about Dave. In fact, I'm beginning to realise you didn't tell me about Dave on several occasions.'

For the second time in as many days Mike felt himself adrift in an argument, reaching out for the words he needed to explain the complicated feelings that were churning around inside him and unable to grasp them. And once again the only person he knew who could help him was the very last person he could ask, the person sitting only feet away from him. 'He was my friend, Rich.'

'He was your *boyfriend!*' For the first time, Richard allowed the emotion that was building up inside him to erupt as he flung himself up from the chair and took his turn to pace around the room.

'Had been, Rich. He had been my boyfriend.'

'So why were you still screwing him, Mike? Or, should I say, why were you still letting him screw you?' Richard paused to look down at Mike. Mike shifted uncomfortably and looked away. 'Right.' Richard went back to his pacing. 'And, most important of all, why weren't you telling me?'

This time, Mike had no hesitation in replying. The answer was simple, the truth undeniable. 'Because I knew you'd be hurt.'

Richard stopped his pacing as abruptly as if he'd been slapped in the face. Slowly he turned to face Mike. 'Right again.' He let himself fall back into the armchair. The two men sat regarding each other. 'So what are we going to do now?'

For a long time, the question hung unanswered in the air between them until, finally, uncertainly Mike leaned forward. 'Come to bed with me, Rich.'

'What?'

Caught in a maelstrom of emotion, Mike clasped and unclasped his hands, needing the warmth of his lover, the comfort of his arms and the sweetness of his love, but unable as ever to put his feelings into words. 'Come to bed,' he said again. 'Please.'

'After what happened to the last guy you slept with? No, thanks.' Feeling rejected and humiliated, Richard had lashed out with a vicious jibe, but the instant it was out he regretted it. 'Shit, Mike,' he muttered. 'I didn't mean that. I'm sorry. Look, I . . .'

Mike shook his head. 'It's all right. It's all right,' he said huskily. There was silence between them. A minute passed. Two. 'It's all right,' Mike said again finally. 'And thanks.'

'What for?'

'For making me answer your question. I was trying to dodge it there for a moment. No, no,' he said quickly, raising a hand to cut Richard off before he could go further with the protests he started. 'You were right. What do we do now? What we do is we have to look at what caused this.'

'It was a heart attack,' Richard said uncertainly. 'The inspector said . . .' He trailed off. How could he say it? Dave Ross had suffered a fatal heart attack only hours after a protracted session of lovemaking with Mike. Richard knew from first-hand experience just how demanding Mike could be. Throw in a flawed heart, a condition possibly made worse by steroid use, and the conclusion seemed inescapable. Even Mike had to have worked it out. How he was going to live with that was another matter. Richard looked closely at Mike, but Mike was shaking his head.

'It was drugs that killed Dave. Illegal steroids.'

Richard waited. Usually, he could follow Mike's thought processes. Nine times out of ten, he could even predict them. But now Mike had him lost. 'So?'

'So we find out where he got them. We find out who gave them to him.' Once again Mike rose to his feet and stalked around the room. Coming to a halt again at last in front of Richard, he placed one meaty fist in the palm of the other hand. 'We find out who killed him.'

I've slipped out of reality, Richard thought. My life has been hijacked and turned into an episode of a TV cop show. Aloud, he said, 'Mike, if it was the steroids that did it, then he killed himself. He was a grown man; he knew what he was doing. He was a bodybuilder, for God's sake. You of all people should know what they'll do to pump themselves up.'

'I don't use steroids!' Mike roared. 'And you know why? Because Dave never used steroids, and that man taught me everything I need to know about this business. So if that shit was in his place, if it was in his body, there had to be a reason for it, and I'm going to find out what it was.'

Richard measured his words carefully. 'Mike, you haven't been with Dave for how many years now? Two? Nearly three? OK, you've been sleeping together.' Mike went to interrupt. 'Just listen to me a minute. You've had sex, but you haven't been together properly for that long. People change, Mike. How can you be sure Dave didn't change?'

Mike heard Richard's words. Part of his mind went back to the previous night to Dave's talk about growing older; his news about re-entering competitions; his magnificent muscles and the sheen of sweat that had stayed on them longer than Mike would have expected. He shook his head. 'I have to know who gave him those drugs.'

'You're not a policeman, Mike.'

'No. PC Plod and his friend back there are, and do you think they're going to put themselves out for some dead Muscle Mary?'

Richard avoided answering that one. 'OK, so suddenly you're Dick Tracy. What are you going to do?'

Mike hesitated. 'I don't know,' he admitted. 'But you're going to help me.'

Richard nodded. Oh yeah. Right. He, Richard Green, was going to help his boyfriend track down illegal drug-dealers to avenge the death of the guy that that boyfriend had been sleeping with behind his back. Of course. Richard pushed himself to his feet. 'I'm going home,' he said.

'Richard, wait. I need your help here.'

'So what am I now? Madonna to your Warren Beatty?'

'You're a reporter. You can make contacts, follow up leads.'

'I write for local papers and the gay press, Mike, not the *News of the World*! If you want a crate of grade A poppers, I could probably find you a good deal, but illegal steroids are way out of my league.'

Mike moved to bar the doorway with his body. 'And if it was one of *your* friends who was dead, maybe one of your former boyfriends?'

Richard looked him straight in the eyes. 'The answer would be the same.'

'And if it hadn't been my former boyfriend?'

Richard went to reply but stopped. Mike had never understood about him and arguments. Just because he was good at them didn't mean that he liked them. He was good at them because he worked hard to end them as quickly as he could, and he did that by trying as far as possible never to say anything without thinking it through first. He'd already made one bad mistake that night. He was damned if he was going to make another. 'I'm going home,' he said. He waited for Mike to move to one side and then ducked past, heading down the stairs without looking back. 'Good night,' he said.

Outside, in an unmarked white car, Inspector Alan Taylor and Sergeant Paul Ferris sat waiting. Taylor chewed slowly on a double cheeseburger he'd had the younger man fetch for him from a nearby fast food outlet. Paul sat staring fixedly out of the car window at the door that served as entrance and exit for Mike Kilby's gym and the flat above. Neither man spoke. Paul was wishing his superior would hurry up and finish his meal. The sound was not pleasant and the smell was making him feel queasy.

At precisely twenty-nine minutes after they had first entered the flat, Richard erupted on to the street.

'Trouble in Paradise,' Taylor said. 'Right. Out you go, and mind you keep him in sight.'

Paul opened the car door. 'You think he's off to spread the word, then?'

Taylor shrugged his shoulders. 'This is how you play the game, lad. You shake 'em up and see what falls out. We've shook 'em up.' He indicated Richard, who was pacing furiously backwards and forwards in front of the gym, as if trying to make his mind up about something. 'And now they've fallen out. True, he'd have to be a pretty dizzy little queen to head straight off to a dealer . . .' He trailed off as Richard, mind apparently made up, headed off determinedly away from the gym. 'But then, perhaps that's just exactly what he is. Get after him, Ferris. If he goes home, then that's probably it for the day and you can turn in. If he goes anywhere else, you let me know.'

Paul stepped out of the car, closed the door and looked back in through the open window. 'And you?'

Taylor shrugged again. 'Duty calls. I'll stick around here for a while longer.' His eyes slid over to the fast food restaurant. 'I may just take a minute or two to stock up on fuel, though.' He pointed after the fast-disappearing Richard. 'Now get!'

Paul got. Even after such a comparatively short wait, it was a relief to be out of the car and doing something. It was a relief to be away from the sight and sound of cheeseburgers. It was a relief to be away from Taylor.

Mike threw himself back into one of the large living room chairs and punched its leather upholstered arm hard. 'Damn. Damn!' The chair arm creaked warningly. Go ahead, said a voice in his head. Smash the place up if it makes you feel better. It's what guys with big muscles and small brains do best.

The voice sounded like Richard.

'Damn!' He punched the chair arm again, twice, and then leaped to his feet to pace the length and width of the living room. 'Damn!' Savagely he kicked at the coffee table, sending Richard's broadsheets and his own bodybuilding magazines cascading to the floor. It was no use; he had to do something to relieve this tension while he still had some furniture left to call his own. He glanced at the clock. It was getting on for nine o'clock. Time to let Andy downstairs go and close the gym up. Then maybe he could burn up some of this confusion and frustration in a hard-core workout, bollock-naked the way he liked to do it. He strode purposefully for the stairs.

Andy was at the entrance desk. That supposed contradiction in terms, a cheerful Brummy, Andy had been with Mike a couple of years now, ever since the time he'd been working in a sports shop and had tried to pick Mike up when he'd come in looking for some new trainers. They never had gone to bed together, but they'd struck up a friendship, and Andy had been only too pleased to come and work in Mike's gay-friendly gym. Not that he was a bodybuilder himself. Too much of a fondness for the nightlife and associated pleasures didn't go hand in hand with the discipline needed for that, but he certainly enjoyed the company of muscular men, and there were several regulars of Mike's gym who enjoyed the company of Andy.

Normally by this time of night Andy would have had his coat on and be raring to be out and hitting the club of choice for that evening. Tonight, though, his coat was still on the peg and he was leaning across the main desk, eyes fixed on a spot some way across the gym when Mike walked in. 'Thinking about overtime?' Mike said.

Andy sighed and didn't look up. 'I could certainly handle a little time and a half with that.'

Mike looked across the gym in the direction Andy had been ogling. The guy was young, kitted out in vest and shorts and heaving some respectable weights. 'Nice?'

'Oh, yes,' Andy affirmed.

'No luck?'

Andy adopted an indignant stance. 'Do you think I try it on with every good-looking guy who walks in here?'

Mike kept a straight face. 'You were the one who came up with the gym's unofficial motto.'

Andy grinned broadly. '"Always an opening for new members." I still say it would look good in neon outside. And no, I haven't had any luck. I think our young friend is one of those who likes 'em big. And I am talking about muscles, here.' He finally took in Mike's unusually sober mood. 'You all right?'

Mike considered telling him – after all, Andy had met Dave a couple of times – but he decided against it. He just didn't want to think about it any more that night. 'Troubles,' he said vaguely.

'Richard?'

'Among other things.'

Andy looked back to the guy across from them. 'Then maybe what you need is a little distraction.'

'I don't think so, Andy. Not tonight.'

Andy walked over to the pegs and picked up his coat. 'Don't be hasty, my friend. Why not wander over, take a closer look and . . . consider your options.' He headed for the door. 'And you can tell me all about it tomorrow. *All* about it.' The door closed behind him, only to open a second later as Andy put his head round. 'His name's Dean. Good luck!' And then he was gone.

Mike smiled ruefully. Not tonight, he thought. He busied himself for a few minutes with tidying up the counter and closing the till. Not after what I've just been through, he thought. He put away a couple of the gym T-shirts that Andy had left out. I don't really feel up to it, he thought. He stopped. The counter was spotless, and everything squared away. There really were no other distractions. OK, so maybe I'll just wander over and take a look, he thought. Just to see what was getting Andy so hot under the collar. He looked around to be absolutely sure there was no one else in the gym and then sauntered over in Dean's direction with a very deliberate casualness.

Dean was sitting on a bench in front of one of the floor to ceiling mirrors, the back fixed at an angle while he worked on his pecs with dumb-bell flye exercises. Mike watched as Dean flung his arms out to either side and then brought them and the dumb-bells back in front of him. 'Like hugging a tree,' was how Mike usually described the action to beginners. A great way to pump up the chest. With each exertion Dean gave a soft grunt, the sort of sound a man made working away on top of another man.

Mike stood behind Dean, looking over the young man's head at his own reflection in the mirror. Well, he was the gym owner, wasn't he, and the chief instructor? Appraising guys' technique and giving them advice was all part of the service. Of course, it was also a great way to appraise the guys.

Dean was young: nineteen, maybe twenty at the most. His sweat-soaked white vest clung to his skin, revealing clearly a good body, chunky if not yet actually muscular. Mike let his eyes travel down to the black cotton shorts the lad was wearing and the broad thighs they left so wonderfully visible. Rugby player, he decided. High school first team. College level, now. Took up weights perhaps a year ago to build himself up for the scrum. And maybe to meet like-minded guys.

Dean carried on with his flyes, grunting softly, regularly, apparently oblivious to the man behind him. Except when Mike dragged his eyes back up from the promising treasure trove of those obviously well-filled shorts, he found the reflection of Dean's eyes fixed on him. For a second they held each other's gaze. Yeah, Mike thought. Definitely to meet like-minded guys. He moved in closer.

'Try to bend your arms a little as you lower the weights,' he said. 'Here.' He reached round from behind to show what he meant, cupping Dean's elbows and pressing up gently. 'Feel the difference?'

Dean nodded. 'Yeah. Yeah, that's good.' He did just one more repetition, then let the weights fall heavily to the floor. He turned on the bench to face Mike directly for the first time. 'Thanks.'

'My pleasure.'

Dean rubbed his hand across his chest, not taking his eyes off Mike's face. 'It really gets you, doesn't it? Here.'

'It certainly does.'

Dean's gaze moved from Mike's face to take in his body at close quarters, and Mike stood silently and let him. He saw Dean's eyes glance to right and left before coming back to him. 'There's no one else here,' he said, as if surprised.

'It's past closing.'

'I was hoping to have a shower before I went.'

OK, Andy, Mike admitted inwardly. You were right. 'No problem,' he said out loud, sweeping his hand extravagantly in the direction of the changing rooms. 'Water's still hot.' He gave it two seconds. 'In fact, I think I'll join you.'

As Dean made for the showers, Mike made for the entrance and dropped the latch. There was no doubt in his mind that he would rather have been with Richard. The sex would have given him some of the release he needed right then but Rich could have given him so much more as well, a deeper comfort he couldn't find anywhere else. But Rich had cut him dead, not entirely unsurprisingly, and Dean was there and apparently willing. It wasn't the workout Mike had planned, but then sometimes you just had to go with the flow. Mike headed purposefully for the changing rooms.

Dean had already turned on the shower and a warm steam was beginning to fill the changing room. Glancing across to the benches, Mike saw Dean's vest and shorts casually thrown to one side over a sports bag. Easing his own T-shirt up over his head, Mike strolled over to the shower area. Dean was standing under the streaming hot water, waiting. Mike smiled at the convulsive jump the sight of his muscular frame caused in the young lad's cock. He kicked his trainers off, pushed his tracksuit trousers down and stepped out of them. He never wore anything underneath them in the gym. He stepped up on to the shower platform, reached for the soap in the dish fixed to the wall, and worked up a lather. 'Need a hand?'

Dean swallowed and nodded once. Mike reached over and began to smooth the creamy foam in long, slow strokes over the boy's wet skin.

Mike worked his way down Dean's body, smoothing his hands across the broad shoulders, over the chest with its light dusting of hair and down the flat stomach. Dean stood, eyes fixed on Mike's hands as if fascinated, his dick lengthening and hardening the closer Mike's hands came to it. By the time Mike touched it, it was bolt upright, foreskin pulled back and helmet gleaming purple in the hot water. As Mike soaped it gently, Dean's breath caught in his throat and he closed his eyes, tilting his head back to let the hot water run down his face and into his open mouth. Mike moved down to the root of the cock, taking the ball sac carefully in the palm of one hand. Very gently he squeezed. Dean gave a soft gasp, much like the ones he'd made when working out.

Releasing the balls, Mike took Dean by the shoulders and turned him round. For a second, the lad hesitated, but Mike firmly though gently insisted and then it was done. Mike stepped in closely, so close his own now iron-hard dick rested against the cheeks of Dean's arse, and then he began the work again of soaping the young man's body, working his way downwards again from the shoulders, along the spine, to the small hollow at its base. He slid both hands along the magnificent pale moons of Dean's buttocks, pausing to enjoy the feel of them and to give the lad a moment to prepare. And then he moved inwards, sliding his fingers between Dean's cheeks and into his arse.

Mike felt the heavy muscles clench against his fingers and the boy pulled away from him slightly. He leaned in closely, lips close to Dean's ear. 'Kind of new to this?' he said softly.

There was a moment's hesitation. When it came, Dean's voice was husky, breathless. 'I've been training for nearly a year now.'

Mike nodded, accepting the deliberate misunderstanding, excited by the confirmation of what he'd suspected. 'It'll be all right,' he said. He turned the young lad around to face him again and sank to his knees. Tenderly, he took Dean's ball sac into his mouth. Dean gasped and his hands reflexively clenched, digging into the thick muscles of Mike's shoulders. Mike felt the urgent tension of the lad's grip. It was a real turn-on. He sucked deep and slow, and felt Dean's fingers dig in even deeper. He'd probably carry the lad's fingerprints there for days. The thought and the sensation made his dick ache for relief.

Finally releasing the balls, Mike turned his attention to the cock itself, running his tongue around the tip of it, bringing on more gasps from Dean. There was just the faintest taste of pre-come, the hot shower water washing it away even as it seeped out. Enough teasing. Mike leaned in hard, taking the impressive length of the boy's meat deep into his mouth. Dimly he heard the boy cry out above him, then seconds later felt hands clamp uncontrollably on his head and pull him hard into Dean's groin. For long minutes Mike pleasured the lad expertly, licking, sucking, working with his tongue, and as Dean moaned, cried out and thrust into him with his hips, Mike reached round behind him, ran a soapy finger down the crack between his arse-cheeks then thrust in and up hard. There was no resistance this time.

Tongue and fingers simultaneously told him when Dean had been pushed to the limit and was about to come. Mike pulled back, panting and laughing. The sound mingled with the splashing of the shower water and Dean's hoarse breathlessness. Instinctively, Dean's hands reached for his own cock, driven by the demand for release after Mike's relentless stimulation. Mike caught both hands in his. 'Whoa there, fella. Not so fast,' he laughed. 'Trust me. Things can only get better.' For a second, pushed to the limit by Mike, it looked like Dean was going to resist, but gradually his startled look gave way to one of understanding and acceptance. He took a deep, shaky breath and then nodded. 'Good lad,' Mike said, releasing his hands. 'And now, if you'd be so kind.'

At first Dean didn't cotton on, but when Mike placed both his hands on Dean's shoulders, the boy understood and after only the gentlest pressure from Mike sank into a kneeling position. Mike looked down, ran his hands through the lad's long wet hair and waited. Dean reached round Mike's muscular butt, closed his eyes, leaned in and took Mike into his mouth. He's never done this before, Mike thought. This is the first time he's sucked off another guy. The thought gave an added spice to the experience that more than made up for a certain clumsiness and lack of

21

technique on Dean's part. His initial hesitancy quickly gave way to an eager enthusiasm and a rapid movement of his head into and out from Mike's groin, running his tongue the length of the bodybuilder's hard shaft. 'Yeah. Oh yeah! Good lad. Go for it!' Mike shouted. Reaching behind himself, he pulled the boy's hands hard on to his arse and soon, with just a little guidance from Mike, Dean's fingers were working at his ring the way he had worked at Dean's. 'Oh, man, yeah!'

He'd just managed to stop Dean at the point of climax. Now it took every ounce of will power he had for Mike to do the same for himself. 'OK, OK. Have mercy.' He laughed, pulling himself carefully back from Dean's hungry mouth.

Dean looked up. 'Did I do something wrong?'

Mike laughed. 'Oh, no. You definitely did something right.' Dean stood. Mike enfolded him tenderly in arms pumped hard by years of brutal, hard-core weightlifting, pulled him in close and kissed him, driving his tongue deep into the eager mouth. Their poker stiff cocks rubbed up against each other, throbbing, dangerously close to coming.

Mike reached over, turned off the showers and led the way back into the main changing room area. From a cupboard he pulled out a huge, thick, white cotton towel and proceeded to dry the young man off, leaving no area unbuffed. When he'd finished, he pulled out another towel and Dean returned the favour, lingering over the heavy pectoral muscles, leaning in at one point to suck hard on one moist nipple, wiping the saliva off with the towel.

Both dry, they stood in front of each other in the warm, heavy air of the shower room. Mike pulled still more towels from the cupboard and strewed them on the floor at their feet, indicating that Dean should lie down. Kneeling at the lad's head, facing his feet, Mike leaned down to kiss Dean's chest, right on that flat hollow at the base of the breastbone, before gradually leaning more and more forwards and pushing his tongue down the boy's body, over the belly, heading for the bush of dark hair out of which erupted that fiercely erect cock. Halfway down, he felt Dean raise his head, felt the boy's hands go up round his arse and then delightfully felt the first tentative probings of Dean's tongue on his arse-ring. 'Yes!' he thought exultantly. He hadn't thought the boy was up to it but he was mightily glad to be proved wrong.

By the time Mike's mouth was round Dean's dick again, Dean's tongue was well into Mike's arse, the lad pushing his face hard into Mike's buttocks. Slowly, Mike pushed his hips back, feeling Dean's tongue pulled out of his arse, his head pushed back to the ground. Mike's cock dragged back over the lad's face. Dean was a quick learner. His mouth closed deliciously over Mike's sensitised member and he began sucking rapturously.

Time lost all meaning as the two men sixty-nined each other on the gym floor. At first Mike was on top, careful not to choke the boy by bringing the full weight of his powerhouse of a body down on him and forcing his long dick past the lad's capacity to take. Then, with a sudden twist that brought on a gurgle of surprise from Dean, Mike flipped them over so that the lad was on top, thrusting down, Mike more than willing and able to take anything Dean could dish out from that angle.

Mike's climax built and built until the pressure was all but unbearable but still he hung on, determined not to shoot until the lad had come. Just as he thought he wasn't going to make it, he felt the uncontrollable spasming of Dean's cock and his mouth filled with hot come. With an inarticulate groan of relief, Mike let go of his own orgasm, both men momentarily lost to the world in the depth of their pleasured release.

It was some time later before either of them was in a fit state to speak coherently. 'That,' sighed Dean, 'was the best workout I have ever had.'

'That, Dave,' said Mike, 'was just exactly what I needed.'

There was an awkward pause. 'My name's Dean.'

Mike closed his eyes and bit his tongue. 'I'm sorry, Dean,' he said. 'I must have misheard. I could have sworn Andy said Dave.'

''S all right.' Dean got to his feet. 'It's late. I'd better be getting on.'

'Yeah,' Mike said. 'I've got a lot to sort out myself. Thanks.'

Dean gave a small smile and walked over to the showers again. Mike wrapped a towel around himself and headed back out into the gym. He didn't go back into the changing rooms again until he heard the gym door close behind Dean.

It was the photo on his work desk that did it.

Richard had stormed home, startling several passers-by with his glowering expression. How dare he? How the hell dare he? Ask him to help with some bloody ridiculous scheme to find out who gave his supposed ex-boyfriend the drugs he used to kill himself! How dare he?

He'd flung himself into the chair at his desk in his cramped living room, intending to work out some of his temper on the keyboard of his computer. And then he'd seen the photograph. Always on the move around Richard's desk, but always in sight, it was at that time rather dangerously perched on a pile of battered envelope folders. A simple enough photo, the mock antique frame holding it something of a joke. It was nearly two years old now, and showed Richard and Mike on their first big holiday together in Seville. They were sitting on the steps of the magnificent cathedral there, Mike a couple of steps above Richard, leaning forwards and down to hug him. There wasn't actually that much of Richard's neck and shoulders visible under Mike's huge biceps. They were both smiling. Richard smiled again now, recalling the Spanish matron Mike had asked to take the photo in halting phrase-book Spanish, and her expression when his boyfriend had thrown his arms around him for the picture. But then she'd smiled too, and when Mike had taken back the camera he'd given her a peck on the cheek and she'd rushed off blushing and laughing. In the bottom right hand corner of the photo were two words, *Love, Mike* and a cross for a kiss. Typically bloody eloquent, Richard thought.

He sighed. Had he been unfair? He tried to look dispassionately at the situation. No, he decided, he hadn't. Mike had let him down and there were going to be repercussions that they were going to have to deal with. But right now, Mike was hurting. He'd lost someone close to him, and there was some heavy guilt to be worked through. Leaving Mike's place when he had had probably been the best thing, before either of them had said things they'd have found hard to take back later, but now maybe the least he could do was give Mike a call.

He picked up the phone and called up the stored number. The phone rang out but there was no answer, not even the daft message he and Mike had recorded. Knowing his boyfriend as he did, Richard decided Mike was probably in the gym working out. He thought maybe he'd give him another hour or so and then go over and see how he was.

Noticing the flashing light on his answer machine, he pressed the playback. Maybe Mike had already rung him while he was walking back home. The florid tones of the speaker made it clear instantly that this was not Mike. 'Hello, Dicky? Harry here. Remember me? We work together. Gerry was wondering if you could possibly pencil us in for a visit some time this year, just in case you might have anything we could use for this week's *Far Out!* You know how the printers hate blank pages. Oh, and if you should happen to drop in, we might just have a little surprise for you. See you. Bye!'

Richard sighed. Typically arch. Typically Harry. The man was a good sub-editor but he could also be a real pain in the neck. As if he hadn't got enough on his plate. Fortunately he was on top of this week's work, and all he had to do was get his notes in order and write them up. He ought to start right away. He stood up and made for the kitchen. He wondered what Harry's surprise was. Probably another boy band revelation he'd be expected to follow up. There was a novelty.

The doorbell rang as he was making a cup of tea. Suspecting that it might be Mike, Richard was surprised to find one of the two policemen he'd seen only a few hours earlier. He looked to left and right for the other, but there was only the one, the younger guy. 'Hello,' he said suspiciously and, he hoped, unwelcomingly, 'Sergeant . . .?'

'Ferris,' Paul said and then fell silent, as if not sure what to say next.

Richard regarded him, puzzled. 'Mike isn't here,' he said.

'I know. I've come to ask you a few questions, Mr Green.'

Richard's brow furrowed even more. 'Me?'

'If you have time, yes.'

Reluctant but curious, Richard pushed the door open wide for the policeman to come in and showed him into the living room. Paul looked around the room he found himself in, noting the contrast with Mike's flat: the prints on the walls, some of which he recognised and some he didn't, the mismatched furniture draped in a variety of throws and blankets that wouldn't have been at all out of place in your average student's bedsit, the large desk that took up much of the valuable floor space, with the computer and accessories and piles of papers and folders, and above all the books, paperback and hardback, on shelves, coffee table and floor, in rows and piles. He'd like to have looked more closely at the titles but that hardly seemed appropriate.

For his part, Richard took a closer look at Paul. He'd not really paid the man much attention back in Mike's flat – he'd had more pressing things to think about – but now he looked he realised that the sergeant was an attractive man. His hair was a light blond but his eyes were brown rather than the conventional blue. A frankly blunt nose and a determinedly square chin kept him from being a 'pretty boy'. Trim waist. It was as he was trying to see what kind of bum the sergeant had that Richard realised Paul had finished looking at his books and was now looking at him. 'Tea?' he asked. 'Or don't you drink on duty?'

'Thank you.'

Richard gestured for him to sit down and went off to pour a cup. Paul looked around for a spot free of books. There were none. By the time he'd cleared himself a space on a chair, Richard was back with a mug. Richard pulled out the office-type chair at his computer, spun it round to face the sergeant and sat down. 'So, Sergeant,' he said, unable to keep an edge of confrontation out of his voice, 'what can I do for you?'

Paul sipped at his tea. There was no sugar. He decided it would be best not to ask for any. 'I thought it might be a good idea to find out a little bit more about the people involved in this case,' he began.

'He didn't do it, you know,' Richard said abruptly, then stopped as he realised what he'd said. 'Listen to me. I'm already sounding like some moll in a gangster film. I mean, Mike didn't give Dave the steroids. He doesn't use them himself, and he certainly wouldn't pass them on to anyone else.'

'Where did you first meet him, sir?'

'Mike? He answered an ad of mine.'

'A lonely hearts type ad?'

Richard snorted derisively. 'I don't think either of us has ever been a "lonely heart", Sergeant, and I think they're called "personals" these days. In any case, it wasn't that type of ad. I'm a writer, a freelance reporter. I was doing an article for the gay press on Muscle Marys and I wanted to interview a few.'

Paul frowned. 'Muscle Marys?'

'Gay guys who get off on being big, muscly. Some are into leather, some are into lace. Muscle Marys are into pecs, biceps and six-packs.'

'So Mr Kilby is a "Muscle Mary"?'

'No.' Richard couldn't help a short laugh when he saw the frown on the young sergeant's face deepen. 'Not really. There's more to it than just the muscles. It's more a state of mind, really.' Paul's frown remained, so Richard attempted to explain. 'Look, for some guys it's all ego one way or another, right? They pump up their muscles because it turns them on, or maybe they want to be physically big to show the world they're like socially big. Some build themselves up to pull guys. Or girls, if that's your thing.' He gestured at Paul, who made no reaction. 'Some want to do it to show the world they're healthy. And health these days is pretty important, if you see what I mean.' Paul nodded, and Richard was glad he didn't have to spell that one out. 'But then there are the others – fewer, but Mike's one of them. They're the real bodybuilders, if you like. For them, bodybuilding is like their art. A bodybuilder's body is his canvas, or perhaps more like his block of marble that he's going to sculpt. In fact, the metaphor of sculpting is one that comes up again and again when you talk to bodybuilders.' Richard stopped and gave a short self-conscious laugh. 'Sorry. As you can see, I got quite into the subject matter. Here –' he spun his chair back round to his desk and leaned down to rummage among a pile of magazines at its foot '– I think I've still got a copy of the magazine that ran my article here, somewhere. Yes.' He pulled out a tattered magazine with the picture of a young lad as naked as the censor would allow on the cover. 'You can borrow this, if you want.' He was handing it over when he saw the sergeant's eye fall on the cover model. 'Or you may not have time,' he suggested.

Paul held his hand out and accepted the magazine. 'All useful background research,' he said. He flicked through the magazine until he came to Richard's article and skim-read it. 'And you obviously did yours.'

'You could say that.'

'So you'll know about Iron?' He asked the question casually but looked up and regarded Richard closely as he waited for the answer.

'Iron? What do you mean? Of course I know iron.'

'I mean the steroid, Iron. It's new, I understand – very new.'

Richard shook his head. 'It's not a name I recognise from when I was writing the article, and I've never heard Mike mention it.'

'You talk about steroids?'

Richard bristled, suddenly wary of some trap. 'Let's not be naïve, Sergeant. Mike runs a gym. He's a competitive body-builder. Yes, he knows people who use steroids, but no, he does not use them himself. Understood?'

Paul nodded but said nothing.

'I presume this was the steroid found at Dave's place?'

'Yes, it was. Quite a lot of it, in fact.'

The sergeant's openness thawed Richard a little. 'Well, like I said – like both of us have said – Mike didn't have anything to do with it.'

Paul flicked through the magazine again, and when he spoke it was without looking up from the pages. 'So is that what you're . . . into, then? Muscles?'

Richard shook his head. 'Not especially.'

'Only I thought –'

'Because I've got a bodybuilder for a boyfriend, that's all I'm interested in? Some of us gay guys do look beyond the body, you know, Sergeant.'

'That's a lot of body to look beyond. No offence meant.'

'None taken. No, I can't deny that Mike's muscles have their . . . appeal, but they weren't the reason I fell for him.' Richard looked directly at Paul, defiantly almost. 'I love him for the person he is.'

'And what kind of person is that?'

Richard was slightly taken aback by the question. 'He's funny. He's caring. Intelligent.' As he said that, Richard's eye fell on the photograph on his desk with its brief message. 'OK,' he admitted, 'he may not have a way with words, but don't let that fool you. There's a good brain in there. It just may run on somewhat narrower rails than some. But then that's the nature of dedication for you. And you need dedication if you're going to be a successful bodybuilder.' He nodded towards the article. 'It's all in there.' Richard lifted his mug and finished his tea. 'Above all, Mike's got heart. That's not easy to find.'

Paul nodded. 'You say a lot of nice things about him. But he was cheating on you, wasn't he?'

Richard put his mug down and inwardly cursed himself. He'd let himself get carried away with his enthusiasm for one of his pet topics, and by his love for Mike. He'd let himself forget this wasn't some cosy chat with a new friend. This was an interview with a policeman investigating a death, a death his boyfriend incredibly enough seemed to be involved with. And just perhaps, Richard admitted to himself, he'd allowed himself to be led on by those warm brown eyes, and that strong jawline with the shadow of a surprisingly dark beard just starting to come through. 'Not "cheating".'

'He was sleeping with another man.'

'We have an open relationship.'

'How can you do that?'

Richard blinked, caught out again by an unexpected change of direction. 'What do you mean?'

Paul leaned closer, intent on the answer to his question. 'I mean, how can two people who are supposed to love each other sleep around? How can you be with one person one minute and someone else the next?'

Where to begin? Richard thought. It wasn't as if he didn't know what to say. He'd read all the books, been to all the workshops and seminars – hell, he'd even led a few, and he lived the lifestyle. But where did you begin to explain it to a straight man? And, he thought, a stab of resentment flaring up at the weird turns this interview appeared to be taking, why the hell should he? 'It's different for us,' he said. Lame. Inadequate. But the only explanation he was damn well going to give.

Paul sank back down on his seat, and for a moment there was an expression in his eyes that Richard wasn't sure he could identify. It was almost like disappointment. Paul drained the mug he'd been holding all this time, looked around for a book-free space on which to leave it, and eventually handed it over to Richard when Richard put his hand out. 'Right, well, I won't take up any more of your time. I'm sure you've got a lot to get on with –' and he indicated Richard's desk.

Richard rose and showed him to the door. As he did so he couldn't help noticing that Sergeant Ferris did indeed have a great bum.

'We'll keep you posted, obviously, sir, about any developments and in the meantime if you think of anything that might help us in our investigation, then do please let us know.'

'I will,' said Richard, 'though I can't think what that might be.'

'Goodbye. And thanks for the tea.'

Alone in his flat again, Richard looked back on the interview and tried to work out just what exactly it had all been about. The more he replayed it in his head, the more he felt like it hadn't been like any police interview he had ever seen on television. Almost from the start, in fact, when the sergeant had asked how he and Mike had first met. Just what the hell was it that Ferris had been after?

Much to his surprise, Richard made another discovery: the memory of Sergeant Ferris's face and that tight arse beneath those official trousers was making him feel extremely aroused. Going over to Mike's now somehow didn't seem quite right. Richard headed for the bedroom and relief of a more solitary kind.

So how am I going to explain this one away? Paul thought as he made his way home. He'd taken things close to the line in the past but always pulled back at the last moment. Now, though, he was going to have to explain to Taylor the next day that he hadn't just left Richard at home when he'd followed him there, but that he'd actually gone up to the door, knocked and gone in for tea and conversation. What reason was he going to give? The truth? Paul gave a short bitter laugh at the thought of that. So he was going to have to fudge things a little. OK, fudge them a lot. He could do it, he knew. He had before. But would Taylor buy it?

Paul walked into the small semi-detached where he lived alone, threw his jacket to one side and himself into an armchair. Why had he done it? The simple answer was he just hadn't been able to resist. They'd been so open in Kilby's flat, Mike and Richard. It had been so easy, so taken for granted. He'd wanted more. And then there had been Richard.

Paul reached for the television and video remote. The tape he'd been looking at last night was still in the machine. He switched the television on and set the tape to play. Yes, Richard. There was something about that student look, the cropped hair, the appearance of almost boyish vulnerability married to a no-nonsense, in-your-face attitude.

The screen in front of him glowed into life and figures took shape. Two naked young men were rolling about on a perfect beach under photographically blue skies. As foam from the waves washed over their flawless bodies, they ran their hands over each other, kissed and laughed.

Almost unconsciously, Paul's hand moved down to the throbbing bulge developing in his trousers and began a slow, firm massage. Yes, Richard. The tempo of his rubbing grew faster and harder.

Three

R ichard dreamed.
He was with Mike. It could have been in Mike's flat, on Mike's bed, though he wasn't certain. It didn't matter. All he could really see was Mike. Mike was so big. Richard was shaving him, all over. Mike's skin was naturally pale, but his hair was jet-black. Celtic colouring, Richard had always thought. Whatever. All it meant for Mike was that the tanning he had to do for competitions was hard, and getting and maintaining the smooth, hair-free body he also needed was even harder. Richard was always willing to lend a hand.

So now in the dream Richard was smoothing rich shaving foam over his lover's body, over the curves of his chest, down over the belly, right down to the crotch.

And then, with the illogic that seems so natural in dreams, the foam became Mike's razor, and Richard was dragging it slowly across the moistened skin, feeling the pull of metal against the bristles of Mike's chest-hairs, seeing the damp flesh left clean and perfect after the blade's passage. Mike lay still, eyes closed, teeth just barely visible through slightly parted lips as Richard eased the razor around the hard buds of his nipples, worked his way down, and down, scything away the thin line of strong black hair that grew, if allowed to, like a pencil line from chest to navel and past that, into the luxuriance between Mike's legs. With the loving

32

precision of a surgeon, Richard drew the silver edge of the razor into the thick growth of hair around the very root of Mike's stiff cock.

And now the razor was no longer the ordinary safety razor he used in reality but an old fashioned switchblade type. Richard had never even seen one in real life, let alone used one, but here in the dream it seemed right and normal. With absolute care, he pulled the blade around the natural lines of his lover's crotch. Not a curl, not a hint of raven black hair could be allowed to peek over the line of the posing briefs Mike had to wear when modelling or competing: only the lion's mane of black on the balls themselves could remain, untouched and natural. Richard held his lover's ball sac gently, and drew his blade deep into his lover's groin.

Mike's cock was erect and hard, wet from the foam and its own excitement. Richard grasped it in one fist, holding it tightly against the slipperiness of the foam. 'You're so big,' he moaned. 'So big.'

'Pump it, Richard. Pump it.'

The voice came from behind him. He turned. It was Mike. He looked back to his fist. He was holding a dumbbell. It was as warm to his touch as Mike's cock had been.

'Pump it, Richard. Pump up those muscles.'

Richard looked down at the weight which hung uselessly in his hand. 'I can't.'

'Pump it, Richard.'

Richard shook his head and tried to release the weight but his fingers refused to obey. 'I can't. I can't do that. I can't be like that.'

'Get big, Richard!'

'I can't!'

And then Mike was in him. Richard was on his face and Mike was pushing down into him, his steel-hard dick spearing into Richard's arse and tearing through his ring. Mike's repeated thrusting was ruthless, the weight of his large body crushing. Richard couldn't breathe. Desperately he twisted his head from side to side, gasping for breath, even as he flexed his arse-muscles, desperately working Mike's huge, implacable dick.

And Inspector Taylor was to one side of them, watching. Apparently oblivious to both his partner's discomfort and the inspector's presence, Mike ploughed on. 'Do you like it, sir?' the inspector was saying. 'Do you like it big? Do you like it hard, sir?'

Mike thrust in deep, much further than Richard had ever been able to take him before. Richard gasped at the agonising pleasure of it and the inspector melted into the sergeant, Paul Ferris. He watched dispassionately as Mike fucked his partner into delirium, making notes just as he had that evening in Mike's flat. 'Like iron,' he said, looking up briefly from his notepad as Richard shrieked at Mike's pitiless reaming. He leaned in closer, his face only inches away from Richard. That clean jawline. 'Like Iron.'

Richard woke bolt upright, covered in sweat, with the dual realisation that he had called out in his sleep and that he had had his first wet dream in years.

Groggily he showered, threw on a sweatshirt and jeans, and then set about stripping the bed and carrying the sheets to the washing machine in the kitchen. It's a happy boy who doesn't have to explain away stuff like this to his mum any more, he thought.

As he worked he tried to piece together the various images that had made up his dream before they faded like dew in the morning sun and were gone forever. What on earth brought that on? he thought. Obviously Sergeant Paul Ferris had made more of an impression than he'd thought, but what was the rest of it all about? He shook his head. It was no good. Already most of it was fading. He'd resigned himself to losing all of it when a single phrase came back like an echo from a distant place. *Like Iron.*

That was the name of the steroid, wasn't it? The one he'd never heard of before. Must have been good if an experienced bodybuilder like Dave was using it. Richard wondered exactly what it did for you. Thoughtfully he headed into the living room, booted up his computer and clicked on the Internet icon. Well, there was one way of maybe finding out. Five minutes later, Richard was absorbed in his search, furiously scribbling down notes as he clicked his way through a trail of weblinks and URLs.

Over an hour later, he logged off and sat back looking at the pages of notes he had taken. 'Shit!' he exclaimed.

Mike stood in front of Dave's gym. Even after the session with Dean and a good two hours' workout afterwards he hadn't been able to sleep the previous night. He'd risen as the daylight had filtered through his bedroom curtains, and for half an hour had stumbled around his flat in a daze, unable to concentrate on the day ahead until the idea had emerged, half-formed and unfocused, that he should go to Dave's place. He had no idea why, or what he hoped to achieve there, but the idea at least gave him something clear to do. He threw himself under a scalding shower, downed the bran and protein supplements that made up his normal breakfast, scribbled a note for Andy to find when he came along to open up the gym later that morning and set off. The drive took nearly two hours, though because of his early start it was still only morning by the time he arrived.

Once he was there, he didn't know what to do. He stood on the pavement opposite, just staring at the entrance. He thought he should be feeling something more, but quite what he didn't know. All he felt was numb, as dulled as he had when he got up.

Dave's gym was about the same size as his own but in a less prosperous area. While, for obvious reasons, they both attracted a high percentage of gay men among their clientèle, Mike's gym also tended to draw in a wider range of punters, from serious bodybuilders to the middle-aged and frankly old businessmen who just wanted to 'keep fit'. Dave's, on the other hand, tended to a tougher crowd: lads who fancied themselves as 'hard' and lads who had to be to survive. Or at least, Mike admitted, it had used to. It had been some time since he had actually been there. Somehow it had always worked out that it was Dave who came to Mike for their 'get togethers' and not the other way around.

He crossed over the street, pushed open the doors and walked in. The gym was empty except for one person, Roy. Less than a partner and more than just a friend, Roy had been for Dave in his gym what Andy was for Mike. He was a former boxer with a lop-sided nose that would be a permanent reminder of his former career. In his fifties now, he still had the wiry figure of a man half his age. A lifetime's training in the use of his fists and a decided 'don't fuck with me' manner made him still more than a match for any kid with attitude, which was handy in that neighbourhood. All the guys respected him and, truth to tell, quite a few were really turned on by him. Stories of his stamina between the sheets were legion, but when Mike walked in now the first thing he was struck by was how small Roy seemed.

Roy was sitting on one of the stools by the entrance desk, simply staring out across the gym. He looked up at the sound of someone coming in and when he saw who it was the expression on his leathery face softened and he walked over to greet him. 'Mike,' he said huskily. 'I kind of thought you might drop in.'

The two men kissed and embraced, simply holding each other for a few minutes and not speaking. When they parted, Roy wiped his crooked nose along his hand. 'No one here,' he said, shrugging his shoulders in a gesture meant to take in their surroundings and his lack of care at same. 'Should've expected it, really, what with the police having been round and all. And I suppose some people wouldn't feel that comfortable like, you know, because, well, it happened up there.' Roy pointed upwards and for one absurd minute, his brain still not up to speed with the day, Mike wondered if Roy was referring to heaven. He wasn't. He was talking about Dave's upstairs flat. This was no longer just the place where Dave had lived; it was also now the place where he had died. 'But then I thought,' Roy continued, 'it's what he would have wanted. So I opened up. Still, no one's come, though.'

Mike looked around the deserted gym. The light from outside came in through grimy windows. The paintwork was unchanged: more scuffed and chipped, perhaps, with the passage of time. The equipment was still laid out in the arrangements he was so familiar with, its dulled chrome showing all the signs of heavy usage and abusage. Everything looked faded and old. It's gone downhill since the last time I was here, Mike thought. Or maybe it was always like this and I just didn't notice. Maybe it had been different because *he'd* been there.

Suddenly, unexpectedly, it all came back to him, the way it had been when he'd first turned up here, drawn by the reputation of a shit-hot trainer who was openly gay. He remembered walking through the door he'd just come through now, hearing the chiming of metal on metal, the grunts and shouts of men pitting their strength against weight, the smells of sweat and liniment. Roy had been there then and had come up to greet the new young arrival, though Mike hadn't really seen him, too busy taking in the sights, sounds and smells.

And then he'd seen Dave. In simple frayed shorts and T-shirt, Dave had been on the bench press across the gym. Mike hadn't been able to believe the size of the plates loaded on either side of the Olympic barbell. As Dave had lain back on the bench, sucking in huge lungfuls of air and psyching himself up for the press, an expectant silence had spread. Men had put down their weights, and looked across to the bench press area. Several moved closer, and Mike realised he had come in on something important.

Abruptly Dave had grasped the bar, let out his last deep breath in a loud whoosh and nodded to the two burly spotters standing on either side of him. With practised speed, they lifted the weight from its hold and released it. Dave had it all. For a second he held it there, arms fully extended, the massive weight as steady as a rock, and then he allowed it to fall, smoothly and controlled to his barrel of a chest, sucking in more air as he did so. At its lowest point it just grazed the cotton of his T-shirt before Dave let the pent-up air in his lungs explode outwards and powered the weight back up.

'Yes!' Mike sensed rather than saw Roy punch the air next to him. His eyes were riveted on Dave. He wouldn't have thought anyone could have moved that weight even once on his own, but now this guy was going into another rep.

The weight fell and rose a second time. There was a spattering of spontaneous applause, swiftly cut off by a savage glare from Roy. The spotters moved forward, ready to take the bar and guide it back on to its rest. 'One more!' The words were gasped out, barely audible. The spotters glanced anxiously at each other over the body of the man lying down between them then glanced across at Roy. Roy nodded and they stepped back. Dave held the bar, arms locked, sucked in a couple of quick, shallow breaths and then let the weight fall an incredible third time.

It reached Dave's chest. It stopped. Mike recalled how he had tensed up his own chest and arm-muscles, willing their strength into the straining muscles of the man on the bench. Slowly, centimetre by centimetre, the bar had edged its way back up again. Veins bulged in swollen biceps, heavy with blood. Sweat erupted from his body with the titanic effort, soaking T-shirt and shorts. Lips were drawn back in a rictus snarl and through his teeth the air hissed out, accompanied by a sound, a keening that grew into a snarling that grew into a mighty bellow until with one magnificent last thrust Dave locked his arms out and screamed his triumph out loud as the gym exploded in cheers and roars of approval.

'You've come in at a record-breaking moment, son,' Roy had said, slapping Mike on the back as if congratulating him for the achievement. Mike hadn't heard him. He was still staring at this magnificent man in front of him. With a crash that Mike felt through the floorboards, Dave let the weights slam back on to their stands and had allowed himself to be helped up by the two very relieved-looking spotters and pummelled and congratulated by what looked like everyone in the gym. It was then that he'd seen Mike properly for the first time. 'Hi!' he'd gasped, his incredibly pumped chest rising and falling, straining the thin fabric of the T-shirt that was plastered against it.

'That was fucking brilliant,' Mike blurted out, then he'd blushed, afraid that he'd let too much of his feelings show, too soon, to someone he'd only just met.

Dave hadn't batted an eyelid. 'Thanks,' he'd said accepting the praise without arrogance. One by one the congratulatory crowd had gone back to their own routines, some still shaking their heads in disbelief at what they had seen. Dave had risen from his bench, and walked over to Mike. He'd wiped his hands on his hips and, following the motion with his eyes, it was then that Mike had seen the generous bulging through the thin material of Dave's soaked, clinging shorts. Dave had seen the direction of his eyes and looked at him. They had both laughed.

'You know what they're saying.'

Jolted out of his memories by Roy, Mike looked round to the older man.

'You know what they're saying killed him?'

'Junk?'

Roy nodded. 'Took a lot of it, they said, from his flat. Don't think they've touched anything else. Don't know: haven't liked to look.'

Mike swallowed, wondering how he was going to ask the next question, knowing that there was really only the one way. 'Was he using steroids, Roy?'

'You know he wouldn't do that.' The reply was as quick and almost as heated as the one Mike had given Inspector Taylor when he'd suggested the same thing.

'I know, Roy,' Mike said, 'but what was the stuff doing up there?'

Roy deflated. His eyes were cast down. 'I don't know, kid. I really don't know.'

Mike put out his hand and squeezed the older man's shoulder. 'Was anyone dealing here, Roy?'

Roy looked up. Mike was glad to see the momentary anger was gone. Roy knew he was only asking the questions he himself had considered.

'You know what he was like about that.'

Mike nodded. Dave hadn't been stupid. In their business and in this neighbourhood, only a fool would have thought kids weren't pumping themselves up with some chemical shit or other, and the local gym just had to be the place to score. But if anyone did it they did it, without Dave's approval, and if he saw anything that even looked like dealing, the guys involved were bluntly told to conduct their business outside the doors and to be clean of the stuff, on the outside of their bodies at least, before they returned. His stance had been an example to many young kids, not least Mike himself, who had thanked providence many a time for the good fortune he'd had to start off his bodybuilding career proper with Dave Ross for a trainer and not someone a great deal less scrupulous.

'But there was this guy,' Roy added slowly.

A guy. Right. Just for a minute, the gym and everything in it seemed to recede into the distance, leaving Mike alone with a peculiar sinking feeling in the pit of his stomach. A guy. Of course there had been. Did you think he kept himself pure for you? Did you think he just didn't have anything to do with sex if he wasn't doing it with you once every month? Right. So there was a guy. It's just, Mike thought, I thought he would have told me. 'He was seeing someone,' he said dully.

'Nah. Nothing like that,' Roy added hurriedly, probably seeing the shadows pass across Mike's face. 'At least, I don't think so. There hasn't really been anyone like that since – well, since after you.' He coughed and ran his hand across his nose again before going on. 'Maybe it's not worth mentioning; it's just that, well, he was the only thing that's been a bit odd, a bit different if you know what I mean.'

'No, Roy,' Mike said patiently, 'I don't.'

'He was so out of place. I mean, he walks in here in a suit and tie, you know, and it's pretty clear he isn't into bodybuilding himself – not really into Muscle Marys either, from the way he looks down his nose at the guys. He just stands there like he's trying not to touch anything 'cause it's all way too dirty for him, and Dave drops whatever he's doing, rushes over and shuffles him off upstairs pronto.'

'How many times did this happen?'

'Just the twice that I saw, but I get the feeling he'd been here before. He seemed to know his way around.'

'Did Dave look pleased to see him?'

Roy wrinkled his already massively furrowed forehead as he thought about this. 'Nah. More like, well, nervous I'd say.'

Mike resolved to store that item of news away for the moment. It might have some connection with events leading up to Dave's death, or it might have nothing at all to do with it. 'Look, Roy,' he said gently, 'I'd like a little time, you know, on my own. Just to have a look around and . . .' He faltered, still not sure what the hell it was he had gone there to do.

'Pay your respects?' Roy suggested.

Mike nodded. Maybe that was it. He was relieved that he wouldn't have to try and put his feelings into words. 'Yeah.'

'No problem, kid. I'll just be behind the desk here. No, I'll go out into the kitchen and make us a cup of coffee, eh? Shouldn't think anyone will disturb you.' He hurried away through the kitchen door behind the entrance counter. Mike took a deep breath of relief. Roy called back from behind the counter. 'And the flat's unlocked. For when you want to, you know, go and have a look up there.' He closed the kitchen door behind him.

Mike turned to confront the empty gym. They'd been together under three years, he and Dave. For over two years he'd lived here with Dave in the flat above. 'If you love a job enough, you'll want to live over it, right?' That's what Dave had said, and it was just one more piece of advice Mike had taken when he went looking for a set-up he could call his own when the time to move on had come.

Mike wandered around the apparatus, rubbing his hands over the chrome and ragged plastic of the equipment. Each piece, each area of the gym brought alive new memories of Dave. He saw again those first real training sessions, just him and Dave after the rest of the punters had gone. It had been such an adventure, a journey of bodybuilding discovery. His horizons then had been the ones Mike had made for himself, and Dave had shown him how to travel way beyond them.

'That's not your body telling you you can't lift that weight,' he'd shout as a straining, exhausted Mike, muscle fibres burning from some ferocious Dave-led workout, had tried for just one more repetition of an exercise. 'It's your brain. Don't listen to your brain. Listen to your body. Listen to your heart!' Mike had listened to his body and to his heart and he had done that one more rep, and then another.

Standing in front of the mirrored wall at the far end of the gym, he remembered now the night that Dave had first told him that what he really liked to do was train naked. Mike's heart had leaped into his mouth. He'd changed with Dave, showered with him, but up until that point he'd been too shy to do more than sneak quick glances, sideways looks at reflections in mirrors. Just the thought of Dave naked made him go hard. Was he ready to make it obvious to his mentor just what an effect he was having on his young protégé?

'Sure,' he'd said, 'why not?' He hadn't needed to be told to listen to his heart this time. It was thundering so loud in his ears he'd been sure Dave could have heard it himself. They'd thrown their shorts and T-shirts to one side. Mike had never felt so vulnerable in front of another man.

Naked, Dave had been superb: the living, breathing embodiment of all those glossy, muscle-mag pictorial fantasies that Mike had wanked over since adolescence. A chest you'd strain to get your arms round but a waist as trim as a young boy's. Arms and legs that literally rippled with solid muscle even as he stood, as he had done then, relaxed and unflexed. In Mike's eyes it had been more perfection than it seemed possible for one man to carry by himself, and yet, for all that, Dave had carried himself totally unselfconsciously. The effect had been to make him even more intensely erotic in Mike's eyes. The young man hadn't been able to prevent himself lapping up the sight of Dave's unclothed body and his first real sight of his teacher's splendid cock, heavy between his legs. Mike had turned away, suddenly embarrassed at the thought of showing the inevitable erection building between his legs in front of Dave but Dave had laughed, reached over, taken his dick in his hand and gently run his hand along its length. 'This is what it's all about, Mike,' he'd said. 'Life. Strength. Vitality. Call it what you want. You don't turn your back on it. You seize it.' He'd reached over with his other hand and cupped Mike's balls. 'With both hands.'

That night, Mike trained harder than probably at any other time in his life before or since. His blood had been on fire at the sight of the other man, at the touch of his hands on his body. Their training had been something else: primal, elemental. To this day, he couldn't remember at exactly what point it had turned from training to the most passionate, intense lovemaking. They had rolled and fucked on the gym floor, surrounded by multiple images of themselves caught in the silvered surfaces of the gym equipment and the floor-to-ceiling mirrors that covered the walls.

To the young Mike, barely out of his teens, every inch of Dave was honed physical perfection, raw beauty bought at the cost of years of brutal effort, and yet he was capable of such tenderness as he touched and kissed and licked his young lover. Mike had arched and moaned, torn between conflicting desires to make this last forever and to give in to the shattering orgasm that was hammering for release. He didn't remember where the condom and lube had come from. What he did remember was lying there, panting heavily, watching in awe as Dave had smoothed the sheath the length of his shaft. He'd been afraid. He wanted Dave in him, wanted it more than he'd ever wanted anything in his life up to that point, needed to feel that rod of muscle powering into his arse and slamming into his prostate. But it was so big, and Dave was such a powerful man. Mike was young, not that experienced. He didn't know if he was ready yet for something so extreme. But Dave had smiled down at him, whispered something – although Mike hadn't quite been able to make out what – and had leaned down and kissed him on the mouth. Mike had known then that no matter what happened, no matter how painful it might be, he had to give himself to this man, totally, completely, without reservation.

It had been painful. Dave was more meat than Mike had ever taken in, up to that point. His muscle-ring was stretched until it burned and Mike thought he would tear but still there was more. He wanted to scream out, to make Dave stop or push in harder, faster – it didn't matter which, so long as it brought an end to this searing hot pain – but he didn't. This was Dave Ross. This was the man he adored. So he bit down on his lip until he tasted blood, screwed his eyes up against the stinging tears and endured. And somewhere marvellous the pain had ebbed away and a tidal wave of unsuspected pleasure had rushed back in to take its place. Mike's being was flooded with the most intense sensations he had ever felt and he had been completely unable to prevent himself coming voluminously on the spot, clamping down hard on Dave in the ecstasy of his release and driving the man on top to frantic explosion.

'I'm sorry,' Mike had said afterwards.

'What for?' Dave had asked, genuinely puzzled.

'I sort of . . . lost control back there. I wanted to make it last longer.'

Dave had smiled and pulled him towards him. 'Well, we'll just have to see what we can manage this time, won't we?'

Mike turned, headed for the stairs that led up to Dave's flat, just as the two of them had gone upstairs that night years ago to make love again in Dave's bed. Mike had moved in the next day.

There was a curious neatness about the flat now that felt wrong. Mike wondered whether this tidiness was an artificial order, left by the police after their search. Furniture and fittings were clean and spare. Dave hadn't really been much of a one for home-making. A sofa was just something you fell into during those odd moments you weren't bodybuilding. Who cared what it looked like? He hadn't been a great one for reading, either. There was the bookshelf of bodybuilding texts, of course, but even those were kept to the minimum 'bibles'.

There was just the one aspect to this room that marked it as undeniably Dave's, and it was a feature impossible to ignore. Trophies. Dave's DIY had extended as far as shelving, and every shelf bore its load of trophies. Shields and plaques, cups and statuettes, they lined the rooms: spoils of victory from dozens of bodybuilding contests over the years and around the country, and some from further afield.

Mike knew them all. Young and hungry for competition success of his own, he'd spent many an hour looking at these symbols of everything he wanted to achieve, holding them, reading their inscriptions, trying to imagine what it would be like to lift one up in victory at a competition. Dave hadn't boasted about them — had hardly ever spoken about them, in fact — but they were all there, dusted, polished, meticulously arranged. Mike looked for one in particular. Yes, it was still there. He walked over towards it, his feelings complex at seeing it again after all this time

It had pride of place on the mantelpiece over the fire. It was smaller than many of the others there, a silvered figure of a bodybuilder in a double biceps pose on top of a small wooden platform. It was the one trophy in the room that Dave hadn't won. Mike picked it up and read the name on the small plinth. It was his. Not the first trophy he'd won, but probably the most significant. It came from the first show where he and Dave had both competed against each other. It was the first place trophy. Dave had come second.

Dave had been pleased. Hell, he'd been more than pleased:

he'd lauded his younger lover to the heavens. For weeks that trophy had been on display downstairs in the gym and when it finally made its way upstairs to the living room it had been put here, the focus point of the room. But Dave's second-place trophy had disappeared, and Dave never entered a competition again if Mike was also taking part. It wasn't long after that contest that they had begun to drift apart and Mike had reluctantly realised that it was time to move on.

Mike held the trophy now, running his fingers over its surface. 'I'm sorry, Dave,' he said softly, maybe to himself.

'Mike. Mike!' Mike was jolted from his introspection by the urgent call from downstairs. He replaced the trophy and made his way back to the gym. Roy was standing by the entrance, the door still swinging backwards and forwards. Roy pointed at it. 'He was here. The guy I was telling you about.'

Not stopping to ask himself what he was going to say or do, responding to the sudden adrenal rush, Mike dashed out of the gym and on to the street, looking quickly to left and right. To his right at the far end of the street, he saw a man in a dove-grey jacket and trousers climbing into a red sports car. 'Hey. Hey, you. Wait a minute. I want to talk to you.'

The man paused, turned to face Mike in the act of climbing into his car. Mike caught the briefest glimpse of a tanned, dark-haired young man, then the face turned away as he climbed into his car and started up the engine. 'Wait!' Mike yelled, charging up to the car. He couldn't make it in time. The car pulled away just as he was almost within reach, its occupant not looking back once. Mike came to a halt on the pavement, panting, unable to do anything other than watch it drive away swiftly into the distance. He trudged back to the gym.

'Did you catch him?' Roy asked as he re-entered the gym.

Mike shook his head. 'What had he come for? Did he say? Did he know that . . . Did he know about Dave?' Roy nodded. 'How was he taking it? Did he look upset?'

Roy considered. 'I'd say he looked angry. Yeah, really pissed off. Didn't want to talk to me. He started to go up to Dave's flat without so much as a by your leave, as if he owned the place. So that's when I said there was already someone up there, and he'd have to ask you if it was all right for him to be there, too, on account of you and Dave had been . . . so close.'

'What did he say to that?'

'He asked me straight out. "Is that Michael?" Not "Mike" but "Michael". I said yes, and that's when he turned around and shot off, without so much as a backwards glance. That's when I called you. So, did you get a chance to see him? Did you recognise him?'

Mike went to shake his head, to say that he hadn't had a chance to get a proper look at the man's face, and that anyway, he didn't know anyone who wore a jacket like that one, but even as he did the memory of that moment when the man had looked back just before climbing into his car flashed across his mind's eye. Hadn't there been something slightly familiar? Hadn't there been some-thing about the man he recognised? He shook his head, dismissing the feeling. He knew for a fact that couldn't be the case. 'Never seen him before in my life,' he said.

So how had this man known him? And why had he so emphatically refused to stop and speak?

'You called on one of the suspects, unaccompanied?'

'I think "suspects" is putting it a bit strong, Chief.'

'All right, then. You called on Richard Green of 6, Alma Road. Unaccompanied. Is that an acceptable way of putting it, Sergeant?'

Paul gritted his teeth and did his level best not to squirm in his chair, sweat or do anything else to reveal his nervousness over this interrogation. And interrogation was just what it was turning out to be. It might have started as his routine morning meeting with Inspector Taylor to map out the business of the day, but the instant that Paul had let drop, with studied casualness, that he had 'interviewed' Richard the previous evening after he and the inspector had parted company, his superior's attitude had changed. Taylor had become cold, obviously suspicious. Paul wondered just what it was he was suspicious of.

Taylor leaned back in his chair, regarding his sergeant closely, but saying nothing. Paul retained his more upright position on the opposite side of his boss's desk, also said nothing and tried to look as if the meeting with Richard had been perfectly normal, or at most only a very slight deviation from usual practice. Part of him was irritated by what Taylor was doing: the classic interrogation technique of sitting back and letting the nervous suspect hang himself. Well, why should he? What had he got to be nervous about? What could Taylor possibly know about why he had wanted to talk to Richard? The other part of him was uncomfortably waiting for the questions he really didn't want to answer.

'Why?'

The word was softly spoken, but Paul had already worked with Taylor long enough to know that the older man was more dangerous when he spoke quietly than when he was shouting. He launched into the answer he had thoroughly prepared before walking into that office. 'Green had gone straight home. He hadn't tried to contact anyone and there was no one else at his flat when he got back. It seemed an ideal opportunity to question him while he was still rattled after our previous interview with Kilby.'

'I don't remember our discussing this beforehand.'

Paul swallowed. 'No, sir.'

Taylor leaned forwards across the desk. Paul caught the faint smell of the man's early-morning cigarettes. 'Fact is, Sergeant, I remember saying you were to get yourself back home for an early night if Green didn't do anything untoward.'

'It was a spur of the moment call, sir. I was using my initiative.'

Taylor leaned back again. 'That what they call it now, is it? All right. So where did this "initiative" of yours get you? Did you learn anything?'

Paul looked down. 'No. Well, that is, no, not really.'

'"Not really." I'm slow in the morning, lad. Run that one by me again and try and make it easy for me, will you?'

Paul leaned forwards. 'I don't think he's mixed up in anything, sir. That is, I don't think either of them are, Green or Kilby.'

'He told you this, did he?'

Paul flushed. 'He seems a decent enough guy. And we know he hasn't got any form. I asked him about Iron and he hadn't even heard —'

Taylor interrupted sharply. 'You told him about Iron?'

'I asked if he'd heard about it. And he hadn't.'

Taylor surged up from his chair and stormed round the desk to look down at Paul. 'Haven't you learned anything about this job, son? You don't go around giving the opposition your best leads. Got that?'

'I don't follow you, sir,' Paul said. 'Iron's a steroid. By his own admission, Green is something of an expert on bodybuilding steroids. I wanted to see what his reaction would be to my referring to it. I didn't see the harm.'

'You didn't, eh? So what was his reaction?'

'There wasn't one. I mean, he was puzzled, said he hadn't heard of it before, and I believed him, but that was as far as it went.'

'I see.' Taylor nodded as if accepting every word he was being told. 'And of course he couldn't possibly have been lying to you?'

'No, sir,' Paul answered, on as much of his dignity as he could summon under this grilling. 'In my opinion, he wasn't.'

'When I want your opinion, Sergeant Ferris, I'll give it to you.' Taylor opened up a desk drawer in front of him, drew out a packet of cigarettes, shook one out and lit up. It was a flagrant abuse of the station's no-smoking policy. Paul, a decided non-smoker, decided it wouldn't be prudent to remind his boss of that. Taylor blew out a long stream of smoke. Coincidentally or otherwise, most of it ended up in Paul's face. 'Look, son, I've seen all this before.'

Paul sat up even straighter. 'All what, sir?'

'You're new to your sergeant's stripes. You're young, you think you've got the answer to everything and one day soon you're going to be Chief Commissioner once all us old farts realise just how clever you are.' Taylor blew more smoke Paul's way. 'Well, maybe you will. But at the moment, as far as I'm concerned, you're still fresh from the beat and wet behind the ears – and if I wanted proof, then what you went and did yesterday gave me all I need.'

'I was eliminating suspects in this case.'

'There is no case.'

Paul blinked, surprised by his boss's words. 'Sir?'

'Open and shut. Death by misadventure. We move on.'

Paul considered what Taylor was telling him. 'But we have a dead man, a case of illegal steroids. Yesterday we were setting up the chief suspects –'

'And today we're moving on. The case, like I said, is closed.'

There was a heavy silence. Paul looked away, trying to see things in this new and unexpected light. Taylor drew on his cigarette and watched him closely. When Paul finally spoke, it was slowly and carefully. 'Would our "moving on" so quickly have anything to do with . . . the type of people involved?'

Taylor replied with equal slowness. 'What do you mean?'

'Minorities.'

His boss gave a dry chuckle. 'First time I've heard bodybuilders called that.' He leaned forwards across his desk again. 'You seem to be taking quite a personal interest in this case, Sergeant Ferris. Are there any interests here you want to declare?'

Paul felt his mouth dry. So here it was: the moment he'd always known would come, sooner or later. Now it was here he had to admit he was really wishing it could have been later. He opened his mouth to speak.

The intercom on the desk between them gave out a piercing squawk. Angrily, Taylor jabbed at it. 'Yes?' he barked, not taking his eyes off Paul.

'Call for Sergeant Ferris, sir. Says it's urgent.'

'We're in a meeting. Who is it?'

'A Richard Green, sir. Shall I put the call through to Sergeant Ferris's office or shall I tell Mr Green to call again later?'

Taylor drew thoughtfully on his cigarette. 'Put it through here. Sergeant Ferris can take the call in my office.' Paul went to protest but Taylor had already picked up the phone receiver and was holding it out to him. 'It's for you,' he said with a cold smile. Feeling like he had just been handed a loaded gun and told to put it to his head, Paul took the telephone. Taylor sat back and watched him speak.

'Sergeant Ferris here. How can I help you, Mr Green?' Pause. 'That's very interesting. Do you have any documentation on this?' Pause. 'Could you bring this down to the station where we can have a look at it?' Longer pause. 'I see. In that case, I'll have to see what I can arrange. I'm afraid I can't do that right at this moment. If you would please give me about another five minutes, I can go to my office, consult my schedule and see what's possible. Thank you very much for your help. I'll get back to you shortly. Goodbye, Mr Green.' He handed the phone back to Taylor.

'Remembered something, has he?' Taylor asked with heavy irony.

'Not exactly, but he says he may have something of interest.'

'Then he should bring it in, shouldn't he?'

'That's what I suggested, but he wasn't that keen.' Paul looked his superior directly in the eyes. 'Apparently he's not too keen on the way police treat . . . minorities. Says he thinks some of them might be prejudiced. I said I'd sort out other arrangements.'

Taylor nodded slowly. 'Very well then, Sergeant. We are here for our public, after all. Make your arrangements, find out what he's got – if anything – and then report back to me. I am fully expecting you to discover that there is nothing that can be of any possible interest to you or me and that our time can be much more profitably spent in other areas. Do I make myself clear, Sergeant?'

Paul kept his voice dead level. 'Perfectly, sir.'

'And one more thing. We'll find the source of these steroids sooner or later, even if it's not going to be because of some ageing Charles Atlas wannabe who should have known better. In the meantime, you keep your mouth shut about Iron. It doesn't help to have bright sparks with initiative mouthing off to all and sundry about case details. Got that?'

Paul nodded. 'Sir.'

'Good. Well, get to it and be quick. You know the sort of cases that tend to pile up on a sergeant's desk if he doesn't keep on top of his work.'

Paul left the office, Taylor's veiled threat all too clear to him.

Taylor watched his progress across the corridor through the frosted glass windows. As he did he slowly ground out the nub of his cigarette in his ash tray. When he saw Paul go into his own office and pull the door to behind him he jabbed again at the intercom. 'Give me an outside line,' he barked. He dialled a number without need of a directory and waited. 'Hello, it's

Taylor. Give me Woodward.' He waited, grinding the cigarette butt harder and harder into the ash tray. 'Blake? It's me. It's about the Ross case.' He looked across again to see Paul already walking out of his office and leaving the station. 'I think we may have a complication.'

Richard didn't have too much faith in 'gaydar'. A particularly embarrassing incident in a public swimming pool with a gorgeous lifeguard during his adolescence had pretty much persuaded him that it was an unlikely ability. Some guys might have it but he certainly didn't. Having said that, when Paul turned up on his doorstep a mere thirty minutes after his phonecall and less than twenty-four hours after his previous visit, Richard was fairly sure he knew.

What surprised him was his own reaction. He'd noticed Paul was cute, the previous night – who wouldn't? – but now he just couldn't help seeing how very good-looking the young policeman was. Maybe it was because he was now seeing Paul as another gay male. Maybe it was because the anger he'd felt after that first encounter with Paul and Taylor at Mike's flat had had a chance to die down a little. Or maybe it was because an unconscious reaction – an immediate attraction, in fact – had had time to put down roots and grow overnight – something his waking dream, among other things, had been trying to tell him. Richard didn't know which, if any, of these possibilities was true, but then frankly he didn't care.

He showed Paul into his living room (taking another good look at that great bum) and waved him to a seat on the sofa. Unlike yesterday, it was now clear of books; in fact there was plenty of room for two. Richard hoped that nothing would lead Paul to look behind the sofa, where he would find the missing books in the untidy pile they'd been thrown into just minutes before the doorbell rang.

'It's not a good idea to call me at the station,' Paul began.

Richard was momentarily distracted from examining the policeman's smooth jawline by this unexpected start to their meeting. He almost laughed. It sounded too much like some

'Don't call me at the office' line a harassed husband might give to his girlfriend. 'Why not?'

'My boss isn't exactly . . . sympathetic to this case.'

Richard felt a familiar smouldering inside. An activist practically since he'd learned to walk, such hints of prejudice were like red flags to him. He'd hoped to chat a little with Paul, get to know him a bit more, and maybe, mentally undress him and shag him senseless on the sofa, but this news spurred him on directly to business. 'Well, perhaps he'll feel a bit more "sympathetic" when you show him this.' He reached over to his work desk, hauled over a pile of printouts and dumped them on Paul's lap.

'What's this?'

'The results of a morning's surfing on the Internet. You say that you think Dave died because he took a steroid called Iron?'

'The test results came through this morning. Positive. What they don't know yet is how long he'd been on the stuff. Chances are it was the first dose that killed him. It's a powerful drug.'

Richard wondered briefly how Mike was going to take that news. Later. He pressed on. 'Do you know how many references there are to "iron" if you run it through your average search engine?'

Paul shook his head. 'I'm not even sure what an average search engine is,' he confessed.

'Shit! What do they teach policemen at police school these days, anyway?'

'Mostly how to arrest people properly.'

The image was an appealing one, and Richard found his mind briefly filled with images of being restrained by Sergeant Ferris. He shook his head and forced himself to focus on matters in hand. 'I entered the word "iron" into the computer this morning and came up with over two thousand hits. That means over two thousand separate websites deal with the subject in one form or another.'

Paul looked interested. 'But they can't all be about the steroid, surely?'

'Course not. You have to start cross-referencing, cutting out the dead wood.'

'And you're good at that?'

Richard hesitated. Was that some kind of personal question? He shrugged. 'Research is part of my job, remember? Anyway, twenty minutes or so fiddling with the parameters whittled it down to what you see here.' He leaned in a little more closely to take Paul through the top few sheets of the pile. The sergeant was wearing a musky aftershave. Richard found it powerfully masculine. He tried to breathe it in as deeply as he could without suddenly appearing to have turned asthmatic.

He was so determined to appear at once businesslike and cool he didn't appreciate that Paul was taking the opportunity of this close proximity to scrutinise him, too. He's your real perpetual student, Paul was thinking. Fresh-faced but worldly wise. A compelling combination of innocence and hard nose. A crusader with a typewriter. Or a computer, he corrected himself. And a boyfriend built like a brick shithouse. What, he found himself wondering, would they look like making love? Richard's slim, boyish body in the massive arms of that gorilla, that tight arse split open by that muscleman's pumped-up dick . . .

'And then, if you poke around a little in some of the . . . less well known sites.' Richard went to move some of the sheets in the sergeant's lap. Instinctively Paul grabbed them tightly, unwilling to let them go. They were the only thing hiding the growing erection that was already stretching the crotch of his trousers. Seeing that Richard only meant to move the top few sheets he smiled apologetically and let him do so. 'You mean,' he said, clearing his throat, 'the illegal ones.' He hoped he'd made that sound light and non-officious.

Richard grinned and Paul relaxed again. 'Yes, well, the Internet is still very new. Several legal areas are still pretty grey.' Richard couldn't resist a small dig. 'Probably because most policemen are still not very up on current technology.' He was pleased to see Paul respond to the barb with a small smile. 'What you come up with is this.' With a flourish he pulled out a single sheet and brandished it aloft. He handed it to Paul who scanned it. THE FELLOWSHIP OF IRON was emblazoned at the top. 'They're selling this stuff practically on the open market. The claims they're making for it are amazing. And, you won't be surprised to see, there's no reference to any possible side effects. Like death, for instance.'

'What are all these?' Paul pointed to parts of the printout.

'URLs. Universal Resource Locators. Links to other websites. They're not important, except for this one.' He pointed to the largest URL. It had printed out in blood red and was right at the top of the list. 'This is the one that takes you to the guts of the site, the place from where you can set up your deals and score your Iron.'

Paul looked anxious. 'So have you?'

'No, Mr Policeman, sir, I have not set myself up for five to ten for illegal drugs trafficking. Besides, I couldn't, even if I wanted to. You click on that URL and you get this.' Richard reached across to his desk and pulled across the last sheet he had been holding back until now. ACCESS DENIED filled the top in large letters. Underneath was the simple instruction, 'Enter your password.'

Paul frowned. 'So how do you get a password?'

'That's the point. You don't. Not unless you send them all the details about yourself and presumably they check you out to make sure you're a safe bet. I'd picked up a few back when I was doing my research, some of them quite high-power. They didn't get me anywhere here.'

'So would it be possible to trace this site?'

Richard smiled at the policeman's enthusiasm and naiveté. 'Websites aren't physical. They're stored on computers that could literally be anywhere in the world. Even if you did find this one, it would be child's play to switch it to another computer thousands of miles away in seconds. That's why the Net is so hard to police. Makes it a great forum for free speech,' he couldn't resist adding. 'No, the only way into this site is with a password, and the only way to get one of those is to apply.' He leaned back against the sofa. 'So what are you going to do?'

Paul, his excitement of a moment ago temporarily abated, handed the pile of printouts back to Richard. 'Nothing,' he said.

'What?'

'The case is closed. Officially.'

Richard flared up, angered by the unexpected rejection. 'You're not going to do anything?'

Paul shifted uncomfortably on the sofa. 'I can't. Even if the case wasn't closed, I don't have access to a computer I can use.'

Richard regarded him narrowly, anger giving way to suspicion. 'You don't have a computer?' he exclaimed incredulously. 'I mean, I know they keep telling us you don't get enough funding these days, but are you really telling me you don't have access to the Internet? Just where is all the public money going to? Smaller cells and better handcuffs?'

Paul hesitated. He was a policeman. Richard wasn't. There were loyalties: some written down, many unwritten. Telling Richard his reasons for not wanting to use the station resources would be transgressing those rules. They were on different sides of the fence. But then maybe that just depended on which fence you were looking at. 'That's not what I said. We're a small station, but of course we're hooked up to computers. What I'm saying is that to use them I'll have to go through Alex, our computer whizz-kid. And if I do that then my boss, Inspector Taylor, will get to know about it. And, just at the moment, I think that's probably not a good idea.'

Richard nodded slowly. He began to see the lie of the land. The explanation was only half there, and instinctively he wanted to know more, to say exactly what he thought about Paul's boss and probably let as much of the world know about it as he could in a blistering series of newspaper articles. But that wouldn't have sat well with Paul. Besides, now that he was cooling down again, the journalist in him couldn't help thinking there might be an altogether different article, if not a substantial feature, to be brought out of this business. If he could get Paul's co-operation. 'OK, then, I'll do it.'

Paul struggled to keep up. 'Do what?'

'I'll apply for membership of this Fellowship of Iron myself, give them my details and wait to be contacted.'

'But you said you didn't want to.'

'Not before I'd told you about it. Now I've told the police, I've got legal cover, haven't I? Now it's just investigative journalism. It's what I do all the time. So, are you in?' He waited a heartbeat before playing his trump card. 'Or do you think your Inspector Taylor is right and that there is nothing more to be done in this case?' He waited for Paul's reply. He found he really wanted to go ahead with this. Here was a new drug with potentially lethal side effects, being marketed in the most up-to-date of ways by a mysterious criminal group. The human interest story focusing on Dave alone was compelling, but the possibility of being the reporter behind the unmasking of a criminal drugs ring was dynamite. And then, of course, even if it all came to nothing there was another consideration. The idea of working as closely as possible with this highly attractive man sitting next to him now was very appealing. He hoped that perhaps a similar idea wasn't a million miles away from Paul's mind as well.

Paul considered. He thought of the information Richard had found. He remembered Taylor's coded warning. He looked at the way Richard's mouth curled up at the ends in a mischievous smile as he used that blatantly obvious piece of psychology against him. He nodded. 'All right. As long as you let me know the minute anything comes through.'

'The very second. Although, if I'm not supposed to call you at the station . . .'

Paul reached into his jacket and pulled out a small card which he handed over. 'Home address and telephone numbers. If I'm not in, there's always a machine to take your call.'

'No one else?' Richard asked as artlessly as he could. 'Wife? Girlfriend? *Partner?*'

'No,' Paul said shortly. 'And it's best not to use the mobile phone number, either.'

'Never know who might be there with you, right?'

'Right.'

Richard tucked the small card into the back pocket of his jeans. 'So we're a team then, are we? Holmes and Watson?'

Paul allowed himself a smile. The sight of perfect white teeth made Richard's stomach turn adolescent flip flops. 'How about Batman and Robin?'

'Fine by me. I've always liked guys who wear skin-tight underwear.' There was a momentary pause. Richard smoothly moved on, unwilling to lose the momentum he sensed was building. 'This isn't exactly orthodox procedure, is it?'

Paul shook his head. 'I suppose sometimes,' he said, recalling an earlier conversation, 'you have to use your initiative.'

'You don't sound much like other policemen I've met.'

Richard's simple words were charged with meaning that Paul knew they both appreciated. Helplessly, he felt his erection building again, shoving blindly outwards in his trousers, and this time he had no convenient wad of paper to hide it. His throat was tight, his mouth dry, so when he spoke his voice was not much more than a whisper. 'I'm not,' he said.

Richard leaned in closer to Paul. The scent of the young policeman's aftershave was warm and heavy. Very carefully, as if worried that abrupt movements might break the moment, Richard moved his hand, placed it lightly on Paul's thigh. Paul's face was slightly turned from Richard, his eyes looking out into the middle distance, as if he was unaware of what the other man was doing, but he didn't protest and he didn't move an inch. With continued care, Richard moved his hand slowly up Paul's thigh, keeping his touch light. When he reached Paul's crotch, the hardness was unmistakable. Gently he pressed. Paul gave a small gasp and closed his eyes. Richard pressed again, harder, then again, his eyes fixed on Paul's face, taking in the flush that was spreading across the smooth skin, the increasing rapidity of the breathing. He wanted to kiss the policeman, wanted to force his tongue between those lips and push it deep into that mouth. But not yet. Instinctively he knew the time wasn't ripe. One step at a time with this one, he thought. He's going to be worth it.

Slowly but firmly, he pulled down the zip of Paul's trousers, opening its full length. The white cloth of Paul's boxers was tenting strongly outwards, wet already with pre-come. One by one Richard undid the slippery buttons. Freed of its restraint, Paul's meaty cock thrust out, hard and gleaming in its excitement. Richard ran his fingers around the very tip, excited himself at Paul's size. Paul gasped again. The knuckles of his hand as he gripped the sofa throw were white. Gently, Richard pushed his hand into the warmth of Paul's crotch, taking the heavy member in his hand, alert for the first sign of protest. There was none. He squeezed. The muscle was warm and solid in his palm. He pushed his hand deep into the crotch, forcing back the foreskin, holding the pressure then slowly releasing it. Paul moaned and thrust his crotch out for further pleasure. Richard pumped again, gradually building the speed, the force. His other arm was around Paul's neck, pulling the man in still closer until their faces were cheek to cheek and Richard could feel the heat of Paul's laboured breath on his skin. The sound and feel excited him almost unbearably. His own cock was surging up powerfully in his tight jeans and he would desperately loved to have torn his zip open and wanked himself off hard at the same time as he was seeing to Paul, but that would have meant breaking off from Paul and he didn't want to do that, not for one second. So while his own tool strained against his denim, he curled his free hand into a fist and pumped Paul harder and faster with the other, practically coming himself just at the sight of the handsome policeman's obvious ecstasy.

It didn't take long under Richard's skilled ministrations for Paul to climax with a strangled groan, and when he did the results were frankly spectacular. Gouts of come shot into the air, spattering liberally his trousers, shirt and even Richard's face. Richard kept up his relentless pumping until the very last drop had been forced out and Paul was left gasping for air. His eyes were wide open now, as if with shock or extreme surprise, but he still didn't look at Richard.

Richard released Paul, reached round the side of the sofa and pulled out a box of paper handkerchiefs. 'For emergencies,' he said, a trifle sheepishly, hoping his preparation wasn't just a little too obvious. Richard passed the box across, sat back and watched. He had a feeling the next few minutes were going to be very important.

Paul cleaned himself up as best he could, stood and zipped up his trousers. 'Right,' he said. He stood for a moment, looking as if he was going to speak, but when he finally did all he said was, 'I'd better be going,' and he reached for his coat. Richard said nothing and made no move. 'I'll call you. Tomorrow. About the Iron business.'

'Right.'

'Right. OK. Tomorrow, then. I'll see myself out.' Paul made

his way to the door and it was only when he was there that he looked back at Richard, who was still on the sofa. 'Thanks,' he said, and then he was gone.

Richard sat, looking at the closed door, hearing the sounds of Paul opening and closing the outside door and walking off. 'Thanks,' he repeated. 'Thanks!'

He pushed himself to his feet. He paced the room. He laughed. He paced some more. '*Thanks!*' he shouted. 'Why do I always get the ones who can't string more than two words together in a sentence?' Wanking Paul off had been even more of a turn-on than he'd expected. Maybe it had been the good looks. Maybe it had been the thrill of jerking off a real policeman. Whatever the cause, Richard found himself literally throbbing with suppressed sexual energy. It was a raging need in his groin that occasional lingering hints of Paul's aftershave did nothing to help. As he stamped around the room like a tiger on heat, he knew that he had to do something about this and it had to be a damn sight more holistic than a video and his own right hand.

Wanking himself now would be like serving up a three-course meal for someone else and eating pot noodle himself.

He turned to the phone. He could call Mike. He hesitated. No, not just yet. Mike was . . . complicated at the moment. (More complicated now than he had been half an hour ago, a small inner voice suggested. Richard ignored it.) No, there was only one answer to the kind of need that was driving him now. Striding to the door, Richard grabbed his leather jacket and headed for the local cruising ground.

It took him less than five minutes to find a pickup in the park used by guys looking for no-strings fun. Wound up as he was, he was in no mood for small talk and was glad to find that the other guy, a young skin sprawled on one of the benches, wasn't either. Within fifteen minutes of leaving, he was back home with his catch, and the skin, who said his name was Baz, was looking around his living room with undisguised amazement. 'Shit! All these books yours?' Throwing off his jacket and tugging at his shirt, Richard nodded. 'You read 'em all?'

'Well, yes.' It had never even occurred to Richard that there might be people who bought books for ornament rather than reading.

'Shit!' The skin turned to him. 'You're not a teacher, are you?'

Richard threw his shirt on the floor and began kicking off his shoes. 'No. No, I'm not.'

The skin seemed vaguely disappointed. 'Shame. I've never been fucked by a teacher,' he said. 'Not even when I was at school.'

Well, thought Richard dryly, I guess that sorts out exactly who's doing what to whom. Alarmed that the lad was showing signs of wanting to inspect his shelves more closely, Richard reached over and without further ceremony began to unbuckle Baz's worn jeans. The skin grinned. 'Yeah, right.' He pulled his T-shirt up over his head and flung it across the room as Richard undid his belt buckle and yanked his jeans down to the floor. He was wearing nothing underneath. 'Ready for action.' Baz grinned.

Without ceremony, Richard took the lad by the shoulders, spun him around and pushed him up against one of his walls. He was already pretty sure that Baz hadn't been out in the park looking for finesse – which was fine by him, right then, as he felt driven way past gentle and sensitive. Sure enough, the skin didn't disappoint him. 'Yeah,' he shouted as Richard pressed him up against the wall. 'Do it. Fuck me. Fuck me hard!'

Richard ran his hands roughly up and down the lad's back. Baz was lean as a whippet. His skin was smooth and pale. He caught hold of Baz's buttocks, kneading them, pulling the cheeks apart. There was a tattoo on one of them, a dragon shooting flame. Richard slapped it hard, the impact like the crack of a small pistol in the confined space of his living room. Baz cried out. 'Shit, yeah! Do it, man! Fucking do it!' Richard slapped his arse again, then again.

Without waiting for lube, he shoved two fingers in and up the skin's hole. Baz yelled out but took it. Richard worked him for long minutes, reaching round and wanking the lengthy rod of Baz's dick with the other. A mingled smell of Baz's sweat and Paul's aftershave filled his nostrils. Feverishly he dragged his fingers out of Baz, ignoring the lad's cry of discomfort, and tugged his own trousers and briefs down, pausing only to pull out the condom and lube in the pockets before flinging them away.

Baz stayed, spread-eagled against the wall, looking round over his shoulder at Richard's cock. 'Come on, then. Stick it in there. Shag me hard. Do it!' To Baz's frenzied encouragement, Richard pulled the condom over the helmet of his pulsing dick. He paused only to smear a token amount of lube quickly over it before turning to Baz and forcing himself right up the guy's arse. Baz howled and beat the wall with both fists. 'Shit! You bastard! Yes! Yes!'

Baz was hot and tight and Richard gave not the slightest thought for the lad's discomfort as he drove hard into him, greedy for his own pleasure. Baz's flat stomach and chest slammed into the wall as Richard fucked him mercilessly, urged on by the skin's own loud cries for harder, faster action. Losing his footing under Richard's frenzied thrusting, Baz slid uncontrollably across the wall and the pair fell to the floor, bringing piles of books and papers crashing down around them, but nothing stopped Richard's urgent pumping or Baz's yells of encouragement. Richard slapped the skin's arse again and Baz's pleasure reached new levels of volume. His muscle-ring clamped down hard on Richard's cock and was repeatedly stretched wide as Richard withdrew and thrust, withdrew and thrust, ramming his swollen dick back and forth over Baz's prostate, shooting pleasure through the skin like sheets of flame.

His orgasm was shattering and Richard made no attempt to hold it back, lost to any thought of waiting for the other man's pleasure, oblivious to anything except the urgent need to shoot hot come deep into this eager, demanding body.

It was another five minutes or so, when Richard began to come back to himself, that his better nature had a chance to resurface, and feelings of guilt at his selfishness began to emerge. He rolled over on the floor to see just what had happened to Baz. He needn't have worried. The skinhead was lying on his back, idly toying with his own nipples, a wide grin plastered across his face. A quick glance made it quite clear that he too had come to a most satisfactory and abundant climax. 'Shit!' Baz said loudly, looking up at the ceiling. He let his head loll to one side so that he could see Richard. 'Thanks,' he said.

Well, the gratitude really is rolling in today, Richard thought.

He'd been a little worried that Baz would want to stay on a while afterwards, maybe even ask him some more about his books, but to his relief the young lad was quite happy to leave after a quick wash and brush-up in the bathroom. 'The day's still young,' he'd said cheerily as Richard had seen him off at the door, and Richard wasn't that surprised to see him heading back out to the park.

Richard took a leisurely shower, then wandered back into the living room with a towel wrapped around him to repair some of the damage his and Baz's enthusiasm had left. It was as he dumped a pile of books on to the sofa that it gave up its very last traces of Paul's aftershave. They hung in the air like a highly stimulating ghost. Richard's cock stirred even now under his towel. 'Oh, hell!' he sighed.

Four

Richard timed his visit to Mike the next day to catch him during his early-morning workout. He knew there wouldn't be many other people in the gym at that time so they would be able to talk without too much interruption. He wasn't ready just yet for anything more private.

He nodded a greeting to Andy, who was manning the front desk. 'Yo, Richard! Still churning out the hack articles?'

'Like a machine. Still cruising nurseries?'

'Like a priest. The big man's over there, working on his tits.'

'Fair enough. He gets on mine often enough.' Andy drew a sharp intake of breath and shook his hands as if suddenly burned. 'Only joking,' Richard said.

'Course you were.' Richard decided that was the point to draw a line under the badinage and made his way across the gym, nodding further hellos to the couple of regulars that he recognised.

Mike was pumping away at the pec deck, pulling the padded levers attached to the weights into his chest as he breathed out, holding them there for a second then releasing them slowly as he breathed in, pulling them back in again the instant before the weights could touch base. The peg fixing the weight was at its highest setting, a target that was just a distant dream to the majority of the men who used that gym but just another warm-up set for Mike. Even so, his concentration, as it always was when he was training, was absolute. He stared directly ahead, eyes not really taking in what was happening in the outside world as he focused inwards.

Richard kept to one side, out of Mike's line of sight, and watched. He liked observing Mike unseen when Mike was working out. It invariably turned him on, though not for the reasons others might have automatically assumed. Even in the loose cotton sweatshirt and baggy training trousers that Mike was wearing that morning, he was a splendid display of sheer male physicality, so absolutely *right* in this gym setting, but that wasn't what was rousing Richard. It was the *focus* Mike exhibited at times like this, the clean-lined simplicity of such moments that struck a chord with something in his own make-up. He knew, even if Mike didn't, that they were both very alike in this respect. Both were capable of a fixity of purpose that they would have described as dedication, although others might have described it as obsession. It was a paradox that had struck him before, that the same quality should point their lives in such different directions, but then maybe if they had been too much alike . . .

There was one other reason Richard could get off on moments like this, a reason a modern, completely out, politically right-on young man like him could only ever admit to privately on rare, secret occasions, and even then he refused to look too closely at what it actually meant. It gave him enormous pleasure to be with Mike in a gym like today, or a club or even just the street, to see the men around them, to see Mike so handsome and physically perfect at his side, and to know that this man, who could be an absolute man-magnet if he wanted to, had chosen him, Richard, as his boyfriend. Not, Richard reminded himself wryly, that men ran screaming in horror from him. Unbidden images of the previous night floated in front of his mind's eye. Baz. And Paul. Mostly Paul.

With the sudden start of someone coming out of a daydream, Richard saw Mike was coming to the end of his set. As he watched, Richard wondered just what scenes were playing inside Mike's head at that moment. Was he thinking of him, of their last less-than-friendly parting two nights ago now? Or was he thinking of Dave Ross? Richard sighed. Who was he kidding? Mike wouldn't be thinking about him or Dave or anyone else. He was at the weights, which meant he would be thinking about only one thing: bodybuilding. Mike had tried to explain to him on a couple of occasions about the mental disciplines of the sport – visualisation, shamanistic technique and the other cornerstones of his training, all of which he'd learned from Dave Ross – but with his limited powers of expression and Richard's even more limited personal experience of physical exercise, they'd never really been able to share what it all meant. Though he'd never said as much, Richard had always blamed Mike for that, but it occurred to him now that, as the one who was supposed to use communication for a living, perhaps more than half the share of blame for that had to be his.

The clank of metal finally hitting metal and the sound of one last whoosh of exhaled breath told him that Mike had finished his set. He stepped forwards. 'Hi.'

Mike blinked, finally caught sight of Richard, and smiled. He clearly hadn't seen Richard come in, but he didn't look surprised to find him there. 'Hi.' He went to get up from the pec deck's seat, but Richard forestalled him by leaning in to give him a quick kiss, then pulling up a bench and sitting down next to him. Mike sat back on the pec deck seat. There was a pause. 'Want to go upstairs?'

For a second, in spite of all his common sense, in spite of all the reasoned arguments he had gone through with himself less than an hour earlier, Richard hesitated. The kiss had been quick but, on top of his covert observation, it had been enough. The thought of Mike's naked body under his training gear and what he could do with it in Mike's bed in the flat above them made him ache with longing. But the time wasn't right yet. 'No, it's OK. I don't want to interrupt your workout.'

The excuse was a poor one but Mike took Richard's message and didn't press the point. 'You all right?' he asked.

'Me? I'm fine. You?'

'Yeah, all right.'

Richard knew he'd say that. Mike could have torn a ligament, twisted a muscle or shattered a bone and he'd most likely have given the same answer. A broken heart too probably would be "all right".

'I've been thinking . . .' They broke off. They had both spoken the same words at the same time. Mike indicated for Richard to go ahead.

'I've been thinking about what you said, about doing something. For Dave.' Richard paused. Mike wrapped a towel around his neck and waited. 'I think there maybe is something we can do.' Quickly and succinctly he filled Mike in about his research on the Internet into Iron.

'OK,' Mike conceded, 'so we know it's out there. I don't really care about that. People want to shoot themselves up with crap, that's down to them. I just want to know who pushed the stuff on to Dave. And he hadn't got a computer, so he wasn't about to get it surfing the Net.'

Irritated by Mike's dismissiveness, Richard nevertheless held back from making the point that he was yet to be convinced that anyone had had to 'push' Dave to take Iron in the first place. 'Look, it's a start, right? I mean, you came up with the idea of doing something. So what have you done?'

Mike told Richard about his trip to Dave's gym the previous day. Richard listened carefully. He was particularly interested in the stranger Mike had chased down the road but was exasperated by the sketchy description Mike gave of him. 'Come on, Mike, that could be one of about fifty million guys. Was there anything else? Any "distinguishing features"?'

'Oh, yeah. He had a missing leg and carried a parrot on his shoulder. What else can you say about someone? Do you want his inside leg measurement?'

'Yeah, well, given another five minutes and I'm sure you could have managed that one.' Richard punctuated the jibe with a quick smile just to show that he was only joking. Given the glasshouse he was living in, it wouldn't do to cast too many stones about the place. 'So what else did you do?'

Mike shrugged his shoulders. 'What else could I? I hung around for a while, talked to a couple of the regulars when they showed up, but they didn't have anything much to say, and I told Roy to give me a call if the guy showed up again.'

'What sort of things were you asking?'

'Whether they'd noticed anything different or odd about Dave.'

'Pretty vague.'

'Well, what was I supposed to ask? I couldn't very well come out and ask if they knew Dave was doing junk and if so could they please tell me who was supplying, could I?'

Richard deliberately moved the conversation on. 'OK. This sharp-dressed runner is obviously significant, but we can't do very much about him at the moment. Maybe when you go back you can ask around a bit more, see if anyone else knows him. Or can at least give a fuller description.'

'I'm going back?'

'Aren't you?'

Mike shrugged. 'Looks like it.'

Richard continued. 'Putting him to one side for the moment, from what you've said it doesn't look as if the Iron was coming to Dave through anyone at the gym, and you say he didn't have Internet access. So what else is left?'

'Practically nothing. The gym was Dave's life.'

'What about pubs and clubs? Was he out on the scene much?'

'No.' Mike hesitated, frustrated to again find himself coming up against the fact that the habits of the man he'd known were the habits of a man he hadn't lived with for years. People change. That was becoming his new mantra. He didn't like it much. 'He didn't used to be,' he amended. 'Not much. Anyway, that's not the best place to go if you want gym junk.'

'I know that,' Richard said patiently, 'but what we're doing here is following whatever leads we can. We haven't got a lot to go on.' He stopped and laughed. 'Listen to me. I'm starting to quote American gangster movies.'

'That's not such a bad thing. The good guys always catch the bad guys in those.'

'Yeah, well, that's in the cinema. In real life, it's a bit harder to tell the good guys and the bad guys apart.' Richard pushed on, afraid he'd begun to sound too heavy. 'So what we do is work with what little we have, because –' and here he adopted a plummy, affected voice, '– "Once you have eliminated the impossible, whatever remains, no matter how improbable, must be true".'

'Thank you, Sherlock Holmes.'

Richard gave a mock bow, mildly miffed that Mike had recognised his quotation. 'So, you go back to the gym, and . . . It is still opening, I take it?'

'Yeah. Roy's keeping it going for as long as he can. I don't know what's going to happen to it in the long run.'

An interesting possibility immediately occurred to Richard, but this didn't seem the right moment to suggest it to Mike. 'All right, so when you go back, as well as asking about the Mystery Runner, you also try to find out if Dave's been on the scene lately, and if so where, especially if he's been going anywhere different.' His voice changed again, this time to mock American. "It's a million-to-one chance, but it might just work." '

Mike nodded glumly. 'OK. It's a good idea. I should have thought of it.'

Richard winced. 'You would have,' he said. 'I mean, I hadn't actually thought about your going to Dave's gym in the first place. In fact –'

'Don't patronise me, Rich.'

Richard's flood of reassurance dried up. 'I wasn't,' he said lamely.

Mike looked down at the floor, but his words carried to Richard with a quiet intensity. 'We both know you're more clever than me. I just wish you wouldn't rub it in, now and again.'

Richard flushed angrily. 'Maybe it's because you've reminded me how far I fall short of your physical ideal,' he snapped.

'What's that supposed to mean?'

'It means I suppose you were letting Dave screw you because his post-fuck conversation was better than mine.' And that, he realised with surprise, had struck much closer to the root of his pain over Mike's infidelity with Dave than anything else they'd yet said to each other.

He remembered how, when he and Mike had first found themselves drawing close to each other, he'd found it hard to accept that a man who devoted so much of his life to achieving perfection of body could even begin to be turned on by someone whose chest and waist measurements were not that dissimilar and whose idea of a workout was a brisk walk to the local kebab shop. As the weeks and months had passed, however, and the undeniable attraction between them had become rooted and grown, Richard had been forced to believe that their apparent mismatch could actually work. He'd even come to think that their differences were not only attractive to each other but complementary. Now he wondered whether he'd just been fooling himself all along.

'I'm sorry,' Mike said.

For what? Richard thought. For snapping at me just now? For not telling me you were still sleeping with your ex? For making me feel like the guy who was always having sand kicked in his face in those old comic Charles Atlas adverts? We need to talk about this. We need to sort it out now, not let it fester until it's out of control. And he knew they couldn't. Not yet. 'Yeah, me too,' he replied. He forced a laugh. 'We're a team, right? Mind and body in perfect harmony.'

'A team, yeah. Like Batman and Robin?'

Richard coughed. 'Maybe more like Morecambe and Wise,' he suggested with a weak smile. Mike smiled back and the difficult moment was passed, for now. Dave's death had put a wedge between them. Richard wondered now whether this joint investigation of theirs into that death might, ironically, be a way of bringing them back together. Or would constantly dwelling on the matter inevitably force them apart forever?

'So,' Mike said with determined decisiveness, 'while I'm doing all this undercover leg work, what exactly are you going to be doing?'

Richard took a deep breath. This part he'd anticipated as being difficult. 'Me? I'm going to order us a batch of Iron.'

'What?'

'Well, in fact, I already have.'

'What?'

Richard took a deeper breath. 'OK, *you* have.'

Mike opened his mouth, realised there was only another 'what' waiting and closed it again. 'Explain this one to me,' he said finally. 'Slowly.'

Richard explained to him about the Fellowship of Iron website – in particular, about how it was possible to 'order' supplies of the drug via the computer. 'They're not going to send it to people through the post, though. That's generally not a good idea when you're dealing with an illegal drug. The website is for setting up personal contacts, and when those have been established and they're happy their customers are genuine, then they open up the supply of the steroid.'

'I'm still waiting to see why it is it's my name that's been tacked on to this deal.'

Richard tapped himself on the chest and then pointed to Mike. 'Mind and body, remember. Chances are that anyone getting a close look at me is going to suss out that I'm not a hard-core bodybuilder looking for the latest wonder drug to give him that competitive edge. I'll take your silence for complete agreement. So what we need is someone who looks the part, has the credentials and has reason enough to let me use his name. Funnily enough, I thought of you.'

Mike nodded reluctantly. 'All right. Use my name,' he said quietly. 'If –' and his attitude became more challenging '– you can just explain to me two small problems that I can see and you seem to have overlooked.'

'Shoot.'

'Firstly, what the hell are we going to do when these drug barons start answering your e-mails? Secondly, and more likely, what are we going to do if the people at the other end turn out to be the police? Do we really want another visit from our friend Inspector Taylor? Do you think he'll believe us if we tell him it was all for a good cause and we were going to give it all back afterwards, honest?'

Richard braced himself. Now they had come to the one detail of the scheme he'd avoided mentioning until he absolutely had to. 'Actually,' he said, 'I have the answers to both your questions. In fact, they're the same.' And he proceeded to tell Mike about Paul Ferris's involvement in their plans.

Mike listened expressionlessly. 'Right,' he said softly, at the end. 'So when did the two of you cook all this up then?'

'Sergeant Ferris came to see me not long after he and Inspector Grisly of the Yard had spoken to us here.'

'And you worked all this out then?'

'No. I didn't get round to searching the websites until the next morning, and then I gave Sergeant Ferris a call at the police station.'

'And you went round there and thrashed it out?'

Richard tried not to make it obvious he could see where Mike's relentless questioning was leading. 'No. He came round to my flat again.'

'Right.' Mike nodded slowly. 'You never did like policemen. At least, you never used to.'

'Yeah, well,' Richard said, 'they're not all the same, I guess.' And then he wished he hadn't said that.

Mike continued nodding slowly as he rose to his feet and unwound the towel from around his neck. 'Well, I suppose I'd better get on with my workout, then. You never know when a gang of Mafia drug bosses might come round to check out my form.'

Richard rose, too. 'No probs,' he said, his accent this time, for no very good reason, pure early evening Australian soap.

'I'll go round Dave's gym again later today. I'll let you know if I pick anything up.'

'Great.'

The two of them stood awkwardly looking at each other. 'Right.' Mike turned to the free weights. 'See you later?'

'Course.' Richard hesitated, looking for that moment when one or the other of them would make a move towards a farewell kiss. It didn't happen. The moment passed.

As he was making his way back to the exit, Mike called out to him. 'I forgot to tell you. Dave's funeral. It's the day after tomorrow. Will you . . . can you come?'

'Of course.'

Mike turned back to his workout and Richard slowly left the gym. They'd exchanged a lot of heated words during that conversation, begun to probe some tender wounds. None of it had hurt

71

as much as that last question, that uncertainty in Mike's voice when he had asked if Richard would support him during what was bound to be a painful experience. Such things should be assumed between partners. Up until only a matter of days ago they had been.

So now he'd gone and done it. Really done it.

Paul Ferris's body sat behind the wheel of his car but his mind was a long way away, and it was only years of driving experience and advanced driver police training that kept him from becoming just another messy statistic on that day's accident report sheet.

There'd been other encounters in the past, but very few, each very brief, and all now a long time ago: furtive glances in the school changing rooms; a spot of rough and tumble with a mate at college that might, just might, have turned into something serious if either one of them had had the courage to say just one word; meaningful looks; loaded, drunken conversations. Just a phase, he'd told himself, all just a phase. And by the time he knew for certain that it wasn't, he was in the force, and 'coming out' went just as far as driving to a city several miles away once a month and stocking up on mucky videos. Until yesterday.

So what was so different? Why did he feel like the Paul Ferris who'd got up, washed, dressed, gone to work today was nothing like the Paul Ferris who'd done exactly the same thing the day before, and all the days before that? He'd been wanked off by a guy. Someone else's hand on his cock instead of his own. Not so very different, really.

So why was nothing the same?

He'd thought about calling in sick that morning. Only an obstinate pride in a hundred per cent attendance record had got him out of the house. On arrival, he was pleased to find that Inspector Taylor had some 'courier work' lined up for him that would keep him out of the station all day. It was pretty low-level stuff, more suited to one of the station uniforms than to him, and it meant the paperwork would pile up on his desk while he was out chasing up and down the county. He suspected it was either a punishment or a warning from Taylor connected with their last discussion, but as things turned out it was the best thing that could have happened. It gave him time to think. Now, if he could just make sense of what he was thinking.

The sudden angry blare of a car horn shocked him back to reality. He'd been stationary at a set of traffic lights and so far gone in his thoughts he hadn't noticed them cycle from red through to green and back to red again. The man in the van behind had noticed and didn't mind letting Paul know. When the lights changed back to green, the van revved itself up and tore past Paul, its driver shouting and gesticulating. You, mate, do not know how lucky you are, Paul thought. On any other day he'd have been nicked well and proper. The incident had, however, been a warning. He'd been driving too long without a break and in his present state of mind that could be dangerous. Paul took the first turning off the main road that he could, pulled in to the kerb and switched the engine off.

For a while he just sat there, oblivious to his surroundings as the events of the past few days whirled round and round in his head. What he really needed, he decided, was some fresh air. He climbed out of the car and sat on the bonnet, looking around. He found himself in some typical, anonymous suburban side road: a few rather stunted trees planted at wide intervals, small detacheds and semi-detacheds along either side with a newsagent and launderette on a distant corner. As he looked about, wondering vaguely where he was and in which direction he should head for his next port of call, his eye was drawn to something else.

Across the road and some five yards along, some minor road work was going on. The pavement was being dug up and battered wooden barriers provided a temporary by-pass into the road for pedestrians. By the side of the already sizeable hole in the ground was one of those small, striped tents road workers used to keep their equipment in. They'd always fascinated Paul as a kid. To this day he remembered being open-mouthed with amazement as he'd watched a stream of men with shovels and picks over their shoulders emerge from one. It had to be so much bigger on the inside than on the outside. It had been years before the literally more down to earth explanation of a manhole within that tent had been explained to him. Paul stood and smiled to himself at the memory. The kid he'd been was further away now than he'd ever been, in so many ways. The tent opened. It was only one man this time, not a procession, but Paul suddenly found his imagination being stimulated even more than it had been as a boy all those years ago.

The guy had to be on a break. He came out of the tent arching his back and stretching his arms wide, presumably working out some of the kinks caused by strenuous work with a pickaxe or spade. He sauntered across to one of the hedges fronting a well-kept garden of a well-kept semi-detached and leaned back against it, arms thrown out as if he owned it, not giving a damn about any damage to the privet his weight might be causing. He was stripped from the waist up, except for one of those luminous yellow plastic waistcoats all road workers were obliged to wear, and as Paul watched he tore open the Velcro fastenings down the front and threw it to one side on the hedge, sprawling back to let the warm sunshine caress his skin. Even from across the road Paul could see how the sweat on the man's chest was carrying away the layer of concrete dust from the shattered pavement, see the honeyed colour of the skin underneath, richly tanned by day-to-day exposure to the sun on roads and building sites. He could even make out, or thought he could make out, a single rivulet of sweat tracing its way slowly down the stomach to the thick waistband of the heavy canvas work trousers.

Some sudden, subconscious alarm dragged Paul from his day-dream of just where the line of sweat was heading and made him look up. He was mortified to see the road worker was looking straight back at him. Shit! This digger was going to think he was cruising him! Abruptly Paul turned his head and stared intently in another direction. Worried that that was too obviously fake, he furrowed his forehead and turned to the other direction as if he was scanning the horizon for someone or something in particular and had only happened to take in the other man by mistake.

All right, he told himself. Count to ten and then have another look. If he's turned away, it's cool. If he hasn't . . . Paul pushed his hand into his pocket and took hold of his car keys, then he casually turned his head so he was again facing the hedge and the basking roadie. He froze. The guy was still looking back at him. He knew! Time to get right out of there before the situation developed into an ugly scene. Paul pulled the keys out of his pocket and then stopped. He'd finally noticed something he'd been too spooked to take in properly before. The man was smiling.

As Paul watched, the road worker shrugged his shoulders. They were broad and powerful, built up by years of swinging heavy hammers and the like rather than being pumped up in a gym. Paul found he liked that. It came across as refreshingly honest by comparison with the gym-sculpted specimens his work had brought him into contact with lately. Slowly, the road worker brought his right hand across to his waist and smoothed it across the wide leather belt of his work trousers. Without pausing, he then moved it down until it came to rest on the zipped ridge covering his crotch and, as Paul watched, in the bright afternoon sunshine, right out in the open, on a suburban street lined by lace-curtained semis, the man moved his hand slowly, deliberately and unmistakably up and down the thick seam at the front of his jeans.

His smile broadened and he nodded at Paul. He looked like he was indicating something, but for a second, his brain still reeling from the sight of a slab of rough miming wanking himself on a public highway, Paul didn't cotton on to what it was. It seemed to be . . . With a hot stab of embarrassment Paul suddenly understood: the hand with which he'd gone for his car keys was back in his pocket. In, out, in again . . . The guy across the road thought Paul was wanking himself, too! In fact, he probably thought Paul had started it!

Paul yanked his hand out of his pocket, and then promptly wished he hadn't. Now he just looked like a prat. Besides, if he had left it in there, then maybe he could have done something about the healthy erection that was building in his boxers. The road worker continued to smile lazily and to rub his hand up and down his crotch. His head now was at an angle, questioning. Inviting.

So what to do? Paul knew what he would have done until very recently. He would have got in his car and driven away. Now, though? Now, as he'd been telling himself, things were different. *He* was different. As nonchalantly as he could, Paul pushed himself up from the side of his car, looked casually to left and right to see that there were no cars coming (and that there was nobody else nearby he might possibly know) and walked slowly over to the grinning roadman. He attempted a confident saunter but, with his heart hammering away in his chest and the whole of his attention focused on the man he was approaching, he had no idea if he succeeded. After a road crossing that seemed to last forever, he was standing in front of the guy, so close he could reach out to touch him. The road worker didn't move an inch from his reclined position on the hedge. His massaging hand didn't miss a beat.

Paul cleared his dry throat. 'Hi,' he said.

The other man nodded in acknowledgement. 'Hi.'

This close to, Paul could see that he was chewing gum.

'Hi.' Early thirties, Paul thought, perhaps a bit younger. Hard to tell with a face weathered by outdoor work and streaked with dust. The unwavering eyes were dark but the hair was light, thinning slightly. On the cast-off plastic jerkin there was a word in simple black letters: GUY. Paul decided that was what he'd call the man, even though for all he knew this was just one waistcoat out of identical millions, and there was an accompanying set labelled GAL.

Guy unhurriedly looked Paul up and down, chewing away at his gum, kneading away at his dick, making no attempt to disguise the fact that he was openly weighing Paul up. Paul stood there in the street and took the man's inspection, for his part noting the curls of light hair across Guy's chest and in one patch round his navel, how his honey-coloured skin looked warm to the touch, and how much the man's arrogance and presumption was turning him on. Too late, Paul saw how he'd made his own interest all too obvious. What would he do now if this supremely self-confident stud judged him and found him wanting – told him, in short, to sling his hook? He suddenly felt very foolish in his clean shirt, tie and neatly pressed trousers. What would this man take him for? A bank clerk? An accountant? What interest could a rough guy like this have in a man like that?

Inspection completed, Guy looked him in the eyes again and

jerked his head in the direction of the small striped work tent set up across the pavement. 'Wanna go inside?'

Not trusting himself to speak and not sound stupid, Paul nodded and stepped forwards. Guy held open the flap of the small tent and, with a mock flourish, ushered Paul inside.

One childhood fantasy died instantly: the tent wasn't larger inside than out. There was barely enough room for the two of them to stand facing each other. In one corner were propped a couple of spades and a pick, in the other a small Calor gas stove, a tin kettle and a couple of mugs. There was the smell of earth and of sunlight on canvas.

Guy drew the flaps of the tent together, loosely knotting a couple of the strings that were all that kept it closed and them safe from prying eyes. Paul wished that he'd tied more of them more tightly. He turned to Paul, undid the stout leather belt round his waist without hesitation, pulled down the chunky zip and let his trousers fall to the ground. His briefs were brief indeed, little more than a hammock for his heavy ball sac, his meaty cock thrusting up out of them, stiff and eager. He carried on chewing and watched and waited. Unable to take his eyes off Guy's magnificent member, surprised to find his mouth literally watering, Paul followed his lead and dropped his trousers.

Without ceremony, Guy pulled Paul's white cotton boxers down. Paul was hard and proud already and he rapidly stiffened still further after the release from his underwear and under the labourer's naked inspection. Paul might have been worried that his appearance earlier would have put Guy off, but he knew that when the trousers were down there wasn't anyone who could complain about the quantity and quality of his dick. He slipped both hands under the thin cotton on either side of Guy's briefs and pushed, easing the briefs down his legs, thrilling to the sensation of the hairy thighs under his palms. To keep in contact with Guy's skin he had to kneel, so that by the time Guy's underwear was round his boots Paul was kneeling, Guy's jutting cock less than an inch from his face. He wanted to lick it, to draw his tongue slowly along the length of its veined solidity, from the base of the ball sac to the ridge of the head and the exquisite sensitivity of the shiny skin at the tip. And then he wanted Guy to do the same, and more, to take his dick deep into his mouth, into his throat, to press his tongue into Paul's shaft and suck him hard, suck him until the come came gouting out uncontrollably. Shakily, a little scared by the strength of these unfamiliar urges, Paul rose to his feet.

Guy seized Paul's cock without words and started to wank him. Paul gasped at the sudden fierce push and pull. This wasn't Richard's skilled, gentle teasing, but its effect was just as undeniable. Guy's broad hand was callused, his grip unremitting, his rhythm urgent and swift and Paul's dick responded eagerly, hot pre-come lubricating the foreskin as Guy pumped the shaft, working it mercilessly back and forth. The questioning Paul had been torturing himself with in the car earlier evaporated like steam. *This* was what was different about his life now. Before Richard, he hadn't really known what he was missing, but now he did and he wanted more.

'Hey.' Unaware that he'd closed his eyes in his pleasure, Paul opened them again. The road worker was still pumping away at Paul's dick with one hand but with the other he was pointing at his own proud member. 'OK?'

'Yeah. Sorry.' Hurriedly, Paul grasped Guy's dick in his right hand. It was already slick from the man's arousal. Paul was amazed by its heat in the palm of his hand. He steadied himself by placing his free hand on Guy's shoulder, feeling the muscles there flexing in time to the man's relentless pumping; then he too began to wank the road worker off. The two men quickly adjusted to each other's position and rhythm. This was no gentle seduction and exploration. It was a mad rush to climax with each man pushing the other as hard and as fast as he could. As they careered closer and closer to orgasm, they leaned in to each other, heads lowering until they were pushing at one another like players in the front row of a rugby scrum, neither slackening the frenzied speed of their shaftwork.

'You OK in there?'

There was a sudden movement at the tent flap, a shadow on the canvas and the sound of someone attempting to enter and then finding the straps done up. Paul twisted in its direction and nearly lost his footing. Shit! He was about to be exposed, literally, with his hand on another man's dick. In the street, for fuck's sake! He went to release the navvy, but the workman only clamped on to his dick even tighter with his large fist, clapping his other hand across Paul's mouth to stifle the gasp at the painful and pleasurable intensity of the vicelike grip. Paul wasn't going anywhere.

'Yeah,' the road worker said.

There was a pause. 'So, you ready to get back down to work, then?'

'Nah.'

When the man outside spoke again, it was in a voice heavy with understanding. 'So, d'you want me to go round the shops again? D'you want some more gum?'

The labourer grinned into Paul's eyes, all that was visible of his face over the wide span of his hand. 'Yeah,' he said. He hadn't stopped pumping Paul's cock for a second.

'OK. Back in ten.' The shadow retreated and footsteps faded away.

Relief flooded Paul's body. He expected Guy to take his hand away from his mouth now but he didn't. He pushed harder into Paul's face, forcing his head back, pressing the flesh of his rough palm into the policeman's mouth until Paul could taste the mingled sweat and earth there, feel the coarsened skin on his tongue, while at the same time he drove into Paul's crotch with redoubled vigour.

And Paul loved it.

The near discovery had shot an adrenaline rush through his system that went straight to his dick. From outside the tent he could hear the sounds of the town, cars passing by, people walking along the pavement, one or two even using the diversions around the tent in which the two men were heatedly jerking each other off, passing within inches of them. The danger of discovery was electrifying! From a secret self-abuser in front of videos at home to doing it in the streets with a bit of rough. Yes, things had changed, all right!

When he came, he didn't hold back anything, his cries of pleasure safely muffled by Guy's broad hand. For his part, Guy clamped down on his gum at the point of climax, grunting primally and rolling his head on his shoulders as his come sprayed into the air and fell heavily to the ground.

The entire episode was all over in less than five minutes.

Paul wiped himself down quickly with a handkerchief. He wondered whether it would be etiquette to offer the sodden silk square to Guy when he'd finished, but by the time he'd drawn his trousers back up, tucked in his shirt and made some effort to restore his tie the workman already had his trousers back on and was undoing the flaps of the tent. He stepped out. Paul followed, blinking in the open sunshine, and looking around swiftly to see if anyone was noticing the sight of such a well-dressed figure emerging from such an unlikely place. But there was no one there.

Guy faced Paul. He was holding something out. 'Gum?' the workman said.

Paul shook his head at the foil-wrapped offering. 'No,' he said. 'Thanks. Bye.'

The workman nodded. 'Bye.' He went back into the tent. A ten year old lad was walking by, regarding the tent with a quizzical expression. Paul couldn't help himself. 'It's bigger inside than out,' he said. The boy nodded and kept walking.

As Paul drove away in his car, he looked back once. He could see the shadow of the workman who had gone back inside as he bent down, presumably to pick up one of the spades.

With a sudden shriek of brakes, Paul stopped the car as a horrifying thought struck him. If he could see Guy's silhouette now, then that meant . . . He gunned the motor and roared away. If any smart-alec bobby on the beat tried to cop him for speeding now he'd pull rank and swear he was on important police business. He just wanted to put as much distance between this spot and himself as he could.

Half an hour later, when his pulse rate had settled down to something approaching normal again, Paul laughed at himself and his reaction. Chalk it up for experience, he thought. More famous people than him had been caught out by sunlight shining through thin material at the most inopportune of moments. Maybe one day it would even make an amusing after-dinner story. 'Yeah, right,' he said out loud. Like who was he going to tell something like this to?

Richard. That was the only person it was even slightly conceivable he could share something like this with. And even that was hardly likely.

Two men. He'd been with two men in two days. Both essentially had done the same thing to him. Why did the experiences seem so very different? With a shamed realisation, Paul had to admit to himself one important difference: at least he'd wanked off Guy. After Richard had pulled him off, he'd walked out. OK, so maybe he had been a bit overwhelmed. That couldn't have been much relief to Richard, though, could it? So why hadn't he asked? Even monosyllabic Guy had managed that. He could have just pointed, as Guy had done, and Paul would have done it. Wouldn't he? But then Richard wasn't Guy, was he? Paul knew he was never going to see Guy again, and that was fine with him. But he was going to be working with Richard. And he knew that he was looking forward to that.

It struck Mike as he was sitting in the pew of the chapel waiting for the service to begin. Everything he knew about funerals he'd learned from television. He had never actually been to a real life one (if that was a proper way to describe such an occasion) until now. Now he was here, he strongly wished he could be at home watching television.

Dave had made his funeral arrangements a long time ago. It hadn't been morbidity, just something he'd believed that 'single' guys should do so that when the time came they could go out with a bit of dignity without being a burden to anyone. Mike liked that idea. It was one more thing that he fully intended to get round to doing. Some time.

Today, though, he was sitting in a chapel he'd never been to before, listening to a vicar who'd never really known Dave tell them all what a great guy he was. He kept calling him 'David' and talked slowly and carefully about 'David's bodybuilding' as if it was just another hobby. If he'd noted that there was only one woman among the mourners, he didn't refer to it.

Recognising very little of the man he'd once known so

intimately in the vicar's words, Mike couldn't help his attention wandering. He twisted in the pew to look around. Richard and Roy were sitting with him at the front. There were about thirty or so other mourners behind them. Richard had read him a poem once – a long time ago now, it seemed – about an Irish wake, which had shown how moments of great sadness were often never more than a heartbeat away from moments of laughter. That was true here, Mike saw, taking in the sight of so many large men, patently uncomfortable in unfamiliar suits and ties, with collars not designed for the bull-like necks of bodybuilders, and jackets not made for chests modelled on barrels. Dave would have appreciated the joke, he thought. Perhaps when he arranged his own send-off he'd stipulate that mourners should all wear gym vests and cut-off shorts. Or maybe he'd insist they all came naked. It could be fun looking down from above at loads of well-built guys trying to look sad with massive hard-ons.

'Who's the old girl?' he hissed to Richard.

With the automatic reflexes of a reporter, Richard had already begun to find out the biographies of anyone there he didn't already know. 'Local newsagent,' he hissed back. 'Dave got his bodybuilding mags from her. She said he was such a sweet man and what a pity it was he never married. You all right?'

'Yeah.'

Richard sighed. Of course he was. Of course Mike wouldn't admit to feeling anything else. He opened his hymn book to the hymn the vicar said and held it out for Mike to share as they stood up to sing.

Am I all right? Mike thought, as he mouthed the words of the hymn. Truth was, he didn't know. That odd moment of gallows humour aside, he just felt empty and numb. He'd wondered in a detached way whether or not he'd cry. He saw no shame in it. He had cried that first night when he'd finally been on his own. But he knew he wasn't going to cry today. That wasn't Dave being talked about by the man at the lectern. That wasn't Dave in the coffin on the bier. It all seemed unreal. There was one thing that was still real, though: the anger that smouldered inside for whoever it was who'd done this. He held on to that, shielding it like a banked-down fire for when he would need it. Richard took the hymn book back and indicated to him that they should sit again.

As the words of the final prayer died away and the priest gave them a few minutes in which to privately say goodbye to Dave, Mike felt a hand take hold of his. It was Roy. The older man grasped his hand tightly, and as the curtains at the back of the chapel opened and the conveyor system drew the coffin out of sight, Roy's grip tightened until it was painful, though his face remained as expressionless as it probably had when he'd faced up to his opponents in the ring. Mike didn't look at him, but kept hold of his hand until the service was finally over.

The mourners trooped away into the nearby Garden of Remembrance. In accordance with his wishes, Dave was to be cremated, and his ashes scattered here. His name would be written in the book that was on permanent display there and Mike had paid for a plaque with Dave's name and dates on to be put up on a wall there for those wishing a more lasting monument.

'There should have been more people,' he said dully to Richard as they joined the others looking through the wreaths and messages attached to them. 'Dave helped scores of guys get on, hundreds. They should all have come.'

Richard glanced round at the mourners. He'd thought for a man with no immediate family it had been a quietly impressive turn-out. He didn't think he could expect so many when his time came. 'Yeah, well,' he said. 'You know bodybuilders. They spend all their lives working at changing something, making it just what they want it to be. Then, when they're faced with something they can't change, well, some of them just aren't good at dealing with it.'

Mike took the specific message behind the sweeping point. 'You are so full of crap sometimes.'

Richard nodded and smiled sadly. 'Yeah. I know.' He put his arm around Mike's waist. 'But the important people came.'

The plan was to spend a few minutes there in the garden before heading back to Dave's gym where Roy had laid on sandwiches and drinks. 'Low-fat cottage cheese on rice cake with mineral water all round, I suppose,' Richard had said with a shudder when Mike had told him – and, given the high percentage of

competitive bodybuilders who'd be there, Mike had been forced
to admit he was probably right.

Richard drew him into a shaded alcove and sat down next to
him on a rustic bench. 'So is there anyone here you don't
recognise?'

From a few feet away, the voice of Dave's lady newsagent
friend drifted across to them. 'He'd have made a lovely father,'
she was saying to Roy.

'Apart from her, no. Why?'

'It could be that someone here is the link to the Iron.'

'At his funeral?'

'Yes, at his funeral. Look, first drug contacts are quite often
made through close friends and family. And it had to be someone
Dave had had contact with recently, so who else is more likely to
turn up here today? Besides –' Richard looked away as he
continued to talk '– whoever gave him the stuff could well be
carrying a lot of guilt. Coming here might be a way of saying
sorry.'

'Or of laughing at us.'

Richard blinked, startled by the sudden bitterness in Mike's
voice. 'That seems a bit strong.'

'Hey, I can play the amateur psychologist as well as you. Aren't
criminals supposed to enjoy returning to the scene of the crime to
admire their handiwork?'

'This is hardly the scene of the crime.'

'Next best thing, and anyway I . . .' Mike trailed off.

Richard regarded him anxiously. 'What is it, Mike?'

'I'm . . . not . . . sure. I thought . . .'

'Mike!' Richard called out after his boyfriend who suddenly,
inexplicably, launched himself from the bench they were sharing
and dashed across the Garden to a point on the far side. The
motherly newsagent was pushed quickly to one side. The vicar
who had come out to join them for a few final words found
himself in Mike's path and was only saved by a display of
commendable agility in jumping out of the way. Richard ran after
Mike, apologising to the victims he left behind him and trying to
undo some of the damage. He finally caught up with Mike at the
gates of the crematorium. The bodybuilder was breathing heavily

and staring down the road. The faint scent of exhaust fumes in the air told Richard that a car had only just driven off. 'What,' he panted, 'what the hell was that about?'

Mike continued to stare out along the empty road. At his sides both his hands were curled into fists. 'It was him, Rich. The guy from Dave's gym.'

'Are you sure?'

'Same car.'

'Did you get a number?'

'What good would that do?'

'I thought maybe we could get Paul to –'

'Oh, yeah, Paul. I forgot about Paul.' Mike turned back from the road and began to trudge up the path back to the Garden. 'No, I didn't get a number.'

Richard followed behind. 'So what did he look like? I mean, what was his expression? Was he laughing or crying?'

Mike shook his head. 'He was too far away again. I couldn't tell.' He stopped so abruptly that Richard nearly ran into him. 'But he was running away, so that means he's got something to hide. So whether he was laughing or crying today, I know what he's going to be doing when I finally get my hands on him.'

Five

    'L o, the merry wanderer returns!'
        'And lo, the merry wanderer leaves, in just under five
minutes – so make the most of me while you can.'
    'Honey, how long have I been waiting for you to say that to
me?'
    Richard rolled his eyes and dumped the manila folder he was
carrying on the desk of the man leaning back in his chair and
rubbing his hands with mock anticipation. 'Well, for foreplay,
Harry, you can start by sorting your way through this little lot.
Three corrected proofs, the rewrite of the cottaging piece, an
outline for a new serial and the notes I've put together for that
interview you thought would be such a good idea. I'll be waiting
for you afterwards if you've still got the energy. Try not to get
the pages sticky.'
    'Darling, you just wear me out. Where is a boy to find the
energy?'
    'Eat plenty of meat, Harry.'
    'I try, Dicky boy. I try.'
    Richard had been working for *Far Out!* since its launch just
over a year ago. His occasional pieces in the national gay press
had drawn him to the attention of Gerry Rayne, a fellow gay
journalist with the ambition to launch a gay paper that was more
than just a collection of pin ups and reviews of 'the scene', and

that also recognised there was gay life outside London. Gerry had drive and he had vision, but more important to the start of their project he also had money, a nest-egg he had scraped together working as Showbiz editor on one of the nationals.

Richard had been flattered and excited to be headhunted by Gerry, a man whose interests and ambitions so closely chimed with his own, even though Gerry had made it clear that *Far Out!* was starting small, and wasn't going to be keeping either of them in the lap of luxury for a very long time – but if Richard wanted to come along for the ride he could promise variety, flexibility and a great deal of job satisfaction. Richard had accepted immediately, and hadn't regretted it since. *Far Out!* had made a solid start and over six months had established enough of a readership base that they'd felt able to increase the editorial staff by one third, that third being the rather portly figure of Harry Collins.

'He may act a little . . . flamboyantly,' Gerry had told Richard, 'but believe me, he's a donkey.'

As Gerry had been blissfully monogamous with his partner James for over fifteen years, Richard assumed he was referring to Harry's capacity for hard work, rather than any physical attributes.

Richard leaned over Harry's desk and helped himself to one of the biscuits Harry kept in his ever-present barrel. 'Gerry in?'

Harry leaned back still further and pursed his lips. 'Oh, yes.'

Something was up, Richard could tell. Harry always pursed his lips like that when he knew something that others did not. Richard could also tell that Harry was dying to tell him. All the more reason, Richard decided, not to ask him. 'Shame you didn't get my messages,' Harry said, as Richard chewed slowly on his biscuit.

'I really must get that machine of mine fixed.'

'Try asking the engineer to plug it in.'

Richard wagged a finger at him. 'Waspish, Harry. Waspish.'

'If you had,' Harry continued, attempting to stand on his dignity and look smug at the same time, 'then you'd know who we have with us at the moment.'

Richard glanced across the small room to the door of the even smaller room Gerry used as his office. Blu-tacked to it, on a small card that Richard himself had printed out, were the words, THE BUCK. Richard sighed. 'OK, who?'

'You'll be surprised,' Harry trilled.

Richard was spared more of Harry's irritating teasing by the opening of Gerry's door and the emergence of the editor himself and another man. 'Greetings, leader,' he proclaimed.

'Ah, Richard. So how was Australia?' The joke was a dry one. Gerry was a seasoned pro who understood there were many different ways to get the best out of your staff. He recognised that Richard was not an office animal like Harry, that he produced his best work when he had freedom to move both physically and intellectually – and as long as he met his deadlines, which he invariably did, then Gerry let him do that. He was honest and intelligent enough to know that it was largely Richard's writing that was starting to earn *Far Out!* its good reputation. Of course, he was also businessman enough to know that it paid to keep Richard on his toes now and again.

Richard winced. 'Didn't have time to look. I was too busy slaving over my word processor.' And he repeated the inventory of the work he'd just left on Harry's desk.

Gerry nodded, looking pleased – and, Richard thought, possibly a bit relieved. 'Well, I suppose it's good luck that you have decided to drop in today. If you hadn't come in, I'd have had to phone you, and I understand your answering machine's been acting up lately.' There was a snort from Harry's direction. He stepped to one side to let the man standing behind him come forward. 'Richard Green, this is Mr Lancaster.'

Lancaster took Richard's hand. 'Devlin,' he said. His handshake was extremely firm. He was probably in his late twenties, Richard thought, although it was hard to tell. His appearance was definitely youthful, his skin tanned and healthy, his hair dark, full and glossy, with not a strand out of place. It was the precision of his grooming, the tasteful but obvious expense of his suit that suggested he might possibly be older. There could be no doubt however about his looks. In the cramped outer office of *Far Out!* magazine, by the side of the rumpled Gerry, the colourful but tasteless Harry and his own 'careless' look, Richard was forced to admit that this man looked good – very good indeed. Richard wondered how unfair he was being to suspect that Lancaster probably knew it.

'Mr Lancaster, Devlin, is entering the publishing business.' Richard thought the man looked more like a model than any publisher he'd ever come across, but he said nothing. Apart from anything else, he was aware of a breathless excitement in Gerry that the senior newsman was trying to keep under control. They'd worked closely for the past year or so. Richard knew it took a great deal to get Gerry as worked up as he was today. Sure enough, Gerry wasn't able to keep his news to himself. 'And he's interested –' Devlin gave him a meaningful look '– very interested in *Far Out!* magazine.'

Now Richard understood Gerry's excitement. *Far Out!* was doing well. They were making a market for themselves and winning some critical acclaim, but in financial terms they were still only just about breaking even. An injection of money, from the right source with no strings attached, was something they had only so far been able to talk about longingly in the pub after each week's issue had been put to bed. If Gerry had actually found such a source in this man . . .

'There's more I'd like to talk about with you yet, Gerry,' Devlin said, 'but I think I can say we both have something to offer the other.' Ordinarily, Richard's hackles would have arisen at the vague pomposity of Devlin's 'business speak', but there was something about the way the man delivered it, a certain self-conscious irony, that made him ready to forgive him. Or maybe it was just the flash of perfect teeth in his smile when he spoke. 'Perhaps we could do lunch?'

Gerry's face fell. 'I'm afraid I have a previous appointment.' Harry pulled a sour face for Richard. They both knew what the 'previous appointment' was. Gerry and his partner James were still very much in love, but if Gerry missed a lunch with him, James showed no mercy in making his life miserable for at least the following seven days. 'But maybe this would be a good opportunity to meet the staff. Harry's been slaving away all day so I'm sure he's ready for an early lunch break, and Richard –' he hesitated '– well, Richard's come in too.' Harry brightened and sat up in his chair. Richard too had to agree that there were worse things he could do this morning than have a working lunch with this man.

'Good idea.' Devlin held out his hand for Gerry's and shook it. 'Gerry, it's been a pleasure. I'll be getting back to you very soon. Harry.' He nodded to the plump journalist behind the desk who looked as if he didn't know whether to stand or stay sitting, hold out his hand or nod his head back. 'And I'll meet you downstairs in five minutes, then,' he said to Richard, and then he was gone.

There was an awkward silence in the room, that seemed curiously smaller and duller now that Devlin had gone from it. Richard smiled embarrassedly at Harry. 'Harry, I'm sorry –' he began.

'Oh, don't mind me,' said Harry, punching his fist into his biscuit barrel and pulling out a handful of Rich Teas. 'Someone's got to keep the place ticking over while all and sundry are off stuffing themselves, haven't they?' He crammed enough biscuits into his mouth to prevent himself saying anything more, although his eyes continued to glare jealously at first Gerry and then Richard. The two men both made further mumbled apologies before making their escapes from Harry's pique.

As Richard was closing the office door, he saw Gerry across the office. 'Good luck!' he was miming from behind Harry's back, and there was a broad smile across his face.

The restaurant Devlin chose for 'lunch' was in town, but for Richard it might as well have been on another planet. For the cost of a meal there, Richard reckoned he could have fed himself at home from Monday through to Friday and still had change left over for takeaways and a bottle of wine with Mike on Saturday. He worried briefly that his jeans and T-shirt would not be allowed past the front door, but he followed in the wake of Devlin's calm assurance that there would be no problems – and sure enough there weren't. The waiters there all seemed to know Devlin and to be pleased to see him, and if they noticed that his companion was wearing something a little less than full evening dress they seemed prepared to forgive it for his sake. The maître d' himself showed them to their seats. A menu was slipped into his hands, and Richard dredged his mind for what schoolboy French he could recall as he chose his meal. Devlin chose the wine.

'So,' Richard said as they waited, 'do you come here often?'

'Only when McDonald's is full,' Devlin replied and smiled.

Richard relaxed. Though he'd never have admitted it, their luxurious surroundings had intimidated him. Devlin's offhand dismissal of them made them seem less threatening and put him at his ease. And he really did have great teeth.

'I was bad back there, wasn't I?'

'Sorry?' Richard said uncertainly.

'Harry. I froze him out, didn't I? I shouldn't have.' Unprepared for such honesty, Richard said nothing. Devlin looked contrite. 'I'll apologise. Later. I'm sorry, it was just an instinctive reaction. You know how it is: you look at someone and think, Do I really want to do lunch with this guy? And then you think . . .'

'No.'

'That's right.' They both laughed. 'I guess he's an all right guy, really.' Devlin waited for Richard to agree. Again, Richard said nothing. 'But maybe I made the right decision?' Richard was nodding before he'd finished. 'OK, but I will apologise – maybe send him something.'

'A packet of Bourbons and he'll be yours for life.'

'What a thought.'

A smart young man in becomingly tight trousers and waistcoat came over with their wine, uncorked the bottle and poured some out for Devlin to taste. Richard was relieved he wasn't invited to taste too. A fine vintage might be all very well, but his knowledge of wines was limited to those that came at less than five pounds a bottle. He doubted if even the cooking sherry in this place came that cheap. With Devlin's approval, the wine waiter served them both to full glasses and left the bottle on the table. Richard watched Devlin watching the waiter's bottom as he walked back to the kitchens. 'Nice?' Richard inquired archly.

'A little young but a good body.'

Richard raised his glass. 'And I'm sure the wine's good, too.'

Devlin raised his own glass. 'To success,' he said. 'Always to success.' Their glasses chimed and they drank. 'So,' said Devlin, putting his glass down and toying with one of the silver knives laid out before him, 'what shall we talk about?'

'Well, there's always the weather. Or I could tell you about some of the work I've done recently for *Far Out!* About some of the ideas Gerry and I have. And Harry, too, of course.'

Devlin put the knife down and leaned across the table. 'How about drugs?' he said in a conspiratorial whisper.

Richard choked as the expensive wine went down the wrong way and ended up being spluttered into a hastily grabbed napkin. As he mopped his lips and Devlin commiserated, he struggled to pull himself back together. Was this it? Was this the contact he'd been waiting for? For the first time in nearly two days he'd managed to forget about the Fellowship of Iron and its complications, and now it appeared to be raising its head just where he'd least have expected it. He'd somehow imagined his contact taking place in a dark back alley, not in the elegant surroundings of a five-star restaurant. This couldn't be it. Could it?

As panicked thoughts flashed through Richard's mind, Devlin leaned back in his chair watching, an amused sparkle in his eyes. 'I mean of course your writing on the subject, Richard.' He raised an eyebrow. 'You didn't think I meant anything else, did you?'

Richard laughed shakily. His stomach felt like it had been on a roller-coaster ride. 'Just the usual.' Devlin's eyebrow remained raised but he made no comment. 'So,' said Richard, making an effort to recollect his scattered thoughts, 'you've read some of my stuff?'

'All of it.'

Richard wondered whether to challenge this but decided not to. Devlin presented this as simple fact, not a boast, and Richard had the feeling he was not a man who made empty claims. 'Did you like it?' he said awkwardly. He didn't want to look as if he was fishing for compliments but they were supposed to be here to talk about *Far Out!* and his work for it.

'Very much,' said Devlin simply. 'Ah, the first courses.'

Their conversation was interrupted by the arrival of more waiters and food. Devlin was unfailingly courteous to the waiters, friendly without being familiar. It would have been so easy for a meal in a place like this to become a stiff, uncomfortable ritual but his charm and easy manner prevented this. Once the waiters had left he resumed their conversation. 'I'm afraid I have a confession to make,' he said. 'I'm here under slightly false pretences. It wasn't really *Far Out!* magazine that I came here for. It was you.'

Glad at least that he hadn't been caught out a second time with a mouthful of wine, Richard wondered where on earth they were heading now. Was this a come-on? Mentally he shook his head and told himself not to be stupid. What he had to acknowledge, though, was that the sudden thought of Devlin's making a play for his body sent a not unpleasant tingling through his whole system, and a flood of arresting images through his imagination. Was the body under those expensive clothes as perfect as those features? 'Oh?' he said.

'Time to come clean.' Devlin held up a well-manicured hand. There was a slim gold band around the base of the thumb. As he proceeded to make his points he counted them off on his fingers one after the other. 'One, I'm a businessman. Two, I'm very good at it. Three, I made my first million by the time I was twenty-four. Four, I want to go on making money, which means expanding into other areas. Five –' which brought him to the thumb and the ring, which he toyed with for a moment '– I think there is more to life than just money.'

'I can empathise with point five,' said Richard, 'although that's largely because I've never had much money.'

Devlin laughed, not unsympathetically. 'Things change, Richard. Nothing stays the same for ever. Which is largely why I'm here. One of my latest business acquisitions is a small publishing house, specialising, would you believe it, in antiques and curios from the nineteenth century. I'm not a fan. I intend to turn the company around, completely change its profile. And hopefully make a tidy profit in the process.' He held up four fingers again. 'Points one to four.'

'Which brings us back to the thumb?'

'Exactly. I believe in community, Richard, our community. I want to use my money to put something back into it.'

Understanding began to dawn. 'You want to start a gay publishing house?'

'Precisely. New authors, new titles, new directions. I've been looking around for some time now with this in mind and that's when I first came across *Far Out!* I liked what you'd written there so I looked around for more. That's when I found the series of articles you'd done on drugs and the gay scene. It's just what I've been looking for, Richard. Writing with a heart and a mind.' Devlin clasped his hands and rested his chin on them as he looked straight into Richard's eyes. 'Will you write for me, Richard? Will you be one of the first authors in my new list?'

Richard leaned back and ran his fingers through his hair as he struggled to take on board just what this man was offering him. It was unbelievable. It was like his most perfect daydream come true. It was what he'd been working towards ever since he'd left university – since before then, even. But to have it land so unexpectedly in his lap in one gorgeous, gift-wrapped box like this. 'Shit!' he exclaimed.

'Indeed.'

Richard shook his head. 'Sorry. That's probably not the most eloquent expression you've heard from a writer who's supposed to have a heart and a mind.'

Devlin shrugged and laughed. 'Conciseness can be a virtue, too.'

Richard forced himself to sit still, although what he really wanted to do was run and shout and maybe turn a cartwheel or two. 'So let me get this straight. You'd like me to write something factual for you about the gay scene, maybe along the lines of those drug articles?'

Devlin spread his hands wide as if to suggest the range of possibilities on offer. 'It's not really a case of what I want you to do, Richard. If that's the approach you want to take then fine, go ahead. But I've read your fiction too and if you wanted to use your articles as background for a novel, then go for it. I think we'd have a winner either way.'

Richard took another gulp of his wine. 'I didn't think publishing houses worked that way.'

'They don't. Until now. I want to change things. Want to come along for the ride?'

Do I? *Do I?* I'd sell my grannies on both sides of the family for this chance. Are you insane? Richard took a deep breath. 'I need to know more,' he said.

Devlin gave a short bark of a laugh. 'Fair enough! If businessmen can get into publishing, why shouldn't writers develop a sharper sense of business?' Two waiters appeared silently at Devlin's elbow and hovered discreetly. 'But I think the main course is here, so how about we put business to one side and just enjoy the rest of the meal?'

Richard nodded. 'Except for one thing.' Devlin looked surprised but waited for Richard to explain. 'You say you didn't really come here today because of *Far Out!* Does that mean you aren't really interested in supporting the magazine?' Richard wanted what Devlin had to offer badly, but he couldn't take it at the expense of Gerry and Harry. At least, he hoped he wouldn't have to.

Devlin put his mind at ease. 'Don't worry, Richard. You're my prize but I meant what I said to Gerry about *Far Out!* His tone softened. 'And I'm glad you said that. I spend too much time working with sharks. I respect your concern for your colleagues. I think I could enjoy working with you, Richard.' He raised his wine glass, Richard did the same and for the second time they chinked glasses.

The two men settled down to their main courses. Richard contemplated polite chit-chat. It wouldn't do to get too controversial or personal with a man who was holding out the prospect of a whole new glittering career direction for him. On the other hand, Devlin was open, warm and friendly and Richard found himself increasingly fascinated by the man. He was charismatic, all right, not at all the cold fish Richard had always imagined businessmen to be. And he was beginning to form a certain suspicion about him and he was dying to know whether he was right or not. He decided to ask; after all, where was the harm? 'So, Devlin,' he said, using the first name, as invited to, though it still seemed somehow daring, 'have you spent much of your life in America?'

Devlin looked startled. 'How did you know? I was pretty sure no one would be able to tell.'

'Oh, don't worry. True blue Brit if ever I heard one, to listen to you. And maybe that's part of it. No, it's not the way you sound, it's the things you say. "I guess" instead of "I suppose". "Do lunch". Very transatlantic.'

'Ouch. I'll remember that.'

'How long, then?' asked Richard.

'Over twenty-five years, now. My parents emigrated there when I was a child.' He spoke easily but briefly. Richard suspected that here at least Devlin was a typical businessman, less willing to talk about himself than his work.

'I'm amazed you don't have a more noticeable accent after that length of time.'

'My British accent meant something to me,' Devlin said slowly. 'It was part of where I came from. I think roots are important. We all need to remember where we came from. My accent was part of that for me. Plus, I have to admit,' he added with a smile, 'a British accent in America is a useful tool. It opens all sorts of doors. So I worked hard to keep it. Obviously I need to work a bit harder. What about you, Richard? What are your roots?'

Richard told him about his home life, school and university, moving swiftly on to his writing and the writers who had influenced him the most. They spent much time comparing authors whom they both enjoyed and moved from there to film, music and art. Devlin was very knowledgeable in all these areas and Richard enjoyed their conversation immensely. He hadn't had such a wide-ranging discussion probably since his student days, and hadn't realised how much he'd missed that until now.

'And any partners?' Devlin asked. Richard told him about Mike.

'A bodybuilder.' Devlin rolled his wine glass back and forth in his hands. 'Is it true that they all have very small penises?'

Richard guffawed, hurriedly pressing a napkin to his face when someone at the next table looked across at him. He was beginning to suspect he'd overdone it with the wine. 'Well, I wouldn't know,' he said, 'I can't say I've had them all. But I can assure you Mike has no problems on that score.'

'I'm glad, for your sake. But isn't it a bit . . . intimidating, being fucked by a bodybuilder? All that muscle and strength. They could do anything to you. And then the drugs. Well, you know all about that, of course. You hear such incredible stories of, what do they call it, '"Roid Rage"?'

'I couldn't be frightened of Mike, no matter how many muscles he's got. I think I'm probably more violent than he is. And he's a natural bodybuilder. He doesn't take drugs.'

'He's never been tempted?'

'Not as far as I know.'

'That must take a lot of dedication.'

'Yes, it does.'

Devlin nodded, as if pleased. 'I look forward to meeting him.'

Richard briefly imagined Mike sitting at the table with them, next to the fluent, widely educated Lancaster. 'Yeah,' he said.

'We could have coffee here,' Devlin suggested when the cheese and biscuits had been disposed of, 'or we could go back to my hotel – it's just round the corner – and have coffee there.'

Richard said that would be pleasant. He was a long way from being drunk, but a cup or two of strong coffee would not be a bad idea.

Devlin paid, left a generous tip, and they caught a taxi to his hotel – one of the best in town, naturally.

The floorspace in the living room of Devlin's hotel suite was greater than that of all of Richard's flat put together. 'Make yourself at home,' he said, sweeping his hand vaguely in the direction of the plushly upholstered sofas, and he left Richard alone for a few minutes. Richard usually enjoyed this moment. He'd found it was something of a ritual. You met a guy, got invited back to his flat for a 'coffee', and found yourself left alone for a few minutes. It gave you a chance to look around, inspect the bookshelves, the video collection, the magazines stuffed under the armchair, the pictures, photos and calendars on the walls. In other words, it gave you a chance to find out a bit more about the person you'd met. This wasn't the same, though. This wasn't Devlin's place. It was just a suite of rooms he was renting. It spoke of wealth, but nothing else. And he really had just come back for coffee. Hadn't he?

When Devlin came back in, he'd taken off his jacket and tie. He smiled and, without asking, poured two large brandies and brought them over to Richard.

'I thought we were having coffee.'

'A shame to spoil such a good meal by not giving it the conclusion it deserves.'

'Do you have brandy after every meal?'

'I wasn't talking about the drink.' Devlin assumed a mock sheepish expression. 'I hope you don't think I'm trying to get you drunk, Richard, so that you'll go to bed with me.'

'No,' said Richard, who had been assuming exactly that.

'Good,' said Devlin, sitting down close to him on the sofa and putting his hand very deliberately between Richard's legs, 'because I would really prefer you not to be drunk when I fuck you.'

It wasn't the fact that Devlin was hitting on him that surprised Richard in the slightest: it was the amazing directness of it. The speed was undeniably exciting and the firm, masculine pressure of the hand on his groin was certainly stimulating. Richard knew from experience that men who knew what they wanted and how to get it generally made for a great session under the sheets. However . . .

'And is this sort of thing going to be part of any contract I might have with you? You know, three thousand words every week and a fuck on Fridays?'

Devlin stroked Richard's cheek with one hand and the front of his jeans with the other. 'I like to think I can get all the sex I want without having to buy it, Richard. Your writing contract will be completely separate from this and will go ahead, even if you say no now. Not,' he added, 'that you are going to.' He kissed Richard on the mouth, nibbling on his lips, probing with his tongue. Richard opened his mouth and met Devlin's tongue with his own. Their kiss tasted of the fine wine they had been drinking earlier.

'You're very sure of yourself, aren't you?'

'You hesitate in business and you're lost, Richard.'

'I thought you said this wasn't business?'

'True.' Devlin undid the button at the top of Richard's jeans. 'Although you could say it is going to be something of a merger. Shall we adjourn to the bedroom?'

The bed was the largest that Richard had ever seen let alone made love in. The sheets, as he had expected, were silk. 'Take your clothes off for me, Richard,' Devlin said softly. 'Start with your shoes and socks and work your way upwards.' Without bending down, keeping his eyes on Devlin, Richard kicked off first one trainer than another. With most other men, he would have felt self-conscious, at least at this stage of the proceedings: but with Devlin he didn't. Devlin, he was discovering, was a man who made things happen, even this. Other people just had to accept that. He fleetingly wondered if there was anything sexual that Devlin might ask for that he would be unable to refuse. If he wanted to. His T-shirt came up over his head and he flung it to one side, standing naked in front of Devlin. He expected the other man to make a move towards him now but Devlin remained in the bedside chair he had sat in throughout and looked at Richard, his eyes moving up and down the body, taking in the sinewy legs, the flat stomach, the chest with the wisps of hair at the nipples, and the swelling cock rising fiercely from the dark hair between his legs.

Richard's skin tingled before this man had even touched it. Devlin's gaze was like a finger tracing itself carefully up and down his body. He felt his cock growing harder at the sensation, the head pushing through the folds of foreskin. It jumped in reaction as Devlin got up from his chair and walked towards him. When the man touched him lightly on the shoulder, Richard couldn't help a sharp intake of breath, so sensitised had his skin become.

Slightly taller than the younger man, Devlin stood before Richard, leaned over and touched his tongue to the top of his neck, slowly moving it down and out along the shoulder, as his hands slid down either side of Richard's body. He cupped Richard's buttocks, while with the tip of his tongue he moved over Richard's face, licking eyelids, nose and mouth. Richard let his head fall back, allowing Devlin to move his tongue from the tip of his chin, along the bony ridges of his throat down the breastbone and into the small hollow at its base.

Devlin stood back, like a sculptor admiring his work. Richard remained where he was, head still back, eyes closed, panting slightly. Pre-come traced a silver strand down the length of his upwards-straining dick. Devlin knelt. Richard swallowed, anticipating the touch of that tongue along his shaft. Not yet. Devlin pressed his face into Richard's thigh, probing the hollow between thigh and ball sac with his tongue. He raised his hand as if to cup the ball sac but did little more than brush along the hairs of it. The tiny sensations were like the prickle of static electricity and Richard struggled against the impulse to press himself hard against the still fully clothed man and rub his dick hard along his body.

'On the bed.' The words were softly spoken, but Richard didn't hesitate. 'Over.' Richard lay on his stomach. The cool smoothness of the silk sheets slid teasingly against the slick head of his cock. He waited, eyes closed, for whatever Devlin was going to do next. He gasped as he felt the tongue again tracing its way up the inside of one thigh, working up and round the cheek of one buttock. There was a sharp, sweet stab of pain as Devlin nipped first one cheek then the other between his perfect teeth. The bed rose as Devlin climbed from it and Richard waited again, face down and eyes closed for Devlin's next move.

'Undress me.'

Richard opened his eyes and rolled over. Devlin was standing to one side of the bed. Richard rose and began to do as he was told, working in the opposite direction from the way he had undressed, undoing the shirt, pulling out the belt of the trousers. Devlin was slim and smooth. His skin was uniformly tanned, no pale trunks-line there. It exhaled the subtle scent of rich oils. Richard was surprised at the musculature. He was no bodybuilder, but defined muscles moved smoothly under the skin, suggesting a hardness at odds with the pampered life style Richard had assumed. A murmured question brought an unexpected glimpse into Devlin's past.

'College wrestling,' he said, with what Richard suspected was a little pride. 'It was quite an eye-opener for a young lad from England to find out just how ready Americans in high school are to jump into lycra and roll about on a mat together.'

'So were you good on a mat?'

Devlin gave a soft snort. 'Of course.'

Devlin sat back on the bed as Richard peeled the socks from him. Richard went to push him back on to the bed, to cover him with his own body, and rub his hard dick against Devlin's cut cock, but Devlin stood and took him by the shoulders. The two men stood naked before each other, touching, kissing. Richard pushed his hips forward, but Devlin pulled back. 'I like to play, Richard. Do you like to play?' he whispered.

Here it was. The point he'd suspected would come. A light-hearted question that they both knew contained heavier meaning. Did he trust this man? Did he care? Would he be able to say no if he didn't like the games Devlin liked to play? 'Yes.'

'Good. On the bed. On your back.' Richard complied. Devlin straddled him and leaned forwards. Richard expected Devlin to press his cock against Richard's face and readied his mouth to take it deep, but Devlin reached over his head on either side and pulled out two long leather straps. The nature of Devlin's game became clearer.

'Thoughtful of the hotel to prepare its beds so thoroughly,' Richard observed. Devlin said nothing, holding out the straps for Richard's inspection, his question obvious in his eyes.

'Yes,' Richard said.

Devlin bound his wrists, not tightly but securely. The job done he sat back to admire his work and Richard. Richard stared back, defiant but helpless. By nature generally the active sexual partner, this submission to another's will, particularly someone as dominant as Devlin, was unexpectedly erotic.

Without explanation, Devlin rolled from the bed and left the room. Richard lay tied to the mattress, wondering what next. He knew some guys got off on leaving their partners bound and helpless. Was that what Devlin was into? All he could really think about was the aching in his dick that the man had worked up. Relief from his own hand would have been so welcome but was now impossible. The realisation only made the aching more pronounced.

When Devlin returned, he was carrying a small bottle. When he uncorked it the air was filled with the scent of mint. Without explanation, he tipped a small amount into one palm, rubbed his hands together and proceeded to rub the oil along Richard's body. It was cold to the touch, but after only a few seconds it set his skin tingling.

'What is that stuff?' Richard asked, turning his head to try and see the label, but the bottle was out of his restricted line of vision and Devlin didn't reply.

Devlin continued to massage the oil into Richard's skin, higher and higher, up Richard's legs, his thighs, passing over the crotch to move across his stomach and chest, pausing only to tip a little more of the liquid into his palms as needed. When he had worked the oil into Richard's neck Devlin paused, leaning over his bound partner to lick at one nipple. Richard closed his eyes and moaned softly. The moan changed to an abrupt yelp of pain as Devlin nipped at the tender, puckered flesh.

'That hurt!' Richard exclaimed, halfway between irritation, surprise and pleasure. Devlin smiled, bent low over Richard again and licked slowly at the other nipple. When the sharp nip came for that one, Richard was prepared. He yelled again. He could see how it was turning Devlin on.

Devlin returned to his bottle, poured more into his hands then tenderly pressed his oiled palms into either side of Richard's eager dick. The cool fire was even more intense on his swollen meat and Richard's mouth gaped like a man suddenly submerged in cold water. Devlin smiled and worked the oil into the hard erection, moving down to the fleshy folds of his ball sac, to the very root of Richard's cock. As he approached Richard's hole, Devlin moved in closer, easing the young man's legs up on to his shoulders to give him easier access to his goal. The pungent oil worked its magic on Richard's ring, setting it tingling, making it hungry. Devlin worked his fingers further and further into Richard and Richard eagerly accepted the penetration.

Again Devlin left the room, and all Richard could do was gasp out, 'For Christ's sake, don't be long.'

When the older man returned it was with lube and some kind of dildo, though Richard could see straight away there was more to it than the average cock-shaped lump of latex. Devlin swiftly resumed the place he had before, leaning into Richard so that his arse was raised from the silk sheets, and open to Devlin's advances. 'A little toy I've picked up on my travels,' he murmured. 'A bit more . . . interesting than anything you can get over here.' Richard strained to see just what it was this man was planning to fuck him with. Devlin laughed at his attempts but made no effort to show him what he was greasing up. 'It's not much to look at,' he said. 'The proof of this pudding is in the eating,' and with the last word he slid the dildo deep into Richard.

Roused by the massage and the oils Devlin had been using, Richard had little trouble taking the whole of the dildo. His sphincter ring was teasingly stretched but it was nothing he couldn't handle and the rigid plastic rubbing up against his prostate triggered the warm waves of pleasure he loved. Richard ground his arse into the toy while Devlin held it steady, watching the younger man pleasure himself. 'Like it?' he asked. 'Good?'

'Oh, yes!'

'Good. Ready for a surprise?'

Richard opened his eyes and looked up at the man on top of him. Devlin had both hands on the base of the sex toy. He was smiling. There was a click.

'Shit! What the . . .? Oh. Oh! Shit!'

'Different, isn't it?' said Devlin. 'Takes a bit of getting used to at first, but once you do they tell me it's quite exceptional.'

The dildo was moving inside Richard, twisting and turning the way a human dick could only do if the guy attached to it was some kind of international gymnast. Richard's hands automatically went to grab hold of the man pushing up his arse but were brought up sharply by the leather straps lashed to the bedposts. He arched his body and twisted his hips to accommodate the writhing sex tool. Devlin bore down hard into his arse. 'It's got different settings, Richard. Want to try the next one?'

Sweat rolled off Richard's body as he writhed on the silk sheets. Devlin pursued Richard's bucking arse mercilessly, forcing the demanding sex toy deep into his body, harder and harder.

'Yes! Yes! Pull me off. Pull me off now!'

Devlin leaned back, relieving the pressure on Richard's prostate. Panting, he looked down at the man underneath him who was begging for relief. The dildo remained in Richard, vibrating quietly. 'You ready?' Devlin teased.

'God, yes! Do it!' Richard ached for a strong grasp of his cock to pump out the orgasm hammering for release in his dick.

Without letting go of the sex toy, Devlin leaned down, brought his mouth close to Richard's engorged penis. Helpless to stop himself, Richard thrust his hips up, desperate to rub his dick against Devlin's face and trigger his climax that way, but Devlin laughingly grasped his hips with both hands and pinned them to the bed. He reached down, bringing his lips close to the pinned man's crotch and very, very gently ran the tip of his tongue around the head of Richard's cock, even as he triggered his device one last time. The resultant climax exploded over Richard's chest, into his face and even the headboard behind him. Somewhere in the coming, Devlin withdrew the dildo but Richard didn't feel it, lost to the ecstasy of his own orgasm.

When he'd come down sufficiently to take in what was going on around him Richard found that Devlin had once again left the room. He lay, sweat and come alike drying and cooling on his skin. He hoped Devlin wouldn't be long.

When Devlin came back, he was wearing a dressing gown. Once again he stood over Richard, looking down at him. For a fleeting second, Richard had the strangest feeling that Devlin wasn't going to release the straps, that part of Devlin's playing was going to involve him begging to have them taken off. He was relieved when Devlin finally leaned over and undid them one after the other without saying anything.

Richard sat up. He reached an arm across to Devlin, and drew him in to kiss him. Devlin's kiss was quick, and chaste. He stood up and moved away from the bed. 'The shower's through there,' he said.

Richard stood up uncertainly. 'But I thought . . . I mean, don't you want to . . .?'

Devlin smiled as he walked away into the living room. 'On a first date? You'd never respect me afterwards, Richard.'

Washed and dressed, Richard found Devlin sitting on one of the chairs in the living room. He had moved the chair round until it was facing the television, although the set wasn't on. He was sipping from a brandy glass.

'I suppose I'd better be getting along, then.'

Devlin stood. 'I left my addresses with Gerry back at the office. Think over what we talked about, put some ideas down, send them to me and we'll get together and talk them through.'

On the threshold of the room, Richard faced him again.

'Thanks,' he said. 'For everything.' He wanted to say more. He would liked to have stayed longer and talked, about anything, but he could also tell that Devlin wanted to be alone now. And somehow, whatever Devlin wanted he got.

Devlin put his arm round Richard's waist and kissed him again, typically unheeding of anyone who might be walking past. The kiss was much warmer than the last one but still only lasted a few seconds before he stepped back again. 'Thank you, Richard,' he said.

Richard made his own way out of the hotel, glowing on one level from the extremely enjoyable sexual exercise he had just gone through, but mildly frustrated by Devlin's not having allowed him to pleasure him in return. Was there something else he should have done? Had Devlin been expecting him to refuse to go? Should he have strapped Devlin down himself and fucked him with his own toy? Or with something else? Was that the kind of 'play' the businessman was into? Perhaps. Perhaps not.

In the end, he thought, with a mental shrug of his shoulders, you just had to accept that it was always going to be a case of different strokes for different folks. Devlin's thing was maybe doing unto others but not being done unto. For all Richard knew, Devlin was busy doing unto himself right at that moment, alone in his hotel room. He wouldn't be the first, Richard supposed. He just happened to be the first that Richard had come across, so to speak. Richard walked up to the ornate hotel doors, waited for the uniformed man on duty to open them for him, and stepped outside.

Back in his hotel suite, Devlin Lancaster sat on his chair in his dressing gown facing the television. The video was playing. On the screen, Devlin watched himself tie Richard down, watched as, while Richard waited for him to return with the oils, the camera closed in on his face, his chest, his cock, before pulling back again to take in his whole body. He wished he'd been able to zoom in on Richard's face while he'd been reaming him with the dildo, been able to capture the savage joy on the young man's features as he'd been fucked out of his mind by Devlin's toy. But of course even he couldn't be in two places at the same time, screwing a young man with a pole of battery-driven plastic and filming it all with a hidden camera.

As Richard's bucking and arching on the screen grew more frantic, his cries of pleasure more animal-like, Devlin's pumping of his own cock beneath his dressing gown became more frenzied. 'If only,' he gasped. 'If only!'

It was as he lay in bed that night that Richard asked himself just what kind of fool he was. He'd fallen for a classic scam. How could he have been so stupid as to take everything that Devlin had told him at face value? It was all quite literally too good to be true. A man that wealthy who was prepared to offer Richard the chance to do exactly what he wanted to do. Richard leapt up out of bed and paced the room furiously. How could he have done it? What was it about Devlin that had made him believe everything he'd said, that had made him fall so readily into bed with him and abandon himself so completely?

Richard headed for his computer and the research he should have done before he'd even gone to lunch with Devlin, let alone allow the man to fuck him nearly senseless.

It took only half an hour on the Internet to find the truth. Devlin Lancaster was everything he said he was. His finger was in enough pies to fill a bakery. Richard even found details of the small press Devlin had spoken of that was to be the basis for his new enterprise. It was true, all of it.

Curiously sobered and excited at the same time, Richard crept back into his bed and tried to fall asleep. The next day, he had a lot of work to start if he was going to prepare material that was going to impress his new benefactor.

With a start, he remembered he hadn't checked his e-mails. Specifically, he hadn't looked to see if there had been any response yet to his message to the Fellowship of Iron website. He returned to his computer and booted it up all over again. There was nothing. He didn't like to admit it, but he was actually relieved. Maybe the whole thing would come to nothing after all, and maybe that would be for the best.

Maybe.

Six

———

Roy was upset, Mike could tell. It took him a while though to figure out why.

Mike had turned up at Dave's gym early in the evening, a good time to catch the serious bodybuilders, the ones who would have known Dave. He'd intended to explain to Roy just what he was about, that he was going to ask the questions Richard had suggested, but the ex-boxer had been busy with one of the punters, sparing Mike only a quick nod before he went back to working out some lad's new exercise routine. Mike had nodded back and headed for the changing rooms, intending to catch Roy when he came out. Roy was busy with someone else when he emerged in his shorts and training vest, so Mike had resolved to see him later when he was free and had set about warming up, casting his eye around the room, and planning his course of action. He'd done his real training that day already, three hours of hard-core action on arms and shoulders that had set the muscle fibres burning with a fire he could still feel. This evening, though, wasn't about pumping iron: it was about pumping people.

First off, he looked for the guys he knew. These would be the bodybuilders he used to hang around with when he and Dave had still been an item. He was disappointed to see how few of them there were now. Most of them, he reflected, would have been Dave's age or even older. No longer on the competition circuit, perhaps no longer even training. Mike never liked to think about that. He didn't like to contemplate a time when he would no longer train his body, push it to its peak. As far as he was concerned, he would always lift weights in a gym.

The old friends he did find were easy to talk to. One or two had been at Dave's funeral, so he didn't spend much time on them. For the others, he wandered over to where they were training, picked up whatever weight or piece of equipment was to hand, did a few reps and said hi. Talk inevitably turned to Dave and condolences were exchanged.

'Training to the end,' Mike would say. 'The man just didn't know when to stop.' Old training partners would nod their heads slowly in agreement and laugh. 'And I hear,' Mike would add, hotly embarrassed at what he saw as the obvious transparency of his ploy, 'that he was getting out and about on the scene too.' Time and again the nods stopped, the smiles turned to looks of mild bemusement.

'I wouldn't know,' one guy said.

'What, Dave?' another had exclaimed, and Mike was left feeling like he had just done something to soil the memory of his former lover.

He moved on to someone he didn't recognise, a lad with blond hair in a ponytail, young but already showing fantastic arm development, although even at a quick glance Mike could see the lack of balance typical of the beginner who wanted biceps he could blast in his friends' faces rather than marks for proportion on a judge's score sheet. He was the kind of kid Dave would have gone out of his way to help. The kind of kid Mike had been once.

'Hi. I used to know the guy who owned this place. Did you know him?'

A shake of the head. Mike moved on.

To add to his discomfort was the fact that it was becoming impossible to ignore that Roy was avoiding him. Mike would approach him only to see Roy walk off and hastily engage himself in conversation with someone, or vanish into the small room behind the counter, conspicuously closing the door behind him. At first Mike had been puzzled. They'd last seen each other at

Dave's funeral, and the memory of the pressure of Roy's hand in his own was still strong. Now it looked like the older man didn't want anything to do with him.

The reason why hit him as the young lad with the arms and the ponytail left his training partner and, after a brief whispered conversation, walked over to him. Mike thought that maybe he'd remembered something about Dave and smiled. The lad smiled back. 'This Dave guy. Did he look much like you?'

'Didn't you see him around? He owned this place.'

The youngblood shook his head. 'Nah. I signed up with the old guy Roy. I train with Phil over there. I haven't really got to know anybody else here yet.'

'Right. No, Dave wasn't much like me. Bit shorter, bit broader. Heavy moustache. He was older than me, too.'

The young guy sat down on a preacher curl bench, his arms hanging over the rest. Flattened out against the cushion like that, the biceps looked even bigger and more impressive. 'I like older guys,' he said with a grin.

Mike was about to remark with a smile that although he wasn't as old as Dave had been he was nevertheless older than this lad, until he cottoned on that that was exactly what the boy had meant. The sensation was confusingly mixed. At almost any other time, Mike would have had no objections at all to flirting with a well-built pup like this, quite probably taking it further than just flirting. But not now, when his thoughts were full of Dave, and not here of all places, where those memories were always going to be particularly strong. Even as it became clear to him that the muscleboy displaying his biceps for him now had mistaken his inquiries for a chat-up, so Mike thought he understood what was wrong with Roy. He'd come to the same conclusion. He thought Mike was cruising Dave's gym. No wonder he was keeping his distance. He was probably as disgusted at the idea as Mike himself was.

The young bodybuilder climbed off the preacher curl seat and came to stand in front of it, very close to Mike. He was flexing his own right biceps, feeling it with his left hand and looking up from it to Mike. 'So, think you could give me any pointers? Show me how to make myself bigger? Harder?'

Mike, looking round for Roy so he could go and explain the mistake to him, turned back to the kid. 'Eh? Oh, yeah. Work more on your back, double your weight on your squats and don't fall for older guys. They always leave you in the end.' He walked away. He didn't look back, but he caught a snicker from the direction of Phil, the training partner. He scanned the rest of the gym for Roy. Again he was out of sight, but this time Mike was determined to track him down and set the record straight.

'Couldn't help overhearing what you were saying there.'

Mike looked round. The voice came from a trainer sitting at the lats pull-down machine. He had twisted in his seat to face Mike.

Mike shrugged. 'Bit of a misunderstanding. Like to say it happens all the time, but I should be so lucky.' He went to walk off, but the man at the pull-down spoke again. 'Heard you asking about Dave.'

Mike stepped back to the man, but by now he had sucked in a lungful of air and started his reps, pulling down the bow of metal suspended above him, holding the bar just past the base of his neck for a count of two then letting it back up, sucking air in as he pulled down, letting it out as he allowed the bar back up. Mike sat down on a bench facing the lats machine and waited for him to finish his set.

He didn't recognise the man. He was older than Mike, maybe in his early thirties. Shaved across the pate and cropped close at the sides, the lack of hair on his head was more than made up for by the hair on the rest of his body. Black chest-hair sprouted over the top of his training vest and along his shoulders. A tattoo on his forearms was all but invisible under the hairs there, and the thighs stretching the shorts he was wearing were possibly even more hirsute. Even sitting down, Mike could see the guy had something of a gut, but there was no denying the power of his shoulders and arms or the respectable nature of the weight he was shifting. Someone who trained for strength rather than appearance. A bouncer maybe, or just someone who liked working out life's frustrations against cold metal and gravity.

The man finished his set and sat for a moment staring up at the ceiling, breathing heavily and waiting for his body to recover.

Mike waited patiently. 'Name's Len,' he said, reaching for a towel at his side on the floor and dragging it across his face.

'Mike.'

Len swung first one then another arm round in large, lazy circles to stretch the muscles. 'Yeah, I saw Dave out and about a few times. Had a drink with him now and again. Quite a wild guy.'

'Yeah. I suppose he could be,' Mike said cautiously. That didn't sound like the Dave he had known, but then that was exactly the sort of thing Richard had told him to listen out for.

'So.' Len reached up again to the bar of the pull-down machine, winding his hands into the strips of cloth wrapped around it to give him a better grip. 'You as wild as he was?'

'Could be.'

Len grunted. 'Good to hear. Used to see Dave at The Buckle. Going down there myself tonight, after this. See you there?'

Mike nodded. 'OK.'

'Denim or leather,' Len said, before turning back to the lats machine and starting his next set of reps.

Mike walked away, uncertain whether he'd just uncovered the sort of lead Richard had told him he would, or whether he'd yet again sent out and received the wrong signals. Maybe, he thought, he should just go back and talk some more to Len when he'd finished his routine. The decision was taken from him by a bitter voice at his side. 'You don't waste any time, do you?' It was Roy.

Mike's face lit up. 'Roy. I've been trying to get hold of you all evening. Look, I –'

Roy cut him short. 'I think this is the man you've been waiting for.'

He gestured to someone who was standing to one side of him. Mike caught a glimpse of a suit and his stomach lurched. His excitement was very short-lived, however. Closer inspection revealed it wasn't the man he'd glimpsed twice before, here and at Dave's funeral. This was an older man, dry with severely cut grey hair.

The man held out a hand. 'I'm pleased to meet you, Mr Kilby,' he said in a voice which suggested nothing of the sort. 'My name is Ratherson.'

Mike shook the hand, looking at the same time to Roy for some clarification. Roy stood, arms folded and lips resolutely sealed. It was obvious he didn't want to do anything to smooth events along.

'I represent Hobden, Bagnall and Grier. Lawyers,' Mr Ratherson added, although he clearly thought the explanation unnecessary. He looked from a bemused Mike to a stony Roy. 'Perhaps there is somewhere we could go?' he suggested.

From behind them came a sudden crash of very heavy metal and the growled 'Fuck it!' of a weightlifter who'd missed his goal. Mr Ratherson's lips thinned. 'Somewhere more . . . private?' he said primly.

'There's a flat upstairs,' Mike volunteered. 'We can use that. Can't we, Roy?'

Roy glared at him, pulled the flat key out of his pocket and stomped out of the gym towards Dave's flat. Mike indicated that Mr Ratherson should follow and he brought up the rear. When Roy had opened the flat door, he slapped the key into Mike's hand. 'I presume you'll be wanting this,' he said, and stamped up the stairs before Mike could ask him what he meant by that.

The three men gathered in Dave's living room. Mike sat in an armchair facing Mr Ratherson, who took the other armchair. Roy remained standing resolutely looking out of a window, as if having nothing to do with what was going on in the room.

Mr Ratherson perched his briefcase on his knees, opened it and drew out sheaves of papers. 'Well, Mr Kilby. Obviously I would have called you at your home but Mr Ross was, shall we say, a little less than diligent about some matters, and giving us an up-to-date contact address or telephone number for you was something he just never got round to.' Mike's ears pricked up at the mention of Dave's name. Mr Ratherson busied himself with his papers. 'And it proved somewhat difficult to find the information through any other channels.'

Mike glanced at Roy, who remained looking out of the window.

'Still, now that you're here, if you would be so good as to sign here, here and here –' he indicated three separate sheets '– then we can work our way through to all the others underneath.'

Mike held up one hand. 'What,' he asked slowly, 'is all this about?'

Ratherson looked from him up to Roy and then back again. 'I'm sorry? I mean . . . You don't know? That is, I thought that . . .' He looked up again at Roy, who tersely shook his head. His lips grew even thinner. 'I had thought that Mr Sanders here would have fully explained to you the purpose of our appointment.' He paused to note the look of surprise on Mike's face at what was, for him, the first mention of any appointment, before continuing grimly, 'But I see that under the circumstances I shall be obliged to explain more fully my reasons for coming here. Really,' he added, as if addressing some junior clerk, 'this is most irregular.'

'Tell me about it,' Roy growled.

Ratherson ignored him. 'As you are of course aware, Mr David Ross sadly passed away last week. Mr Sanders here had been appointed executor of the will, his job –' and the lawyer's tone gained a distinct edge '– being to facilitate such matters as we are dealing with now. You, Mr Kilby, are the sole beneficiary of said will.'

Mike's mind went blank. Something inside refused to accept the full meaning of what was being said.

'He means you've inherited,' snapped Roy. 'Everything. Lock, stock and fucking barrel.'

Mr Ratherson's lips practically disappeared. 'Quite. You are now, Mr Kilby – or will be, as soon as you sign these papers here, here and here, and allow me to do my job of processing the requisite paperwork – the legal and –' he glanced at Roy '– sole owner of this . . . establishment.'

Mike laughed mirthlessly. A little of what was going on had begun to sink through, just enough for him to see the grim irony of it.

'I'm sorry?'

Mike lurched to his feet and paced the room, motion an outlet for his churning feelings. 'Look, I may not be the brightest guy on the planet when it comes to legal goings on and "requisite" paperwork, Mr Ratherson, but I do know something about buying and running gyms. They're expensive. They're full of costly equipment. You don't buy one without borrowing money. I did it. Dave did it. So just how much of this is mine, and how much belongs to the bank?'

Mr Ratherson regarded him calmly. 'There is no mortgage, Mr Kilby. No loans, no debts. The property and its contents are all paid for. And they are all yours.'

Mike shook his head. 'No, that can't be right. There's got to be some kind of mistake.'

Mr Ratherson bridled. 'I assure you, Mr Kilby, that there is no error. Hobden, Bagnall and Grier are not known for their mistakes. The arrangements are thorough, precise and accurate. All that they require,' he said pointedly, 'is your signature. Here, here and here.'

In a dream, Mike took the pen Ratherson held out and did what Richard was forever telling him he shouldn't: signed on the dotted line without reading the small print. Or any of the print. Ratherson took the papers from him before the ink had dried and slipped them into his briefcase. 'Thank you,' he said crisply, snapping the locks and rising to his feet. 'Thank you very much. I'll make sure everything is processed as quickly as possible and any further important paperwork is sent your way. I trust I may now safely address it to this residence?' There was a silence from the other two men in the room. 'Very well. I wish you both a good day. Please don't trouble yourselves. I can see myself out.' The lawyer left.

Neither Mike nor Roy made a move until he had gone.

'I didn't know,' Mike said finally.

Roy didn't look round. 'Right.'

Mike walked over to him. 'I swear to you, Roy, I didn't.' He reached out to put a hand on Roy's shoulder. Roy shrugged it off and stalked over to another part of the room.

Mike could see that he was struggling with his feelings and wisely waited for him to spit it all out as best he could.

'It was his fuckin' gym. He could do what the fuck he wanted to with it. I'm not saying he owed me anything.'

'I know,' Mike began soothingly.

Roy turned on him with surprising savagery. 'No, you don't know!' he snapped. 'You don't know fuckin' anything. How

114

could you? You were never here. Once a month, sometimes maybe two months you'd get together with him and have your little fling and then it was back to business as usual for you. Very nice. But what about him? Did you ever stop and think about Dave? He was never the same after you left. There wasn't anyone else. Flings, OK, yeah, but nobody who meant anything to him the way you had. And he still lent you all that money. Do you know how hard that was for him? Do you?'

Mike shook his head in dumb misery.

'Course you don't. Things were tight, very tight for that first year. But I don't suppose he ever let on to you, did he?' Mike shook his head again. 'No. He worked his balls off. And I was here with him. Good old Roy. Just like ever. Clap on the back and "see you tomorrow".'

Mike listened as the older man's bitterness and hurt poured out. The more he heard, the more the world he thought he'd known changed. He'd believed the past was fixed and gone. He saw now how it could be revisited and seen again through completely different eyes. He'd always acknowledged Dave's generosity in loaning him the money to get his own gym off the ground, but Roy's words made it clear he'd never really understood Dave's sacrifice. Had he never really appreciated the depth of love behind it? Had there still been enough love there to save their relationship if they'd worked at it?

And what about Roy and Dave? Mike had always assumed they'd slept together, that they might even have had a go at being a couple before finding a truer level with a close friendship. But now he saw beyond the banter and male camaraderie that had always seemed to characterise Dave and Roy, saw this broken-nosed, craggy-faced ex-boxer sticking by Dave as first he hitched himself to a younger man, and then put his livelihood on the line when that younger man took off. And then he got nothing when the man he'd loved died.

Mike had never really thought about what would happen to Dave's gym after his death. Hell, Dave hadn't been fifty. But looking at it now he knew that part of it, all of it probably, should have gone to Roy. That would have been *right*. That would have been what a man like Dave would have done. What had in fact happened was wrong. 'I didn't know,' he said again miserably.

Roy sank down on to the sofa. Mike wanted to take his hand, hold it the way Roy had held his at Dave's funeral. He couldn't.

'You'd better go,' Roy said eventually. 'You've got a date.'

'Roy, it's not what you think. I –'

'I know what you were doing,' Roy rasped. 'I'm not stupid. Do it. Find out who killed Dave. If you can.'

Mike stood up uncertainly. 'Yeah, right. Thanks.' He started walking towards the door. 'Roy? You will still . . .? I mean, this is still your place, you know. You will stay, won't you?'

There was a sound that might have been a laugh. 'Got nowhere else to go, have I?'

Mike was uncertain how to answer. In the end, he left without a word. Before he stepped out of the flat he left the key on the hallway shelf for Roy to find. Maybe he'd ask him for a copy later.

In the end Mike went for denim. A few years previously there had been a fad in bodybuilding competitions for 'fantasy' rounds with contestants dressed up as barbarians, superheroes and the like, anything that showed off their muscles in new and unusual ways. Neither Dave nor Mike had been particularly keen on this fad. 'Why not just go on bloody naked and stop pratting about?' Dave had said, and Mike had agreed. So they weren't disappointed when such novelty rounds quite quickly went out of vogue – largely, it was suggested, because straight competitors felt they just couldn't begin to compete with the creativity, exoticism and risqué costumes of the gay bodybuilders. The more flamboyant gay bodybuilders resigned themselves to plain posing pouches, and kept their competition costumes for the dance scene.

While the fashion had lasted, though, Dave and Mike had had one costumed outing. They'd gone as a pair of Vikings, all leather straps, sheepskin jackets and horned helmets. In the end, they'd been beaten by a pair of aliens in blue body paint and very little else, but the costumes had sparked an intense session of fantasy lovemaking that night when the two Dark Age warriors had locked horns to determine supremacy, the victor getting to dock his longboat exactly where he wanted to. Now Mike thought there might be enough left of his outfit to pass muster at The Buckle that evening.

With a certain amount of quiet pride, however, he found he had put on much more muscle since he'd last worn the leather straps and what had been tight before would have been agony to wear now. Instead, he settled for a pair of close-fitting Levis with a broad black leather belt and a white T-shirt cut high at the arms to show off his swelling biceps and deltoids, and tight everywhere else to leave nothing to the imagination. A little cloney, perhaps, but then that wouldn't exactly be out of place where he was going.

He thought about asking Richard to go along with him – after all, this had been Richard's idea in the first place – but he had a feeling that that might not be completely appropriate. Len had invited him, not him and a partner, and Mike wasn't so naïve as to guess why that might be. Still, it made sense to let someone know where you were going when the venue was a bit risky, so he decided to leave a message on Richard's answering machine. 'Sorry, Richard Green can't help you at the moment, he's out saving the world, but if you'd like to leave your name and number after the beep he'll get back to you just as soon as we're all living in a socialist utopia.' Mike sighed and left his message.

Just over an hour later, he was standing outside The Buckle. Typically featureless from the outside, the club's door was manned by two equally typical expressionless doormen. He recognised one of them, a guy who'd been on the competition circuit until a while back. He nodded and said hello.

'Hiya, Mike,' the doorman said. His companion cleared his throat and frowned. Obviously cheery greetings were not the order of the day for Buckle doormen. The doorman ushered Mike in with an apologetic smile. 'Catch you later, maybe,' he said.

Mike filled in a 'membership' form, paid his money, bought a beer more for appearance than to drink and walked out into the club.

By far the majority of the clientèle was into leather. They sat and stood in groups, bottles in hands, talking, eyeing up the new meat as it came in. Mike could feel the eyes moving over his bulging T-shirt and tight arse. Not a vain man, Mike nevertheless got off on the attention of so many guys. A man who made his living displaying his body in nothing more than a glorified G-string found nothing threatening in close inspection when he was fully clothed, even if the motive behind it was blatant sexual hunger. The Buckle was wall to wall men, all of them using their bodies to attract other men and not caring who knew it. Mike couldn't help responding to the raw honesty of it.

Mike wandered in the gloom, searching for Len while attempting not to make it look like he was trying to pick up. Twice he had to refuse offers of a drink and once of a 'good shag up the back way'. Mike shook his head wordlessly each time, pointed to the bottle he was carrying, smiled and moved on. He suspected as much as anything that the smile put the guys off. A broad grin in The Buckle was as much a contravention of the dress code as a gingham frock.

He finally spotted Len in a dark corner by the bar and moved over to join him. He was sitting on a bar stool talking to two young lads when Mike approached, but at a few muttered words the boys took off leaving Mike to take his place at the bar.

'Drink?' Mike pointed again at his bottle.

Len nodded and tipped up the bottle he had himself until it was empty and then held it out to Mike.

Mike took the hint and the bottle and bought Len another. He'd guessed he'd find Len in leather, not denim. Len's jacket was open to the waist, displaying the abundant black hair of his chest and belly and a glimpse of the harness he was wearing underneath. Mike found himself excited by the unaffected, aggressive maleness of it.

Len accepted the drink without thanks. 'So what is it you're really after?' he asked after he'd downed half the bottle.

Mike was startled. 'What do you mean?'

'You come into a gym you don't normally use and start asking everyone there questions about Dave Ross. Like I said, what is it you're really after?'

He'd been right. His questioning had been clumsy, obvious.

118

Now though he had no choice but to press on. Maybe he should have brought Richard. 'Dave was my friend.'

'So much so you didn't know he used this place?'

'We'd . . . been out of touch.'

'Sure.' Len looked him slowly up and down, rubbing the cool bottle of beer against the crotch of his leather trousers. 'So, what do you use?'

Mike mentally gritted his teeth. 'The usual,' he said.

Len nodded. 'Working?'

'Not as well as I'd like.'

Len nodded again and raised the bottle to finish the beer. Mike waited. The silence drew out. Mike knew that the next move was being left to him. With a silent prayer that he was doing the right thing and that Richard hadn't dropped him in more shit than he knew how to cope with, he broke the silence. 'You got anything better? Anything that Dave might have used?'

Len put the bottle down on the bar. 'Maybe. Ever heard of Iron?'

This was it. 'Yeah. I think Dave might have mentioned it.'

'Might have! Yeah, I just bet he might have. So, you ever heard of the Fellowship of Iron?'

'Yeah.'

'Well, here's where you get your chance to join, boy.' Without standing, Len reached out and grabbed the crotch of Mike's jeans. 'If you've got the balls.'

Without taking his eyes from Len's, Mike grasped his hand and removed it firmly from between his legs. 'I've got what it takes.'

Len grinned, about the only type of grin that would have been accepted at The Buckle: the grin of the predator that believes it has cornered its prey. He pointed to a place behind Mike. 'Back room.' He stood and moved off. Mike followed.

The corridor Len led Mike down was illuminated only by a series of dim, unshaded bulbs. They passed several doors, muffled groans and shouts coming from behind most of them. The door Len was leading Mike to was right at the end of the corridor and some way away from all the others. Len stopped, opened the door and stood to one side, waving Mike in with mock chivalry. Mike hesitated, gritted his teeth and walked in. As soon as he was past the threshold he turned to see what or who was behind the door. There was no one. Len snorted, walked in behind him and closed the door.

The room was small, lit by two naked bulbs in wall recesses, and bare of anything except for two solid wooden posts the height of a man and four feet apart. In each post, at just below shoulder height, was set a large iron ring. There were two other men already waiting, both leathermen. Len indicated each in turn. 'Rick and Sam.' The two men regarded Mike with arms folded.

'Nice to meet you,' Mike said, sarcastic as much as anything to hide his nervousness. His flippancy didn't even dent their stony stance.

Rick was in his late twenties, a tall, blond biker, his hair hanging down well past his shoulders. Under his leather waistcoat he was bare-chested, his spare, pale flesh covered with tattoos of skulls, burning angels and other biker motifs, the twining reds, blues and blacks extending along both arms as well. He was wearing black leather gloves and impenetrable black shades. Shaven-headed Sam was older, shorter and stockier, built like a rugby player. A leather harness stretched across his barrel of a chest, its steel circlet buried in wiry hair. Through his leather chaps Mike could see a sizeable pouch, heavy with its contents.

One by one the three men began to circle Mike, inspecting him, running their eyes the length of his body, from the broad shoulders down to the slim waist and hard arse to the powerful legs. Mike stared straight ahead, catching the eyes of each man only as he passed in front of him, determined to appear calm. The room was warm and close, the heavy scent of leather filling it like musky perfume. The only sound was the soft creaking of the leathermen's gear and, in Mike's ears, the pounding of his own heart. He'd heard guys talk of the leather scene but had never really understood the fascination. Until now. The combination of sights, sounds and smells had roused him more than he had anticipated.

It was Len who finally spoke. 'So how badly do you want it? The Iron, I mean.'

'Badly enough.'

The three men stopped circling and stood, arms folded, an

inwards-facing triangle with Mike at the centre. 'Take your clothes off.'

'Why?'

'Because if you want to join the Fellowship, first you have to do what the Fellowship tells you to do.' Len flipped a finger at Mike's tight jeans, his T-shirt which fitted him like a second skin. 'Besides, could be anything under that, right, lads?' The others nodded humourlessly. 'Guns, wires. Could be undercover police, for all we know.' His voice lost its mocking tone and took on a harder edge. 'So, take 'em off. Or leave.'

With his eyes fixed on Rick, the man now standing in front of him, Mike kicked off his trainers and peeled off his socks. He reached down to the hem of his T-shirt and with deliberate slowness pulled it up his body and over his head, throwing it at Rick's feet and staring challengingly at the man. Rick didn't move. His shades fixed unwaveringly on the stripping body-builder, reflecting back twin images of Mike's naked pecs and abs. With more teasing slowness, Mike undid the buckle of his jeans and let them fall to the ground. He kicked them to one side and stood with the natural poise and confidence of a man used to posing in even less than the black cotton tanga he was now wearing. But this was unlike any other competition pose down he'd taken part in before. In a room bare of everything except three men in fetish gear and one near-naked bodybuilder, the examination was cruder, more hungry, more frankly sexual than any Mike had experienced. There was no point in denying the powerful excitement it exerted over him. The stretched material at the front of the cotton tanga pouch made that clear for all of the men there to see.

The men circled again, pausing twice so that each one of them could take in the sight of Mike from front and behind. It was Len who finished standing in front of Mike this time. He stepped forwards, leaned down slightly and without warning cupped the tanga pouch in the palm of one hand. He looked up at Mike, waiting for a sound, a reaction.

Mike looked down coolly and said nothing. His cock stiffened still further at the pressure of another man's hand.

Len nodded and stepped back. A test had been passed. But only the first. He pointed to the tanga. 'And that.'

Mike eased the thin cotton past his hips, down over his thighs and let it fall past his knees to his ankles, keeping his eyes on Len all the time. When he kicked the underwear away, it landed on Len's boots.

Len didn't look down but fixed his gaze on Mike's proud shaft, rising unhindered now to stand solid and erect against the smooth, flat skin of his belly. 'No wires,' he said. 'But quite a gun.'

'Seen enough?'

Len stepped forward and jabbed a finger at him. 'You keep quiet, boy, until you're spoken to. You understand?' Mike kept his face as expressionless as his inquisitors'. The three leathermen began their circling one last time as Len explained the final stages of the evening's entertainment. 'You want to join the Fellowship, boy, you got to take a little test. You man enough for a little test?'

There was a sniggering sound from one of the others. Mike was pretty sure it was Rick.

'Yes.'

'You man enough for all three of us?'

The adrenaline was racing through Mike's veins. Its message to his brain was primitive, simple and undeniable: Fight, flight or fuck! There was no doubt in his mind which it was going to be. Now it was he who turned to look at each one of the men in turn, subjecting them to the crude inspection they had been putting him through. When he came to the end, he was facing Len again. 'Are you three man enough for me?' he said.

Len snorted again. 'Let's see, then, shall we?' He indicated the iron rings fixed to the posts. 'Rules are simple. You take these and you hold on. You don't let go until we've finished. All three of us.' He lifted one of the rings, holding it up for Mike. 'You let go, you go. Without the Iron.'

Mike took the ring, inspected it, measured the distance between it and its partner with his eyes, before looking again at each of the three men, drawing out the moment, notching up the tension. Even if there hadn't been so much at stake, he was hot for it, his manhood stoked by the surroundings and the challenge, but he wasn't going to make it look like he was begging for it. When he finally grasped the one ring and reached across to take the other, there was a sound like a sigh of relief from Sam. The test was on! Mike took a good grip on the cold metal of both rings, readying himself for his initiation into the Fellowship of Iron. 'Who's first?'

It was Rick. While Len and Sam stood in front of Mike, drinking in the sight of this powerful young man opened up for their pleasure, Rick approached from behind. Mike heard the soft sound of his leather trousers falling to the floor, followed by the clunk of his heavy belt buckle, the rustling sound of a condom being broken out of its packet, followed by the silence as it was rolled down Rick's cock and lubed. Mike forced himself not to turn round. Instead he stared at Len and Sam. The latter had loosened his chaps in anticipation of his own fun, and the large leather pouch now clearly visible was bulging impressively. Mike's cock ached and he waited in keen anticipation for the cool touch of lube on his ring prior to Rick's entry. There was none.

The hardness of Rick's swollen dick-head pressed up against the cheeks of his buttocks and the coldness of Rick's leather gloves on his hips was the only preparation Mike was given before nine inches of stiffened cock was forced into and up his arse. Mike instinctively yanked down on the iron rings and bit back the cry the sharp pain would otherwise have forced from him. He was damned if he'd give the leatherman the pleasure of knowing he had hurt him. The burning faded quickly as he accommodated the meat, but he could already feel Rick withdrawing most of his long tool prior to thrusting again and again, heedless of Mike's pleasure, perhaps even turned on by the thought of the discomfort he was causing.

In front of him he could see Len and Sam grinning at the sight. Len's arms remained folded across his hairy chest. Sam's hand was inside his pouch, wanking himself as he watched his friend drive into Mike's muscular body. 'That's Rick!' crowed Len. 'In like flint.' Rick pushed his hands round Mike's hips, the leather of his gloves rasping against Mike's skin as his tattooed arms clasped the bodybuilder in a bearhug from behind, pulling Mike's powerful body in closer to his own, the better to force himself deeper into Mike's arse.

JACK STEVENS

Rick's screwing was a one-way street, his own pleasure his only goal. His convulsive grip on Mike's waist and the frenzied thrusting of his groin were the desperate means to his own orgasm. Under other circumstances, Mike could have got off on it, providing that he'd known his partner would indulge him with a little reciprocal role play after. And if he hadn't got two other leathermen lining up to be satisfied as soon as this guy had finished. As it was, he hung on, letting the posts take some of the weight of his body, squeezing hard on Rick's meat when at its deepest in his arse, forcing the man to pull hard to withdraw each time, working the leatherman closer and closer to his climax. All too soon, Rick found he had pushed himself too far, too soon. Mike heard the gasped, 'Oh, shit!', felt the momentary hesitation as the fucker tried to hold back, and he struck, tightening up on Rick's hot meat as hard as he could with a savage grin. He felt the man's body buck behind him, heard the repeated, 'Shit!' shouted out in mixed anger and pleasure this time, and felt a rush of success that set his heart pounding.

Rick withdrew, gasping. Mike took his weight on his feet again, fired up by his sexual victory, glaring defiantly at Sam and Len in front of him. 'Next,' he said, with provocative cockiness.

Sam already had the lube in his hands and was squeezing a generous length along his fingers. He came up and stood to one side of Mike as he pushed his fingers into Mike's punished hole, watching the younger man's face as he lubricated the raw muscles. The pressure was at first hard to take after Rick's hectic attack, but the coolness was pleasant. Mike allowed Sam to push the slipperiness deep within him. 'You're gonna need lots, boy,' Sam whispered to him, squeezing still more lube on to his fingers and applying it liberally. 'Trust me.'

When he had finished, Sam stood in front of Mike again, loosening the ties of his chaps, pulling them to one side with a flourish and throwing them off across the room. The pouch beneath was tied along both sides. Sam undid the laces and it fell away. Mike couldn't help swallowing at the size of the throbbing tool revealed. It was shorter than the far-reaching Rick's but much, much thicker. Sam stroked it proudly in front of Mike.

'Good thing these stretch,' he said as he forced a condom over his cock-head, watching Mike all the time to take in his reactions.

It took Sam some time but, completely covered at last, he stood with both hands round his shaft, emphasising its girth. 'Wanna pull out now? Before I have to?' Mike shook his head. Sam reached up and took his chin between thumb and forefinger, pinching it as though Mike were a child. 'Good boy,' he whispered, and stepped behind Mike to set to work.

Len and the slightly recovered Rick, who had replaced his leather leggings, stood silently in front. Mike could see the expectation in their eyes and also the question: would he be able to take Sam? Mike closed his eyes and forced himself to relax as thoroughly as he could. If Sam was as brutal as Rick had been, this might be the test that saw him rejected by the Fellowship of Iron.

Sam's entry was slow and remorseless. Mike felt his ring stretched then stretched again, further than it had ever been before, and then still further. Rick leered. Len leaned in closer. 'Say if you can't take it, boy.'

'Fuck you!' Mike gasped.

'I will, boy. I will.'

Mike hung on to the iron rings, casting his mind back desperately to the first time he'd been penetrated by another man. He'd thought he couldn't take that, thought he'd never be able to, couldn't believe that the burning, tearing sensation could ever possibly give way to pleasure. Had it been worse than this? Unable to help himself, he gasped as Sam continued his slow penetration. Rick was grinning now. Nothing could have been as big as this.

Just as he thought he would have to cry out to make Sam stop or at least pull back a little until Mike could relax more, he felt the warmth of the man's stomach against the small of his back and knew he held Sam's full length within him. Mike forced himself to take deep breaths, adjusting to the prodigious shaft within him, and Sam let him, reaching his arms round him to rub his hands over his chest and stomach, leaning in close to move his mouth up and down the sides of Mike's body, gently rubbing his teeth against the skin. The unexpected light touches after the brutality of the penetration worked their magic. Mike felt his crotch and arse melt into pleasure around the stocky man's hardness. When Sam finally ground his hips into his buttocks, Mike took the pressure and returned it, working the man's thick dick with his sphincter ring, eager to give as much pleasure as he was now receiving.

Len and Rick circled the pair as they fucked, Mike all but oblivious to their presence, leaning forwards to let the posts again take his weight, spreading his legs so that the shorter Sam could step inside them and lean into him to power his hefty tool into his arse. The bald man was grunting now in time to his thrusting, near to his climax. With a stab of panic, Mike realised that he was too. If he came now, he doubted he would be ready for Len immediately afterwards, and then he would have failed the test. He had to hold back even as Sam's delicious reaming was growing faster and faster, tipping them both towards orgasm.

Sam's coming was accompanied by a great roar of pleasure and a hefty whack of Mike's buttock. Mike gasped and held back, forcing himself to breathe deeply, to think about anything other than the keening demands of his ball and dick. All he had to do was let go, release the rings: then he could grasp his cock and pump that fucker harder than it had ever been pumped before.

Mike held on.

For several seconds Sam clung on to the younger man, his shaven head resting on his shoulders, gasping into his neck, his dick still deep inside Mike. If it was shrinking down after its exertions Mike couldn't feel it, and for a second he had a horrible suspicion that either he'd been wrong about the climax or the man was going to go straight in for another fuck. He was hugely relieved when Sam slowly and carefully withdrew from him.

Sam stepped round in front of him. Sweat beaded down from his gleaming skull to his chest and leather harness. Once again he reached out to take Mike's chin, pulled his face towards his own and kissed him, thrusting his tongue in once hard. When he stepped back, he patted the side of Mike's face. 'Good boy,' he said.

Mike was two-thirds of the way through his initiation.

Len was already stepping up to Mike from behind. Twisting his head, Mike saw Len's cock erect and already in its sheath. For all he knew, the man had put the condom on while Sam had been screwing him. It was obvious he wasn't planning on giving the initiate any respite or chance of recovery. Mike braced himself.

Though mercifully not as wide as Sam, Len was hard as a ramrod and speared Mike deep with his first thrust, pushing his bone-hard dick right past Mike's enflamed prostate, setting the muscles at the base of his ball sac spasming dangerously. Mike had already been pushed to the brink of coming and Len was just starting! Mike gasped. 'Come before me, boy, and you're out!' Len growled.

Mike lost track of time as he screwed his eyes shut and fought back the climax Len was relentlessly pumping him towards. Damn it, the man was good. Hard as steel with a piston rhythm that showed no sign of slackening. If he could have borne down on him like he had with Rick, Mike might have stood a chance, but the exertion itself would have pushed him over the edge. His defeat was imminent. It would be shatteringly sweet, achingly, desperately marvellous, but it would be defeat nonetheless. Len growled in his ear. 'Come on, boy! Take that dick. Take that hard cock. Come for me, boy! Come on! You know you want to. Give it up!'

Keeping one arm around Mike's waist, pulling him in again and again on to his pumping member, Len abruptly raised his other arm. Around his wrists he wore leather bands and he began now to rub the one wrapped round his right wrist over Mike's face. 'Like it, boy?' he breathed huskily. 'Like the smell of leather? Like the taste?' The rhythm of his thrusting increased as he did this, and through the gathering tension of his building orgasm Mike saw his chance for victory.

He opened his mouth as Len rubbed the leather over his face, bit and sucked at the leather, groaned as Len rubbed it harder and faster across his eyes, nose and mouth. It wasn't all pretence. Fucked hard by three men, his senses were working at their limits. The scent and taste of the leather, the cold points of the studs on Len's leather harness as they slid over his sweat-slicked back, the urgent hot thrusting of Len's pitiless dick were driving him helplessly past the point of restraint. Turned on by Mike's responses to his torment, Len's fucking was wild, his breathing a series of ragged gasps. He was going to come. But it was too late! Mike couldn't hold out any longer. It was impossible. It was . . .

There was a long drawn-out howling from somewhere in the room. It took Mike some time to realise it was him. His come was as forceful as foam from a fire hydrant, spraying uncontrollably out from his body into the room, catching Sam and Rick across the chest as they stood in awe before it. He'd lost. He'd lost! But, by God, the release was fantastic!

It was only as the spasms finally passed, and after what seemed like hours of extreme erection his muscular dick began finally to subside, that Mike realised Len had stopped pumping him, that the other man had in fact withdrawn. Wearily, still hanging from the posts, Mike turned his head to see behind him. Len was standing against the far wall, breathing heavily, face upturned to the ceiling, eyes closed. The condom hung heavy on his subsiding cock. He had come and Mike was still holding the iron rings. Mike had won.

Drained but triumphant, Mike at last released the rings. Sam came up to him. He held out a towel, Mike's tanga and his jeans. Mike accepted them, wiped himself down and dressed. By the time he'd got round to recovering his T-shirt, the other three guys had also dressed again, or at least replaced as much of their leather gear as they needed to return to the club outside.

Len had something more. 'Congratulations,' he said. He handed over to Mike a small cardboard box. 'Welcome to the Fellowship of Iron.'

Mike shook the box. It rattled. He opened it and looked inside. 'This is it?' he said. 'One tablet?'

'Consider it a taster,' Len said. 'Like I said, you could have been police. Wasn't going to take a chance being caught with a load of gear on my hands, was I?'

'You're sure now I'm not police?'

Len snorted one last time. 'Not met a pig yet prepared to go as far undercover as you've just gone. Nah, you're straight. In a manner of speaking.' He nodded to the box. 'You want more, you go to the address inside. Tomorrow at eight. You'll get what you want.' He reached out as he had before for Mike's crotch.

Mike caught his hand in his own before it could touch him and pushed it away. Len nodded. 'Right. See you around.'

One by one, the three members of the Fellowship of Iron walked from the room. Sam was the last to go. In the doorway he stopped, turned round and winked once at Mike before leaving him and closing the door after him.

In the now empty room, Mike stood and waited: one second, two, three. When he had counted to at least twenty, he let out a great whistle of released breath and sank to the floor. He'd had ball-breaking workouts that had left him less tired than that night's exertions. He held up the box with its single tablet. Were people really prepared to go that far for such a small thing? Had Dave gone through this? Mike couldn't see it somehow, but then as events unrolled more and more he believed he knew less and less about his erstwhile lover.

He waited at least another ten minutes to give the others time to leave the bar or at least lose themselves in the crowd before he ventured out. A young black guy in a G-string and spiked collar was leading an older guy on all fours along by a choke chain. 'Room free?' the master inquired.

'All yours,' Mike said, and stood aside to let them pass.

It was only after he had left the club that he looked inside the cardboard box to see just what it was he had won. Along with the pale-blue, surprisingly small capsule was a screwed-up piece of paper. Mike unfolded it, smoothed it and held it up to a street light to see what it said. He squinted, pulled it in close to make sure he was reading it correctly. Was this some kind of joke? Then he realised that after all, dismay him though it did, it did make a kind of sick sense. Weary and dispirited, he made his way home.

Seven

It was Richard who chose the venue for their next meeting. Under the circumstances, his flat seemed the most neutral location. Mike arrived first. They embraced and kissed, but Richard thought Mike had been reluctant. Or had it been him? Now that he and Mike had been sexually estranged from each other for nearly two weeks, Richard found it difficult to tell him about just what and who he had been up to. He also realised, and the thought made him uncomfortable, that the encounter which in many ways had been the most innocent, the brief sweet interlude with Sergeant Ferris on the very sofa they were now standing in front of, was the one he was least willing to talk about.

What he couldn't know was that Mike was feeling more or less the same. How did you tell your boyfriend that although you haven't slept with him recently, you have managed to take part in what was essentially an S&M orgy with three other guys?

They were saved from the complications of small talk by the doorbell. Now things get even trickier, Richard thought.

Paul was on the doorstep. Two steps back from the doorstep actually, Richard noted with faint amusement. He wondered whether that was so he couldn't be hugged and kissed for all the world to see. When they entered the living room, Paul hung back in the doorway, looking from Richard to Mike, uncertain about just what this formidable-looking man knew and what he felt about it.

'Sergeant Ferris,' said Mike. He'd seated himself on the sofa. He didn't get up. He didn't hold his hand out.

'Paul,' said Paul. He didn't extend his hand either. Casting his eyes around he was relieved to see that Richard had cleared the single armchair of its piles of books and papers, and walked over and sat down on that.

Thinking quickly, Richard pulled out the office chair from behind his desk, twirled it round and sat on that so that he could see both of them and have access to his computer for what he had to show them shortly. 'Tea? Coffee?' Paul politely declined, Mike waved a hand to pass. Richard sighed. 'Down to business, then. Gentlemen, we have contact!' His dramatic statement was met by two pairs of unamused eyes and a silence waiting to be filled by explanation. Richard sighed again. He twirled his chair round to face his computer and with a jab at the mouse banished the screen saver program. 'Voilà!' The inbox of his e-mail set-up sprang into view. The cursor was fixed at the latest message. 'F.o.I.' proclaimed the header. 'An acknowledgement of the details I sent to the Fellowship of Iron,' Richard proclaimed. 'And an invitation.' Paul rose from his seat to walk over and get a closer view.

Beaten to it, and unwilling to join the sergeant at the screen, Mike sat back. 'What does it say?' he asked Richard.

'A time and a place,' Richard said gleefully. 'Spencers', the old glove factory outside town.'

'That's not far from here,' Paul said, returning thoughtfully to his seat.

'Yeah. About a ten-minute drive, maybe.'

'Convenient.'

'Yeah.'

'No, I mean "convenient". Very. You say this Fellowship is a national organisation?'

'At the very least. I haven't looked further, but some of the links suggest it could be fairly wide-spread internationally.'

'And they set up a meeting for you almost round the corner.

Most global businesses aren't that accommodating. It also suggests,' he said, leaning forwards, 'that they've done their research well. They know where you live, Richard.'

Richard could see what Paul was driving at, and he could also see the alarmed look coming into Mike's eyes. 'Your problem,' he said to Paul, 'is that you think establishment. Police brainwashing in the ideology of conformity to the existing societal structures.'

Paul didn't bat an eyelid, but he didn't smile either. 'I haven't got a clue what you're talking about,' he said evenly, 'but I do think we need to be very, very careful. We're talking about people who are peddling an illegal drug. People like that are quite capable of hurting people like you. Badly. And they won't be put off by long words.'

Richard bridled at the change from 'we' to 'you', with all its implications. 'We're talking about a bodybuilding steroid here, not crack cocaine.'

'In Glasgow, there were gang wars over sales pitches for ice-cream. It doesn't matter what's being sold. If there's enough money involved, there are people who'll kill for it.'

'This isn't Glasgow.'

'And you're deliberately missing the point.'

'He's right, Rich,' said Mike.

Richard spun his chair round to face his boyfriend. Irritated at being ganged up on, he couldn't help also seeing the amusing irony of the situation. He'd known very well that the meeting between Mike and Paul was going to be difficult, given the circumstances of their first meeting and the suspicions he was fairly sure Mike had about what had already taken place between him and Paul, and he'd known he was going to have to work at getting them to like each other if they were all three going to work on this Fellowship of Iron business. Now, though, he saw that even without his help they were finding common ground, and he was the one being left high and dry. 'Well, unless you have anything else to go on it's the only lead we have.'

Mike dug into the pocket of his jeans and pulled out the spoils of his recent victory, the cardboard box and its contents. 'As a matter of fact, I have.'

Richard took the box, inspected it and passed it on to Paul. 'Tell us all.'

Mike told them. His account was clear and detailed, except for the time spent with three leathermen in one small room and what exactly happened there. Throughout his account, it was Richard's reactions he was following. He could tell that Richard was listening closely, as a journalist and as a man who knew him intimately. He knew really that he didn't have a chance of hiding everything that he'd done the previous night. He hoped, though, he could at least limit the damage for the time being.

It was Paul who asked the first question. 'You say this man Len only had the one tablet on him because he'd been worried you might have been with the police?' Mike nodded, his eyes on Richard. 'So, why did he decide he could trust you?'

'There was . . . a test.'

'A test? What kind of test?'

Richard gave Mike a couple of seconds to squirm before he supplied the answer. 'You had sex with him, didn't you?'

Mike nodded. 'Yes.'

Paul glanced at Richard to see how he took that. This was like a replay of the first time he'd met the pair of them. He was surprised to see how calm Richard was. 'Any . . . specialities involved, Mike?' Richard asked levelly. 'The Buckle does have a certain reputation, after all.'

'We'll talk about this later,' Mike said, with a none-too-subtle nod of the head towards Paul.

Paul shook his head. 'This doesn't sound right.'

'I told you before,' Richard began in a brittle voice, 'things are different –'

Paul interrupted him. 'No, no, I don't mean that. This meeting, this place, the . . . test . . . and the one tablet leading you on to somewhere else. This doesn't sound like any other set-up I've ever heard of before. And it doesn't fit in with this global network you keep saying is selling itself on the Internet. It's wrong. Something's . . .' He shook his head as he tried to work out just what it was that was making him unhappy. He gestured to Mike. 'You're just one guy out on the street, and you're having to go through all this to get your supply. Who else is going to have this sort of motivation?'

'Bodybuilding's big business, these days. And for some guys it's a way of life. They can get pretty desperate. Steroid pushers know that.'

Paul looked unconvinced. 'Maybe, maybe. But making your customers work this hard isn't exactly good business sense. It's like there's a whole other level of the selling chain that's missing somewhere.' He looked up. 'You didn't pay him for this, did you? No money changed hands at any point?'

Mike found he was actually quite pleased to be able to tell a simple truth. 'No. Not a penny.' It hadn't really struck him as odd that money hadn't been mentioned at all until Paul made the point.

'There was payment in kind,' said Richard coldly.

'All right, then. That's good. That there was no money involved I mean.' Paul looked as if he didn't quite completely believe Mike, but he had no choice other than to take his word. 'We have got to be very careful here. Things are happening fast. If money had changed hands, your legal situation could have been tricky. Remember that when we go out tonight. Don't take any cash with you, not even a penny, and no credit cards.'

'We?'

'Yes, we. You need me there for your own protection.'

'I can look after myself.'

Paul took in Mike's powerful build. 'I don't doubt that for a minute,' he said, 'but I'm not talking about your physical well-being. Like I said, you've got to be careful about your legal situation. We know you're going to meet a drug dealer for the good guys. A judge and jury might not be so trusting.'

'If that's the case, then maybe we should take this to your boss, Inspector Whatshisname, and get the real police involved. No offence meant,' Mike added.

Paul tried to picture Inspector Taylor's reaction to what he had heard from these two so far. He felt uncomfortable, very uncomfortable with the way things were developing. Information gathered from a distance over a computer was now turning into meetings with live criminals, and he could see a very real danger of them ending up in some very nasty shit. But could he tell Taylor he'd been working behind his back on a case that had officially been declared closed? Especially when all he had to show for it so far was one tablet and some stories from men the inspector clearly despised? If, however, Paul could be in on the collar of an actual dealer . . . 'Not yet,' he said reluctantly. 'We just haven't got enough. If we want to make anything of this we have to go further.'

'All right.' Richard adopted a brisk tone. 'So we go first to the contact that I've got lined up here –' he tapped his computer '– and then afterwards we go with Mike to the contact he's got lined up. I assume it's nearby, too. Where is it exactly?'

Mike handed over the small piece of paper with the address on it that had so surprised and depressed him the previous night. Paul took it and read it out. 'Walker Street.' He sensed something passing between Mike and Richard, some kind of recognition. 'Does that mean something?'

'It's the street Dave Ross's gym is on,' said Richard.

Paul looked thoughtful. 'Well, if Mr Ross was involved in the distribution of this steroid –' he stopped, aware of the dangerous ground he was walking on to. 'Yes, well, that's what we're trying to prove, isn't it?'

'Actually,' said Richard, taking the paper from Paul and handing it back to Mike, 'I think it's what we're trying to disprove. Anyway, like I said, first we go to Spencers' and then bomb like hell across the city to Walker Street. It'll be tight but we can just about make it.'

Paul shook his head with professional firmness. 'No. You can't rush something like this. We're going to have to prioritise. I don't like this Internet contact.' He raised a hand to forestall Richard. 'Don't ask me why, but it doesn't feel right. Quite a lot of things don't but that's the worst. No, we'll go with Mike's contact. Mike's trusted; whoever's there won't be expecting trouble. Mike says hello, the guy gives him the stuff, I come along and arrest him. End of story. I'll bring a wire from the station.'

'End of story, all right. You'll have one dealer locked away.' Richard tapped his computer screen. 'There's hundreds of them out there.'

'I know that. And I also know there's not a thing we can do about it. What were you expecting, Richard, that you could step in and sort out problems the slow old British police force hadn't been up to? This is the real world. Don't let yourself get carried away.'

Richard refused to let the sting of Paul's rebuke show. 'OK, so I go along to my contact and check out the scene, and when you two come back from playing cops and robbers we can follow up on that.'

Again Paul shook his head, even more emphatically this time. 'No way. It wouldn't be safe for you to go on your own. They tell me even thugs can use computers these days. You don't know who's likely to be waiting for you at the other end. If anyone.'

Richard glared at him. Mike knew from long experience what was going on inside Richard's head right at that moment, the ruthless examination and re-examination of facts before he spoke. Much to Mike's surprise, though, Richard sank back into his computer seat and nodded curtly. 'All right. I'll come with you.' Mike frowned briefly. He'd never been able to best Richard so easily in an argument.

Paul took a deep breath before this last and highest hurdle. 'No, you'll not. You'll be staying here.'

'What?'

'It's not safe, Richard. This isn't some game or some television programme. Police don't get to take their friends on jobs with them.'

'You mean, because I'm not a pumped-up killing machine like Mike here?' Richard exploded, too angry to register that use of the word 'friend'.

'I mean because you'd be an untrained civilian going up against some very nasty customers. It just doesn't make sense for you to come. No way, and that's final, or this "operation" we seem to have got ourselves into doesn't go ahead at all.'

Mike waited for Richard's reaction to that one. He had noticed that use of his boyfriend's first name, and the use of that word 'friend'. Now part of him was, he had to admit, looking forward to the attack Richard was bound to launch at this patronising policeman's decision, even though the other part heartily agreed with it himself.

'All right,' said Richard through gritted teeth. 'I'll stay. But I won't like it.'

Both Mike and Paul took a few seconds to fully accept what they had heard. Both waited for the surely inevitable conditions. When none came, they briefly glanced at each other to check that the other hadn't heard something he'd missed, but when Richard continued to sit simmering in front of his computer, they finally allowed themselves to relax. 'OK,' said Paul. 'Good.'

Mike regarded Richard closely. Richard glared back but said nothing. He continued to say nothing as the other two made their plans and arranged when and where they were going to meet later that evening, except to ask bitterly whether they would like him to make himself useful and put the kettle on. They both declined the offer. When their arrangements were finalised, they both sat back. Mike waited for Paul to make his excuses and leave. Paul didn't. Fair enough. He would just sit there and wait until the policeman got the message. 'Don't you have training you need to be doing?' Richard snapped. 'I mean, your exertions the other night at The Buckle must have taken a lot out of you.'

Goaded by his boyfriend's words, Mike rose and headed for the door. 'I'll see you later,' he said stiffly to Paul. Paul nodded. 'And I'll see you –' he looked across at Richard, who was still sitting sulkily at his computer, making no effort to accompany him to the door '– I'll see you whenever. Bye.' He had gone before Richard could reply.

Richard got up from his swivel chair, crossed to the sofa and threw himself in it. 'Oh, shit!'

'Angry?' Paul ventured.

'Yes! But not in the way you think.'

'He's been with another man. Again.'

'Another one?' Richard laughed. 'Let me take you to The Buckle some time. If you get out of there after only one shag, it's been a poor night.'

'Is that all it is, then: shagging?'

Richard looked across at the policeman on his armchair, trying to gauge the tone of his question. 'Sometimes, yes. Not always.'

Paul rose from his chair and walked across the room. He thought of Guy back in his small plastic tent, Guy's hand on his cock, the breathless excitement of being wanked off in the street. It didn't make his heart pound the way the memory of Richard's hand gently but firmly working him to climax did. It didn't excite him as much as the thought that Richard was here again in front of him and he could perhaps repeat the experience. He hesitated in front of the settee. Had he judged this right? There was still so much he didn't understand. Richard said he accepted Mike's infidelities, and had not been backwards in coming forwards himself last time, but was this really the moment, only minutes after his boyfriend had walked out after such a difficult meeting?

'You going to stand up there all night, or am I going to have to drag you down to my level?' Richard asked.

Paul sank on to the sofa, his arms reaching out and enfolding Richard, pulling him in closely, his mouth on Richard's. 'I thought –' he finally said, pulling back a moment from Richard's eager mouth.

'Don't think. Don't talk. I've had enough of both today,' Richard said angrily, and he pushed his mouth savagely over Paul's again, thrusting his tongue in deep, leaning over the policeman's body and raising his knee to rest it in the policeman's groin, making Paul gasp at the sudden unexpected pressure. Wildly, the two men ran their hands over each other's bodies, Richard tearing at Paul's tie and the buttons down the front of his shirt, Paul roughly pulling up Richard's T-shirt, rubbing his fingers hard over the nipples beneath, surprised and exhilarated by the cries of pleasure this brought from Richard.

'I want more than just a hand shandy this time, you fucker,' Richard whispered. He felt the other man falter.

'I don't . . . I mean, I haven't . . .'

'Don't think! Don't talk!' Richard pushed hard at the policeman's crotch, delighted by the undeniable hardness and size there, scattering all of Paul's rational thoughts.

'Oh, God, yes!'

Something small and heavy slipped from one of Paul's pockets and fell to the floor. 'Was that a mobile phone, or were you just pleased to see me?' Richard gasped, even as he tugged at Paul's belt.

Paul didn't answer, didn't even laugh, too lost in the sensations flooding his body. Eyes closed, he was squeezing Richard's solid cock, as blind and urgent in his need as a baby sucking milk. It was several seconds before either of them registered that the phone that had just fallen to the floor was ringing.

'Ignore it,' Richard gasped, throwing Paul's belt to one side and starting on his fly buttons. 'Probably banged something when it fell on the floor.'

Paul struggled to sit up against Richard's efforts to rip his trousers from his legs. 'No,' he gasped. 'No, I can't.'

'Ring back later. Ten minutes. Five even!'

Paul shook his head and leaned forwards, falling to his knees as his trousers were halfway down his thighs by now. 'It might be important,' he shouted. He jammed the small machine to his ear. 'Ferris. Yes?'

Richard sat back, breathing heavily. On any other occasion, the timing of this damned call might have been comic. Now, it made him want to scream out loud with frustration. He moved forwards as if to carry on with the removal of his guest's trousers, even while he was on the phone. Paul pushed him back sharply with one hand and a fierce expression. Richard subsided and watched. Whoever was calling Paul wasn't giving the other man much of a chance to speak. Paul sat on the floor and listened. Richard watched as his flushed skin went first pale then an angry red. When the call finished, Paul snapped the machine closed without a word to whoever had called. He stood and, with his back to Richard, pulled up his trousers before looking around the room for his belt.

'Who was it?'

Paul found the belt and began threading it through his trousers again. 'My boss,' he said tersely.

'What? You mean Taylor?'

'*Inspector* Taylor.'

'So what is it? Some emergency?'

Paul hesitated. 'Not in the way you think.'

'Then I don't get it. Where are you going? And why have you got to go now?'

Paul turned to face Richard as he was pulling his jacket on. 'He knows I'm here, Richard. He knows I'm with you.'

For a second, Richard was literally speechless as the implications sank in. 'How the fuck could he? Are you all tagged these days? Does big Chief Inspector Taylor get to follow you all around all day on some giant screen back in the Bat Cave?'

'He's not a chief inspector, and I don't know how he knows. But he does.'

'So? You don't punch a clock, do you? Why shouldn't you be here? It's not like there's an official case or anything. He's seen to that.'

Paul started for the door. 'I've got to go.'

Richard moved to bar his exit. 'I say again, Paul, why? You're not doing anything illegal. They stopped burning people for this a long time ago, you know.'

Paul raised a shaky hand to his forehead, eager to get out, to avoid this unpleasant discussion, shaken much more than he'd care to admit by the unexpected phone call. Richard was right; it raised very many issues. He wasn't sure how many of them he wanted to confront, or how closely. He knew he didn't want to confront them with Richard there. 'It's not right,' he said finally.

Richard reached out with one hand and stroked the side of Paul's face. 'What's not right? This? Does this feel not right to you? Did what we were doing a minute ago seem not right? Don't listen to other people, Paul. Especially not people at work.'

'It's not just "work". And . . . And you've got a boyfriend, for God's sake.'

'We've been through that. I told you, it's cool.'

Paul looked him straight in the face. 'Well, it doesn't look cool from where I'm standing.'

Richard withdrew his hand. Without a word, he stood to one side and let Paul pass. 'I'll let you know how things go tonight,' Paul said.

'You're still doing that with Mike, then? Not afraid to let the big bad inspector find out about it?'

Paul stood on the top stair leading down to Richard's front door. 'That's different.'

'Yeah, right. Mike's probably not going to kiss you. If he does, remember, he likes to play bottom.'

Paul flushed, went to say something, but ended up shaking his head and leaving.

Richard gave him ten seconds, counted out a second set of ten, then let out an almighty yell, purging himself of the bitter, confused feelings that were welling up inside him. He didn't care if Paul heard him. Point of fact, he didn't particularly care what Paul thought about him at that moment. Or Mike, either. Pair of patronising, self-obsessed bastards that they were. Treating him like a kid. Who the fuck did they think they were?

He flung himself down at his computer desk, the violent action jarring the mouse and knocking off the screensaver program that had kicked in again while he and Paul had been thrashing about on the sofa. Once more the message from the Fellowship of Iron glowed on his monitor, the message he'd waited so long for. Richard stared at it for long seconds and knew what he was going to do. It was stupid. He knew it was stupid. And yes it was probably dangerous. He knew that too. He rose and headed for the bedroom and his rucksack. But he wasn't a kid, he was an investigative journalist, damn it – a good one, who'd just been head-hunted by someone with more money than God. You didn't get successful by staying at home and letting your boy-friends do all the dirty work. He paused for a second. 'Boyfriend. Singular,' he corrected himself. He'd show them. He couldn't help a bitter laugh. Now that really did sound childish.

Outside his flat, Paul Ferris climbed into his car and drove off without a backwards look. Three seconds later a black transit van with mirrored windows pulled out and followed him.

The old glove factory would have made an ideal cruising ground, Richard thought. Far enough out of town and off the beaten track to avoid unwanted attention; enough nooks and crannies for a clandestine shag; close enough to the bright lights and more comfortable beds of civilisation if such was preferred. He wandered around the derelict buildings, kicking at loose stones and clumps of weed, waiting for his contact from the Fellowship of Iron to show his face. If all that did come out of this was an offer of a quick screw up against a wall, Richard wasn't sure in his present mood whether he'd say no or not. 'You're a professional, Green,' he muttered to himself. 'Make the contact first, then if he's good looking ask if he fancies a shag.'

There was the sound of footsteps behind him. Punctual, Richard thought. He took a deep breath, forced himself to look a lot calmer than he felt and turned round. In an instant, he felt as childish and foolish as he'd accused Paul and Mike of making him feel. Stupidly, short-sightedly, unforgivably idiotically, he had assumed there'd be one contact. He could cope with one contact, couldn't he? He knew how to look after himself. Now he found himself confronted by three.

In the gathering gloom of early evening, it was hard to make out details of faces. All three were in leather jackets. One was shaven-headed, one had long, shoulder-length hair and shades. They sauntered towards him, hands in their pockets. There was no hurry; equally, there was no hesitation. There was no doubt that Richard was their target.

Richard looked around him. No one about. Of course not. That was the whole point, wasn't it? Should he run now? Don't be stupid. Why should he? OK, so there were three of them. It was cool. It would be all right. He eyed up his escape routes as they drew nearer, just in case.

The three new arrivals came to a halt. Two stood in front of him; the third, the guy with the long hair, walked behind. Paul turned, trying to angle himself so that he could be facing all of them at the same time. The guy behind moved again, keeping himself right in Paul's blind spot. The shaven-headed guy shifted slightly to the right, and Paul found himself in the centre of a triangle. His escape routes were as useless to him now as if they were miles away.

'Looking for Iron?' said the guy Richard assumed was their leader.

'Yeah.'

'Looks like he needs some,' came the voice of the long-haired man behind him.

'Doesn't look like much of a bodybuilder,' said the shaven-headed man, folding his arms across his chest. His leather jacket moved slightly and Richard caught a glimpse of naked chest underneath.

'I'm buying for a . . . friend,' said Richard.

The leader nodded ironically. 'Sure you are.' As he spoke, he was pulling something from his jacket pocket, a strip of some material. He proceeded to wind it round his knuckles, round and round. When it was done, he tied it off then made a fist, looking down at the material stretched across his knuckles and smiling. To one side of him, Richard could just make out the shaven-headed guy pulling something from his jacket. There was motion behind him as well. 'Only problem is, there's kind of a test you have to go through first.' There was a low chuckle from one of the others.

The blow to his head was like an explosion in Richard's skull. Blinding yellow light and searing pain shot through his brain. When his sight had cleared enough for him to once again be able to see, he was somehow on the ground. The three men were standing over him, grinning. The long-haired guy was holding what looked like a crowbar, tapping it reflectively in one hand. In an oddly detached way, Richard noted the red stickiness at the end of it. 'Here's your Iron, kid. Take it like a man.' The three men closed in on him.

Was it policemen or buses? Mike wondered. Something about never one around and then all at once three turned up at once. He stomped his feet angrily on the pavement and shoved his hands into his jacket pocket. It was buses. Policemen were supposed to be there to tell you the time and look younger every day. Not to move in on your boyfriend. 'Where the hell are you?'

He'd turned up at the small car park just down the road from Walker Street half an hour before, as arranged, and then he'd waited for Paul to turn up. Time ticked on but no Paul. When it was only one minute to the rendezvous time, Mike left his car with a curse and crossed to where he was supposed to be waiting. The young sergeant had made such a fuss about security and getting this right, and now the wanker hadn't even turned up. That would be something to tell Richard when this caper was over. Maybe he wouldn't be quite so star-struck when he found out about this. A nasty thought suddenly occurred to Mike. What if Ferris had deliberately not turned up? If anything happened to Mike, then it wouldn't be his fault and the field would be clear for Richard.

He shook his head and stomped some more on the pavement. Paranoia, Mike, he told himself sharply. The cop has cocked up so you're going to have to go on alone. Play it by ear. Maybe Ferris would turn up in time to make this arrest he was so looking forward to. Yeah, right.

''Lo Mike.'

He'd been so absorbed in his musings he hadn't heard the approaching footsteps, hadn't noticed which direction they had come from. It was Sam from The Buckle. He smiled openly at Mike, warmly even. Strangely, Mike found this friendliness more difficult to cope with than any of the more hostile encounters he'd envisaged. 'Hi. You're late.'

Sam sauntered closer. 'Bit of unfinished business to take care of, first.'

Mike looked behind him, then behind himself. 'Either of the others with you?'

Sam shook his head. 'Nah. Thought I'd like to do this one myself. Alone.'

By this time, the grin on Sam's face was unmistakable. Oh great, Mike thought. Not that the thought of Sam's club cock forcing its way up his arse wasn't an appealing one. Mike felt himself stirring at the memory and at the thought of just what they could do if he was free to use his hands. It just seemed bad manners to lead a guy on, maybe even shag him and then set him up for arrest. Not, he thought, that it looked like that was going to happen that night. There was still no sign of Policeman Paul. He played for time. 'Got my stuff?'

Sam unzipped the front of his leather jacket and held the flap open. Poking out of an inside pocket was another cardboard box, similar to the one Mike had already earned. This move also made it clear that Sam was bare-chested under his jacket. 'Want to come and get it?'

Mike forced a smile on to his face, stood his ground and held

144

his hand out. Sam shrugged and handed the carton over. Mike took it, opened it and shook out the contents. Two pale blue capsules tumbled into the palm of his hand. 'What's this?' he said, holding them out accusingly.

'On the house, Mikey boy. Just like the last one. Iron's powerful stuff. The three you've got now should see you through the month.'

'And after that?'

'You see me again and you pay for another load. Or –' Sam stepped closer '– you see me again and you don't pay.'

Mike turned the capsules over in his hand, as if inspecting them while he considered Sam's offer. 'Must be hard finding someone who can take that donkey dick of yours.'

'You have no idea. The things we could do, Mikey boy.' Sam abruptly stopped and stepped back as if he'd caught himself getting carried away. 'And I don't just mean sex.'

Mike looked up from the capsules puzzled. 'What do you mean?'

'Iron's new shit. We're getting in on this on the ground floor. The Fellowship of Iron is really going to go places. You could be with us. With me. So, what do you say?'

You're under arrest. That's what he wanted to say. But he couldn't. Paul hadn't turned up, and without him it was just his word against Sam's as to what had really happened and been said here this evening. Besides, even if he did try to arrest Sam, what about the others? He'd never get them. But if he read Sam right, the leatherman was offering him another opportunity to nail all three of them.

If he read him right.

Running right through Sam's words was an undeniable sexual hunger. His voice, his eyes, his stance all made it crystal clear that what he really wanted to do was ram that mammoth cock of his between Mike's legs again. Was that all there was to the offer? Did the rest of the Fellowship even know about it, or was this just a little private enterprise on Sam's part? 'I need to think about it,' he said.

To his relief, Sam didn't look surprised. 'OK, Mikey boy,' he

145

said, zipping up his jacket again. 'But don't leave it too long, eh?' He patted his crotch and grinned. 'Be seeing you again soon.'

'How can I reach you?'

Sam was already ambling away. 'Don't call us, we'll call you.' And then he was gone around a corner.

Mike leaned back against a cold brick wall and let out his feelings in one long whistle. This was getting crazier by the minute. He stayed leaning against the wall to let his racing heart slow down to something like normal again. He wondered if police work was like this, whether guys like Paul got off on the excitement. For that matter, maybe Richard got something like this from following up leads for his writing. It was heady stuff. On the whole, though, he thought he'd stick with bodybuilding. It had to be healthier in the long run.

It was as he leaned there coming down that he saw the light. Maybe it had been there all along and he'd been too wound up to notice; maybe it had only just come on. Either way, it shouldn't have been there at that time. A light, in Dave's gym. His gym.

Mike crossed the road and walked up to the main entrance. The doors were open. Mike entered. There was no sound from within, none of the familiar clanking, grunting sounds. Cautiously, he stepped further inside, scanning to left and right of him. No one on the desk, no one at any of the equipment. He stood in the centre of the main workout area. 'Roy? Hello, Roy? Is that you?' Silence. 'Sam?' No reply. 'Who is it? Who's there?'

There was a sound behind him, a door opening. He whirled round to face it. Standing in the door that connected the gym to the flat above was the man he'd only glimpsed twice before, the man who'd run from him twice – first from this gym and then from Dave's funeral. Well, he wasn't running anywhere now. Mike stood between him and the exit and there was no way he was letting the man escape without some sort of explanation. The man himself seemed to realise this. At any rate, he didn't look as if he was planning to run away again. He stood in the door frame regarding Mike coolly, defiantly even.

'How did you get in?'

'I have a key.' And the man held the key up in front of him to prove his point.

'What are you doing here?'

'That's my business.'

Mike shook his head. 'Wrong. This is my gym now. It's my business.'

'Oh, yes. It is, isn't it? You must be very pleased with yourself.'

That wasn't the response Mike had expected. The voice was sharp with sarcasm and hostility. But why? He didn't even know this man. Did he? Again Mike was struck by an eerily familiar quality to the face. And more. He couldn't shake the feeling that that face and these surroundings went together. If he'd met this person before, it had been here, among the chrome and mirrored surrounds of Dave's gym. But that was crazy. He just knew that had never happened. 'Who are you?' he demanded.

The intruder straightened slightly, as if drawing himself up for a formal introduction. 'My name,' he said, 'is Devlin Lancaster.'

The name meant nothing to Mike. 'I'm –'

'You're Michael Anthony Kilby. I know who you are.'

Mike took two steps towards the stranger, angered by his attitude. 'All right, Devlin Lancaster, I've had just about enough of you appearing then disappearing, turning up where you're not welcome and not saying why. I'll ask you again, what the fuck are you doing here, and what do you know about the death of Dave Ross?'

Far from being cowed by the potentially threatening advance of a mountain of a man like Mike, Devlin Lancaster came out of the doorway to meet him halfway. 'What do I know?' he said, voice rising in anger. 'That's rich coming from you, you bastard! Yes, I've been following you. Yes, I've been finding out about you, and now there's just one thing I want to ask you.' He jabbed a finger at Mike's broad chest, apparently too furious to care about any possible consequences. 'Why did you kill Dave Ross?'

Mike's jaw dropped. The question was like a physical blow to the stomach. But Devlin hadn't finished with the surprises for that evening. He took another two steps forwards until the two men were practically nose to nose. 'Why did you kill my father?'

Eight

First there was the pain, a great deal of pain. Shards of glass were stabbing into his skull. Clubs of molten metal were beating his arms, legs and chest, and someone was turning a knife between his ribs every time he breathed. Curiously though, it was all a long away off, his sensations and yet someone else's. Not something he had to worry about. All he had to do was float in this vast nothingness. Just float . . .

Then there were the sounds, many sounds. People talking urgently, much movement, electronic sounds he couldn't place, and a voice calling: 'Richard? Can you hear me? Richard?' That was his name, wasn't it? He thought so. But it didn't matter. All he wanted to do was float. Richard could answer the call. He would just float . . .

And then came the light. A dim red dawn that he slowly realised was light seen through closed eyelids. He opened his eyes and was blinded by the brilliance that shone in, igniting fierce pain deep in his head. He screwed his eyes tight shut again, the very motion of doing so causing still more agony in his skull. He wanted to go back to the dark and the warm, to float away from this pain, but the voice was there again calling his name. 'Richard? Richard? Are you awake?' Tentatively, very tentatively he opened his eyes again, just a fraction this time. A man's face looked over him, dark against the brightness behind him, distorted by his tear-blurred vision. 'M . . . Mike?'

The looming face gave a small, rueful laugh. 'No, it's Paul.'

Richard went to lift a hand to wipe his eyes clear but shooting pain and Paul's gently restraining hand prevented him, and he accepted the policeman's dabbing his eyes with a paper tissue. When he could finally see he took in what he'd instinctively already worked out. He was in a hospital room, starkly and antiseptically white with Paul Ferris sitting next to his bed on a chair. He looked around as well as he could without moving his head. 'No flowers?' he said weakly.

'You're supposed to say, "Where am I?"'

'Well, unless you've kidnapped me, dragged me home to wreak terrible sexual pleasures on my body and have very strange tastes in bedroom décor, I think I've worked that one out.' Richard's forehead furrowed, then smoothed again as he realised the pain that even that small involuntary gesture caused. 'The only thing is, I can't quite remember how I got here.'

'Don't worry. The doctors say that's quite normal. You've had several blows to the head, among other things. You're still in shock. It might take a while for things to come back to you. Just relax.' Paul knew the injunction was a waste of time. He could see in Richard's face that he was struggling to put together the events that had brought him to this bed.

'I went to make the contact.'

'Like you were told not to.'

Richard ignored him. 'And I was met. Somebody came . . .'

'Some bodies.'

'That's right! There were three of them. I remember them standing there. I remember thinking this might have been a mistake, and then –'

An expression of despair crossed Richard's face as he struggled to recall exactly what had happened after that. Impulsively Paul reached out and took the young man's hand as it lay there on the bedsheet. '– and then you proceeded to have the shit kicked out of you.'

'Oh, yeah. I knew there was something I'd forgotten.'

From outside the room came the sounds of a hospital at work.

JACK STEVENS

In the room itself there was a companionable silence. Richard, eyes closed again, kept his hand on the bedsheet. Paul kept his hand on Richard's. Slowly Paul leaned forwards, trying to see if, as he suspected, Richard had lost consciousness again.

Richard spoke without opening his eyes. 'I'm just trying to work out how to do this without feeling like my head is going to come off.'

'Think yourself lucky it's still attached to your shoulders. The doctors say you're going to have one hell of a headache for a few days and some spectacular bruises for some time longer, but you're damned lucky it wasn't a great deal worse.' The young policeman squeezed Richard's hand. 'You could have been killed, Richard. I think . . . I'm pretty sure that was the intention.'

'So why wasn't I?'

'Like I said, you were damned –'

Richard opened his eyes again and shook his head slightly, even though the motion brought tears of pain to his eyes. 'How did I get here, Paul?'

'I brought you here.'

'You followed me?'

'Not exactly. I . . . I had a pretty good idea you'd ignore what I said about not going. I decided it would be a good idea to go along and just make sure, before I met up with Mike.'

'Thought you said the two meetings couldn't be done?'

'Yeah, well, good thing for you I tried. I got there just as your Internet friends were starting to lay into you.'

'Took 'em on all by yourself?'

Paul smiled. 'Actually, no. They ran as soon as they saw me.'

'You're a frightening guy.'

'More like they didn't know I was on my own.'

'You're still my hero.'

'All part of the job. Do it for anyone.'

'Would you, Paul?' Richard turned his hand until it was no longer just covered by but was holding Paul's hand. 'Would you?'

Paul swallowed. 'I . . .'

Whatever he might have been about to say was interrupted by the opening of the door into the room. Paul snatched his hand back and got rapidly to his feet. Detective Inspector Taylor stood

150

in the doorway. He looked from his sergeant to the man in the bed and then back to Paul again. 'A word, Sergeant Ferris,' he said. He turned his back and walked off, not waiting for an acknowledgement.

'I'll be back,' said Paul.

'Mmm,' said Richard. His eyes had closed and he could feel himself drifting back into the comforting warm numbness of unconsciousness. Paul envied him.

Taylor was waiting in the corridor. With a curt gesture he indicated that they both go into a nearby deserted waiting room. Taylor did not sit down. Paul knew better than to suggest it. 'Explain,' he said.

With the professional brevity of a policeman giving evidence in court, Paul told his superior about the attack on Richard, his rescue and the transport here. He did not tell Taylor what Richard was doing alone at such a spot at such a time, and he did not tell him why he had been there to rescue him. The omissions were glaring. He braced himself for Taylor's questions and the inevitable repercussions.

To his surprise, Taylor's tack was a different one. 'Am I to assume, Sergeant, that your involvement at this juncture is pursuant to the case you and I dealt with some weeks ago?' The inspector too had slipped into formal language. It was, Paul knew, a bad sign.

'The death of David Ross, yes, sir.'

'And did I or did I not inform you that that case was closed?'

'Yes, sir, but –'

'Don't "but" me, Sergeant. Were you or were you not told by your commanding officer that that case was closed?'

Paul gritted his teeth. 'Yes, sir, but I have some new information about the matter. There have been –'

'No, Sergeant, I have some new information to tell you.' Taylor silenced Paul. 'Firstly, I remind you that the death of Mr David Ross is officially and irreversibly closed. Secondly, what we have here is a completely separate incident. And let us look a little more closely at it, shall we? A young man of known . . . persuasions is out by himself at night in a remote area of town where he is attacked. Bashed, you might say. Questions will of course have to be asked about what he was doing there at that time on his own. Questions might well be asked of anyone who was hanging around that spot at that time. Don't you agree, Sergeant?' Taylor continued without pause and without giving Paul a chance to reply. 'So there really is no need for you to stay here any longer, Sergeant Ferris. You have done your civic duty. I'm sure the young man in there was very grateful. Now it would be better for all concerned if you turned around, went and left this to be dealt with through the proper channels.'

Paul flushed, part impotent rage and part embarrassed guilt. He'd noticed that edge Taylor had put on 'grateful'. Had he seen Richard holding his hand? 'Sir —' he began.

'Sergeant Ferris!' Taylor's bellow overrode Paul's words and brought startled looks from a couple of passing nurses. 'In case I haven't made myself absolutely clear, I am ordering you to leave this matter well enough alone. It will be dealt with in the proper manner.'

'Like the death of Dave Ross was "dealt with"?'

Taylor's face darkened at the younger man's insubordinate comment. 'Get out, Ferris,' he said in a low whisper. 'Get out now.'

One thing that had always been important to Paul about the police force was its structure, its discipline. There were rules, there were codes. You knew where you were. When so much else in his life had seemed confused or uncertain, they'd given him stability and security. It was difficult now therefore to challenge them. He just didn't know how. Impotently, he could see no way to deal with his superior's blind opposition. 'I have to get my coat,' he said, 'if that's OK.' He left the room without waiting for an answer.

Back in the small private room, Richard was stirring again. Even in his drugged state he could see that something was wrong. 'I've got to go,' Paul said, snatching his coat.

'No goodbye kiss?'

'That . . . wouldn't be a good idea.'

'Paul, wait.'

Reluctantly, Paul turned back to face the hospital bed.

'How did the rest of it go? With you and Mike, I mean?'

Mike! The shock of what had happened to Richard had driven the evening's other operation completely from his mind. Should he tell Richard that, though? Already he could see the beaten young man slipping back into unconsciousness. Wouldn't it be kinder to let him sleep thinking that all was well? 'Fine,' he said. 'It all went fine. I'll tell you about it tomorrow.'

Paul left the hospital, quickly determined to find out what had happened to Mike that evening. He hoped to hell he'd been right.

'Your father?'

Devlin Lancaster pointed to one of the floor-length mirrors they were standing in front of. 'Don't you think there's a resemblance? We did. I don't exactly have my father's physique, but I try to make up for it in other ways.'

Mike was shaking his head. 'You can't be. You just can't. He never said –'

'It doesn't really matter what you think, Mr Kilby. I know who I am and that's all that matters. Now I'm asking you again: why did you kill my father?'

'I didn't.' Mike's voice was little more than a whisper. He felt like he was caught up in some horrible nightmare. 'I didn't,' he repeated more loudly. 'Dave died because he took some stupid drug, some fucked-up concoction called Iron.'

'I'm not stupid, Mr Kilby,' Devlin snapped. 'I'm well aware of the circumstances of my father's death. What I want to know is why you gave him the drug in the first place.'

'Me?' Mike's head was spinning. 'I didn't give him the damn stuff.'

'Then who did?'

The question hung in the air between them. 'That,' said Mike slowly, 'is what I am trying to find out. I thought you might have something to do with it.'

'Me?' This time it was Devlin's turn to look as if he'd been struck by a thunderbolt. 'Do I look like someone who pushes bodybuilding steroids?'

'Do I?' demanded Mike.

Devlin took in the broad chest, tapering waist and overall physique of the man standing before him. 'To be frank, yes.'

Mike went to make a blistering reply, then stopped. Of course he did. He was nearly fifteen stone of hard muscle. How was someone like Devlin to know that every ounce had been gained through punishing weight-training and rigorous attention to diet? And if he thought Mike used steroids it was only a logical step to assume that he'd push them on to others.

Mike's anger, stoked for weeks now, ebbed as he began to see how matters must look from the other man's point of view. 'Well, I don't.' Compared to the spirited denials he'd made in recent days, his words now lacked fire, but they contained a conviction that carried. He saw the hostility in Devlin's handsome face soften, saw the first suggestions of doubt. 'Maybe we should talk.'

Devlin nodded. 'Maybe somewhere a little more comfortable? I've got a hotel suite not far from here.'

'Fine.'

The two men moved out of the main area of the gym. Mike switched out the lights and Devlin locked the door behind them. He didn't offer to give Mike this key to the gym he hadn't known about and Mike didn't ask for it. Not yet.

Behind them in the darkness, the telephone on the main desk rang out four times before the answering machine clicked on. 'Mike! Mike, are you there? It's Paul. Sergeant Ferris. There's been . . . an accident. Look, if you get this message, call me at the number I gave you and I'll explain. Call me before you call Richard. I'm sorry I missed our meeting but you'll understand why when we speak. Call me.'

The phone went dead, the answer machine's message-window blinking red neon over and over in the darkness where no one could see it.

Mike was impressed. He'd been impressed by the sleek, powerful car. He'd been impressed by the hotel Devlin was staying in, far grander than anything he'd ever stepped into before. He was impressed by his suite, its space and luxurious fittings. And he was impressed by the man. Devlin had confronted him when many another would have been too intimidated by his size. He was rich, there was no doubt about that, but he wasn't soft. Already Mike could tell that this was a man who had earned his wealth and who wasn't afraid to go for what he wanted. Mike could understand and admire that.

There was something else about the man, too, some feeling that he couldn't pin down. It had to be the resemblance to Dave. He'd tried to cast his mind back to photos he'd seen of Dave when he was younger, about Devlin's age now, to see if he could pinpoint the resemblance there. It hadn't worked, possibly not helped by the fact that about the only times Dave had ever bothered to have his photos taken was when he was wearing little more than posing pouches, sometimes not even those, and Devlin was definitely wearing more clothes than that. Mike narrowed his eyes thoughtfully as Devlin turned his back a moment to pour them both a drink. Not that the thought of seeing Devlin without clothes on wasn't attractive. Actively looking for the resemblances didn't work, but when he wasn't looking for them, he thought he caught them: there in the eyes, the way the mouth curled, the tilt of the chin.

'Drink?'

Devlin was holding out a glass and Mike blinked embarrassedly and took it, aware that he'd been scrutinising his face more closely than might have seemed polite. If he noticed, Devlin didn't make any comment. Mike suddenly wondered how far his genetic inheritance ran. The thought was a confusing but strangely exciting one, and it was as he accepted that that he understood the nature of the other feeling he was experiencing. He found Devlin Lancaster very attractive. Was that just because of the resemblance to Dave?

'Thanks.' He tipped his glass at Devlin, who reflected the gesture, and took a good swallow of the large measure of spirit Devlin had poured him. Smooth. Devlin took a smaller sip and then put his glass down on a table. 'So you're telling me that all the time I knew Dave, he had a son?'

'Yes and no.'

'Meaning?'

Devlin sighed and leaned back in his chair. 'My parents were both very young, very young indeed when they had me. Let's be honest, Mr Kilby . . .'

'Mike.'

Devlin bowed his head in grateful acknowledgement. 'Let's be honest, Mike, my father's time with my mother was probably not much more than the sort of experimentation so many of us go through before we learn to accept ourselves as we are.' Mike said nothing but took note of that 'we'. Score one for the theory of inherited sexuality. 'I don't know the exact details of what happened back then. I can only imagine it was very difficult for all concerned. Things were not quite so liberal in so many ways. All I do know is that my father and mother split up practically as I was born. I'm not even sure if my father saw me as a baby. My mother met someone else, someone more . . . congenial, and we emigrated to America some months before my first birthday.'

'You don't have any accent.'

Devlin smiled. 'That is something people have remarked on. I prefer to keep to my roots. Which, in the end, is why I'm here. I left my family as soon as I was able.' Mike wore a quizzical expression. Devlin dismissed it with a wave. 'Things with my stepfather weren't so comfortable in the long run. Possibly because I took after my real father in too many ways. If you see what I mean.' Mike understood perfectly. 'I spent some years making my own way in the world and achieved a certain measure of success.' Unselfconsciously, he indicated their plush surroundings. 'Then, when I had time, I set about finding out more about my roots, tracking down my real father, finding out if the apple had after all really fallen that far from the tree. When my researches and certain other business projects coincided in bringing me to England, I couldn't have been happier. I came, I saw . . . and I met my father.'

Mike tried to picture the scene, Dave meeting the son he'd never known. 'How did he take it?'

'It was . . . difficult at first.'

'Did he believe you?'

'Funnily enough, yes. Without hesitation. I suppose there are some things you just know. In any case, I had all the relevant documentation, a final parting gift from my mother. I still have them, by the way, if you want to –'

Mike waved aside the offer. Later perhaps, just out of curiosity. For the moment, he was content to accept the evident truth. As Devlin said, there were just some things you knew. He wondered though if Devlin knew everything. Mike looked into his drink as he spoke. 'You know about your father and me? I mean, you know we were –'

'Oh, yes. We spoke of many things. He spoke of you a great deal.'

Mike looked up again. He so badly wanted to know what his former lover had said about him in those last few days. Finding Devlin like this was like having a second chance to talk to Dave, to find out things. To ask for forgiveness. His throat tightened. Not yet. He couldn't ask those things yet. 'And . . . you don't mind? I mean . . .'

Devlin leaned forward. He put his hand on Mike's knee and shook it affectionately. Mike felt the lump in his throat tighten still further. That was precisely the sort of playful gesture Dave himself would use. 'Not at all,' Devlin said levelly, looking deep into his eyes. 'You made my father very happy. Which made me happy.' He stayed where he was, hand on Mike's knee for fractionally longer than was necessary before sitting back. 'I think perhaps if you'd still been around in his life, then maybe he wouldn't have died.'

The words were so softly spoken, yet they cut through Mike's heart like the sharpest of knives. 'Why do you say that?'

Devlin looked at him closely, obvious concern in his eyes. 'I'm sorry, I can see this is hurting you. Do you think perhaps we should –'

Mike shook his head. 'I have to know,' he said huskily. 'Do you think I could have prevented it?'

'Perhaps,' Devlin agreed reluctantly. 'More to the point, I don't think he would have wanted to use drugs if you'd still been together. I didn't fully understand everything he told me.' Devlin paused for a minute, head bowed over his drink although he didn't take any more of it. 'We had such a short time together. But I had the impression there was something there to be proved, some issue not fully resolved between the two of you. That trophy – the one he kept on the mantelpiece, I mean – does it mean anything to you?'

Mike nodded, unable to speak. His first-place trophy.

'He was forever picking it up, looking at it.' Devlin shook his head with incomprehension. 'And of course there was his age. I suppose having a twenty-seven-year-old son turn up on your doorstep does tend to bring home your mortality. Not an experience we single men have to face too often.' His voice became thoughtful. 'I guess building himself back up to what he'd been in his heyday was his way of turning back the clock. And he saw Iron as a way of helping him do that quicker. Make sense?'

Mike thought back to that final conversation, Dave's worrying about his age. It all fitted together. He nodded.

'So do you know where he got the drugs from?'

Devlin's question brought him back to the present, the hotel room and the drink in his hand. He took a second heavy pull of the smooth spirit. 'No.'

'I thought, you being in the business –'

'I never use them.' Mike softened his tone. 'Sorry. Bit of a sore point.'

'No, I'm sorry. I understand. You've been through quite a rough time, these past few days. We both have.'

'But I am trying to find out where Dave got the drugs.'

Devlin looked interested. 'Any luck?'

'Of a kind.' Mike told Devlin all about his encounters so far with the Fellowship of Iron, about The Buckle, his initiation and the meeting with Sam just hours earlier that was supposed to have led to an end of the matter but which had instead opened up a whole new can of worms.

Devlin sat silently throughout Mike's story, hands folded in his lap, drink untouched at his side. Without going into explicit details, Mike was nevertheless more honest and open than he had been with Richard and Paul. It seemed surprisingly natural to be like that with Devlin. Much as he would have been with Dave. Devlin made no comment, gave no sign that he was judging.

When Mike finished, Devlin was silent for a minute. 'This is quite a situation,' he said finally.

'Yeah.' Mike waved aside Devlin's offer of more drink. The emotions and alcohol were beginning to tell on him. 'You could say that.'

'I need to think about this a while.'

Mike looked up puzzled. 'What do you mean?'

Devlin fielded the question. 'This policeman you say was supposed to have helped you, Sergeant Ferris? You don't know what happened to him?'

'I can make some guesses,' Mike said bitterly. 'But I don't know for sure.'

'Perhaps you should give him a call now? You have his number?' Devlin passed the telephone over to Mike. 'Would you like me to . . .?' He indicated another room.

Mike shook his head. 'You're very welcome to hear anything I have to say to Officer Paul.' He keyed in Paul's mobile number. He was connected immediately. The call was brief and not at all as expected. Devlin watched as Mike's rather bleary belligerence turned to alarm and then relief, edged with concern. 'I'm going there now. I don't care. I'm going.' Mike hung up and stood, reaching for his coat. 'It's Richard,' he said.

'Richard?'

'My boyfriend. He's been attacked. Bashed. Mugged. I don't know what yet. He's in hospital.'

'Is it serious? I mean –'

'"Could have been worse", that's what they're saying. He'll be OK. Look, I'm sorry, but –'

Devlin nodded and stood to show Mike out. 'Of course, of course. Would you like me to drive you there?'

'No, no. It's all right.'

'A taxi, then. You shouldn't drive at the moment, Mike. You're too –' Devlin paused and searched for a tactful word '– worried.'

Mike gave him a sheepish grin. 'Thanks.' He hesitated for a moment. Did he shake this guy's hand? Give him a hug? Just say goodbye.

It was Devlin who leaned forward and kissed him on the cheek. 'The taxi will be waiting for you by the time you get to the lobby. Call me tomorrow. Now go.'

★

Devlin stood in his hotel room after Mike had left, reflectively stroking his lips. He ordered the taxi for Mike and then sat down by his untouched drink, his fingertips still on his face. Yes, indeed. He had much to think about.

Mike hated hospitals. He'd kept away from them as much as he possibly could. Once he'd put a shoulder out doing dead lifts. He'd endured the pain for three days, assuring everyone it was 'getting better', until Dave had practically carried him into A&E. When a smiling young doctor had pushed it back into place, he'd nearly passed out.

It was the smell. It was the look. It was the hushed sounds. It was the sheer unhealthiness of the places. But now, for probably the first time in his life, none of this registered as he pushed through the doors and dashed round the labyrinth of corridors to find the room with Richard in. When he finally located it, Richard's duty nurse wasn't keen on his going in and disturbing her patient's rest, but the sight of Mike's determined expression and imposing build had made her back down, muttering darkly. Mike entered the room slowly and carefully approached Richard's bed.

His boyfriend was lying, eyes closed, in the stark light of the antiseptic white room. Mike knew it was wrong but he wanted badly to wake him, to hear him speak, to say something to him. He wanted to touch Richard. He edged closer to the bed, standing over and looking down at his boyfriend, taking in the cuts, the bruises, the bandages round the head. How many times had he seen Richard asleep? And yet now he couldn't tell if his breathing was shallower than normal or not. They'd wasted so much time, these past few weeks. His fault. He'd make it up to Richard. He'd take him home, look after him, make sure nothing like this ever happened to him again.

'Rich,' he whispered, unable to help himself.

Richard stirred, muttered something Mike couldn't hear. Eagerly, Mike leaned forwards. 'Rich?'

'Paul?' Richard said, voice slurred with drugs, eyes half opened and half-focused. 'What've you come back for?'

★

160

Len, Sam and Rick stood in a row and waited for their judgement. Sam's face was as impassive as a rock. Len tried for the same but the nervousness in his eyes could be read by the man in the chair. And Rick. Rick shifted uneasily from foot to foot, darted nervous glances at the others, who studiously avoided him, and threw his long hair back over his shoulders in quick nervous flicks. It was irritating their employer.

'You fucked up, boys,' he said.

'We didn't know the other guy would show up,' Len replied defensively. 'You said . . .' He dried up as their employer fixed him with a cold stare. 'Sorry,' he muttered, dropping his eyes to the floor.

'I said we should have taken him, too,' Rick said. 'We could have done it, both of them.'

'But you didn't. So now there are two witnesses: Richard Green, well enough to sit up tomorrow and give detailed descriptions of all three of you, and a police officer. Excellent work, gentlemen.'

Rick stepped back, his attempt to curry favour having backfired.

The man in the chair looked at Sam, silent throughout all this. Sam looked back at him. Was there insolence there? No. Not a trace. Even powerful Sam wouldn't dare. Good. He liked that. 'Have you fuckwits any idea of how you've screwed my plans around? Of how careful I've got to be from now on?' He scanned each of them. Only Sam could return his gaze. Very wisely, none of them answered. 'No, of course you haven't.' He lapsed into silence, let them stew for a few moments, let them wonder just how he was going to react. 'But you'll be relieved to know,' he said finally, as if he hadn't broken off at all, 'that I think I can salvage something from the shambles you've left matters in.'

Rick grinned nervously, looked as if he was going to say something, but was silenced by a savage glare from Len. It was Sam who finally spoke. 'Do you want us to go for the boy again?'

The figure on the chair in front of them considered. 'Perhaps later. It's a possibility. I wanted him hurt more and I wanted him unconscious longer – all of which, I remind you, you assured me was well within your capabilities. However, at least he's in hospital and out of the way for the moment.'

'So is there anything else you want us to do for you tonight?' Rick asked with fawning eagerness.

'Oh, yes. I think there is, Ricky.'

Words ripe with suggestion and meaning, perfectly understood by the three leathermen. The charged atmosphere in the room changed. With silent amusement, their employer watched the subtle changes in the three hard men he'd recruited. Len was standing taller, raising his head to look him directly in the eye. Sam's arms remained folded across his barrel chest, but now he had pulled back his leather jacket and was stroking one exposed nipple with his thumb. Rick, as ever, was more blatant. He was fingering his crotch, giving him the come-on with his eyes. Poor Ricky, his employer thought. He still hadn't got the picture, had he? 'Do you want to please me, Ricky?'

Rick smiled, giving his companions a triumphant look, feeling that he had scored over them. Sam and Len, more aware of the ways of the man they worked for, didn't respond, and waited. 'Yeah,' said Rick.

'Good. Take your clothes off.' With a cocky smile, Rick began slowly to remove the leather jacket he was wearing. 'Don't bother trying to tease me, Rick; just take your clothes off.' Slightly nonplussed, Rick did as he was told, quickly standing stark naked with no self-consciousness in front of his employer and co-workers. Top or bottom, on their own or in front of the others, it was all the same to Rick. He ran his hands provocatively down his smooth chest and stomach, gripping the sizeable rod of his dick and pulling back the foreskin, smiling.

His employer didn't rise from his chair, but nodded, satisfied. 'All right, Sam,' he said. 'Fuck Rick.'

Rick's smile failed him. 'Aw, shit,' he said, stepping back.

'What's the matter, Rick? Think you can't take it?' Their employer's tone took on a threatening note. 'Something else you think you can't do for me?'

Rick squared up to the chair again, torn between a fear of angering this man and his understandable qualms about Sam's massive dick. 'I can do it.'

'Show me.'

Sam had removed his jacket. He dropped his trousers and cast away the black thong he was wearing underneath. 'Don't worry, Ricky,' he said. 'I'll be as gentle as if you were my own.' He stroked his massive member, rousing himself for action.

As Sam stretched a condom over his swollen meat, the man in the chair gestured for Len to lube Rick up, then to stand facing him. Rick took hold of Len's shoulders and braced himself. He looked up into Len's face. Len saw the mute appeal in his eyes. Len flashed his predator grin down at the younger man and grabbed hold of his heavily tattooed upper arms.

When Sam was ready, he walked up to Rick, rested one hand on a pale shoulder, used the other to guide his ramrod to the point of entry, and then stood waiting for their employer's word. The man in the chair savoured the scene, Rick's whiplash-thin body leaning into Len, eyes tight shut, dick pressed up against Len's jeans, arse and belly-muscles taut with anticipation, and Sam with his rugby player's build, the incredible meat of his cock poised on the crack between Rick's pale buttocks, ready to thrust between them and up into his fellow leatherman. He nodded.

Rick gasped into Len's face as Sam began the work of pushing his cock-head through Rick's tight sphincter. Len pushed back, forcing the lad on to the engorged tool. Rick's hands gripped tight on his shoulders as he bowed down, fighting to accommodate Sam. Len could see over his shoulder, right the way down the back with its ridge of backbone and trails of coloured tattoos, down to the base of the spine, the beginning of the smooth cheeks of his arse, and Sam's thick cock slowly forcing itself centimetre by centimetre out of sight and into Rick.

'Take it, boy,' he said, part encouragement, part excitement at the sight.

Rick sobbed once, a sound that could have been pleasure, could have been pain, and then buried his head in Len's chest. Len could feel the young man biting hard into the leather of his jacket the way men under surgery would have bitten into a leather strap before the invention of anaesthetic. He wondered if his jacket would have teethmarks before Sam was through. The thought was powerfully erotic. He shifted his hands on Rick's shoulders, maintaining the pressure and enjoying the sensation of the small muscles there working under his fingers.

When Sam was finally in, Rick lifted his head, like a diver coming up for air. His face over Len's shoulder, he gasped out, 'Do it, man, quick! Quick!' His prostate thrilled to the ruthless pressure of Sam's hefty club cock, but his ring burned under such unaccustomed extension. He threw his arms around Len's neck as Sam pumped at his arse. Len leaned into Rick, sliding one hand up his shoulder and twisting it into his long hair, burying his own face in Rick's neck, licking, biting, rubbing his own cock, fiercely erect in his denims, hard against Rick's naked dick while Sam thrust in again and again.

Arse reamed by Sam, cock-head rasped by Len's denim, Rick came quickly, his come soaking the front of Len's jeans. Grimly he hung on as Sam worked his way to his own release, blind to Rick's increasingly frenzied cries. When finally Sam reached orgasm, he pulled Rick into him and held him there as his pulsating dick shot load after load into the thin latex of the condom. When he was finally spent, he withdrew roughly, wringing one last gasp from Rick, who collapsed like a puppet with its strings cut against Len.

Len gave him five seconds before roughly pushing him upright and stepping back.

'Fucking ruined my jeans,' he said. The wide damp stains on the outside soaked inwards to mix with the ample quantities of come he had expended on the inside.

Throughout the sex session, their employer sat back, watching, expressionless except for the burning pleasure in his eye. Now he laughed at them coldly in their various states of post-coital relief. 'Maybe you do have your uses,' he said. 'Now get out of here and clean up.' One by one they left, leaving him alone with his thoughts and his plans.

Nine

'So where the hell were you?'
      'I was busy. Making sure Richard wasn't beaten to a pulp.'
   'And what were you doing with him in the first place?'
   'I had a hunch he'd try something like that. Why, would you rather I hadn't?'
   'Maybe I'd rather you just kept your nose where it belonged and out of other people's business.'
   'And maybe I would if people like you didn't take it on themselves to play junior detective.'
   'Well, maybe we have to because the police apparently don't want to get their hands dirty in cases involving people like me.'
   Mike and Paul glared at each other across the room in Mike's flat. Paul had rung earlier that morning, suggesting they meet to discuss what they should do next. Mike, gritty from a sleepless night and sour from a frustrating evening before that watching Richard slip in and out of consciousness, had grunted something that Paul had decided to take for agreement. They had been at each other's throats almost from the second Paul had stepped into the flat.
   'They are doing something. We are.' Paul noted Mike's raised eyebrows. 'I'm not on this case.' He pressed on before Mike asked awkward questions even he wasn't sure he had the answers to yet. 'They'll be getting descriptions of his attackers from him as soon

as he's able to concentrate for long enough. I've already given mine. Between the two of us, it should be fairly easy to get a match.'

Mike slammed his fist into the back of his sofa. 'I want the bastards who did this to him.'

'So do I.' Mike looked up sharply at Paul's heartfelt expression. The policeman pressed on, adopting a determinedly professional tone. 'We will get them.'

'That's not what I mean.'

'I know what you mean, but it's what you're going to have to accept. You can't take the law into your own hands.'

'I thought that was what you'd been helping us to do.'

'You're right. And maybe I was wrong.'

'Now you say. Pity you couldn't have decided that before my boyfriend ended up in hospital.'

Paul knew he could easily have challenged Mike's unfair words but he didn't. 'I don't think the Fellowship was behind Richard's attack.'

Mike frowned. 'Why not? He got the message from them to go to that place and then three guys turn up and beat the crap out of him. You're saying that's a coincidence?'

'Maybe. It doesn't make sense that it should have been the Fellowship. What was the point? Why should two people who contact the same organisation receive such different treatment?'

Mike punched the sofa again, feeling the rising of the familiar frustration, the impossibility of dealing cleanly and simply with matters that couldn't be reduced to kilos and reps, the difficulty of being a man who measured his life by physical challenges, but who lived in a world that was much more complicated. 'Is that what your precious Inspector Taylor thinks?'

Paul's eyes narrowed. 'We haven't discussed this.'

'Why not? He did come to see you yesterday, didn't he?'

'How did you know that?'

'Richard told me.'

'He told you that I visited him?'

'Is there any reason he shouldn't have?'

'Of course not.'

'So what did your boss have to say to you, then? Running after queers wasn't a good way to get on the fast track for promotion?'

'Of course not.'

'But it wouldn't be, would it? A nice easy arrest of some two-bit dope dealer wouldn't have looked bad on the records, but now the whole thing's got messier and more confused, you're backing out, aren't you? Aren't you?'

'If I might possibly interrupt?'

Both men spun round to the sound of the new voice. A figure stood in the doorway. He stepped forwards confidently, hand outstretched to Paul. 'Devlin Lancaster,' he said. 'I hope you don't mind,' he added, turning to Mike. 'Your young man downstairs said it would be all right to come up.' He gave a small laugh, a deliberate attempt to break the tension in the room. 'And I think he tried to pick me up.'

Mike couldn't help a small smile at Devlin's mock surprise. 'That's Andy for you. He tries it on with everyone. No offence,' he added rapidly.

'None taken,' Devlin replied smoothly. 'He definitely wasn't my type.' He glanced first to Mike than to Paul, waited, and then when nothing was said seated himself on the sofa and waited again. Rendered out of place, Mike and Paul shuffled to the two armchairs and also sat down.

'Forgive me,' Devlin went on, 'but I couldn't help hearing what you were talking about as I was coming up. In fact,' he added, 'I rather think a number of people in the gym downstairs could hear what you were talking about. And I've been doing some thinking of my own. I think I may be able to help.'

'Excuse me,' said Paul, half relieved by Devlin's calming influence on the situation, but half irritated by being made to feel like a sulky adolescent, 'but if I may just ask, who are you?'

'I'm Dave Ross's son,' Devlin said, as calmly as if he were describing the weather, 'and I've come to see if I can make up for an earlier mistake.' Clearly and precisely, he brought Paul up to speed on his involvement in the situation and his error in thinking Mike had been responsible for Dave's death.

'I'm surprised your connection to this case didn't come to light earlier,' Paul said.

Devlin shrugged. 'There was no reason why it should and, in any case, from what I've seen, the police investigation of my father's death has not been exactly thorough. Although I can see that is no fault of yours,' he added quickly.

Paul stood stiffly, stung by Devlin's words no matter how swift the qualification had been. He could see Mike smirking at the barbed comment. He decided it was time for him to leave. 'I think you will find, Mr Lancaster, that the police are proceeding with all due expediency and that the person or persons –'

'Yes, yes, yes,' Devlin said, waving the words aside. 'Forgive me, Paul – I may call you Paul, may I? Forgive me, but when people slip into official jargon, I know that their brains have shut down and there's no point in listening to them any longer.'

Paul's face whitened. 'I think I'd better be going.'

'Your problem,' Devlin continued, 'is that you just haven't taken the right approach. Either of you.'

Paul stopped in the act of walking out, drawn back by the look of surprise on Mike's face at Devlin's double accusation.

'Don't get me wrong,' Devlin went on. 'By working together you've gone a long way – about as far as you can. But you've lost sight of what this Fellowship of Iron is all about. It's a business.' He held his arms out as if holding himself up for display. 'And if I am anything, I am a businessman.'

'You can't buy answers to crimes, Mr Lancaster,' Paul said acidly, fascinated in spite of himself by the man's silky delivery and boundless self-confidence.

'Ah, but that's where you're wrong, Inspector.'

'Sergeant.'

'My mistake. Can't you see the pattern that is being played out for Mike here? The initiation at The Buckle? The meeting with this Sam character? You're not being strung along as just another customer, Mike. You never were. Paul said it felt like there was a whole level of organisation missing. He was right, and that's exactly where this trail of crumbs has been leading. This Fellowship is looking to recruit you into that level, as management, not just as another consumer. With your clout, your reputation and two gyms, you're a real catch.' Devlin was on his feet now, pacing between the two men, addressing them as excitedly and determinedly as if they were chairmen of multinational companies he was trying to win over to some vital financial deal. 'You're already in much deeper than you thought. You've got to strike now, hard, while you can, before this window of opportunity closes and the deal's off.'

Mike shook his head. 'But what does that mean? What the hell am I supposed to do? What comes next?'

'What always comes next. What business always comes down to.' Devlin clapped his hands together and rubbed. 'Money!'

'But I haven't got any. Not real money.'

'You've got two gyms, now,' Paul pointed out. 'I should have so little.'

'Yeah, but . . .' Mike went to speak about his mortgage, about the outstanding debts on Dave's gym, but then he remembered. All Dave's debts had been paid.

'It's OK,' Devlin said. 'You may not have the sort of ready money you need to get you into any worthwhile deal with the Fellowship.' He paused, eyes flashing, smile fierce. 'But I have. Let me help. With you up front, me underpinning the deal and Sergeant Ferris as cavalry-in-waiting, we can blow this Fellowship apart from the inside, nail the bastards who really killed my father. And you —' turning to Paul '— should at least get a promotion.'

Paul bridled, uncertain as to the extent of Devlin's irony.

'You'd do that?' Mike asked slowly.

Devlin looked straight at him with those eyes which were so eerily reminiscent of Dave's. 'It's like I said. Roots are important. Family is important. Even if you find out too late.'

Knowing they were going to hate him for it, Paul moved in to break up the dream. 'No. It's too dangerous. You're going in too —'

'How soon can you get the money?'

'It's a phone call away. It can be wherever we want it as soon as we need it.'

'We have no way of contacting the Fellowship, though.'

'They'll be in touch again very soon.' Mike gave Devlin a quizzical look. 'Trust me. Multimillion dollar corporations, ladies' knitting circles and drug cartels. They all operate according to the laws of business. Forget physics. Money really is what makes the world go round, and it makes it go round in very predictable ways.'

'And how many drug cartels have you been involved in?' Paul asked sourly.

'I was part of a team that bought out an aspirin packing factory, once,' Devlin replied glibly. 'Talk about financial headaches.'

'Jokey answers don't make this idea any safer. The answer is still no.'

'Your answer, maybe,' said Mike. 'But not mine.'

'You can't go through with this.'

'Who's going to stop me?'

'You're talking about dealing with illegal drugs pushers.'

'True,' said Devlin, moving to take up a position behind the chair Mike was sitting in so that both men were facing the policeman. 'And who was it who agreed to be with Mike when he last met them?'

Paul went glacial. 'Your point?'

'My point is you can hardly turn us over to your Inspector Taylor now for something that we haven't even done yet, without making it very clear to him just what you've been up to with the local chapter of the Friends of Dorothy. And you'd have nothing to show for it, anyway, apart from a widening circle of new and interesting friends. Not the sort of thing you want whispered about at promotion board meetings, now, is it?'

Paul fumed. Devlin was threatening him, albeit in a roundabout fashion, and there was nothing he could do about it. Not here, anyway, but maybe there was another way. He started once again for the door. 'I'll be in touch,' he said to Mike. 'Don't do anything stupid before you hear from me.' The door slammed to behind him.

'Oh, dear,' said Devlin after a short silence. 'I've done it again.'

Mike let out a pent-up breath. 'I'm glad you're on my side,' he admitted.

'I'm afraid I let my instincts take over. When you get one guy like that who's holding up an important deal, you use everything that comes to hand to slap him down and make him toe the line.' He gave Mike a sheepish look. 'I guess that sounds kind of ruthless.' Mike made a noncommittal gesture, unwilling to agree that Paul had been harshly treated. 'I'll make it up to him later. Buy him a drink. Take him out for a meal. Shag him.'

Mike spluttered at the bluntness of Devlin's suggestion, delivered apparently straight but with that mischievous turn of the lips that was pure Dave and that set his heart racing at the memory. 'So, what do we do in the meantime?'

'You go about whatever it is magnificent specimens like you do to stay magnificent.' He clapped his hands together again, as if gleefully preparing for physical exercise himself. 'And I shall go to my bank to make the way clear for our imminent dealings. I'll see you later to fill you in on the details.'

'Here?'

Devlin considered. 'I'd quite like to meet back at my father's gym, if that's all right with you,' he said slowly. 'I don't suppose I'll have that many opportunities to visit it in the future, and, well, you know . . .'

Mike nodded. He knew.

'You're looking better.'

'What? Better than when you last saw me or better than when you first saw me?'

Paul laughed and sat down in the chair next to Richard's bed. 'And now I know you're feeling better if you can ask questions like that. Here, these are for you.'

'Grapes. How . . . how clichéd.'

'I like them,' said Paul, helping himself to three at one go.

'So I see. Well, thank you anyway. I didn't know that gifts of fruit were part of the service our wonderful police force offers these days.'

'Yes, well, they aren't. I mean, this isn't. I'm not here in an official capacity.'

'I rather hoped you weren't.'

'No, I mean I can't be involved with your case at all.'

Richard held out his hand for a grape then toyed with it. He hated them but didn't want to hurt Paul's feelings. 'Taylor?' Paul nodded. 'You've told him . . .?' Richard left the question dangling.

'Good God, no!'

'Good God, indeed,' Richard murmured and put the grape in his mouth without thinking. He had to work hard not to gag.

'But I think Taylor's guessed something. I got a warning, in no uncertain terms, to keep my official nose out of things.'

'So, no more help with the Fellowship?'

'I can't, Richard. It could cost me my career.'

Richard nodded noncommitally. The grape had left a sour, acid taste in his mouth. 'And have you told Mike this?' Paul nodded gloomily. 'I shouldn't imagine he took it very well.'

'Not very. But right at the moment, he doesn't think he needs me or the police any more.'

Richard struggled to sit up. It was still beyond him. 'He's going to do something on his own? You've got to stop him.'

'He's not on his own. He has a new partner. A business partner,' he added hastily. 'And I mean that literally. Would you believe Dave Ross had a son?'   ·

Richard laughed incredulously. 'You're kidding me? Dave strayed on to the straight and narrow? When was this?'

'About thirty years or so ago, I should say.'

Richard couldn't help smiling at the thought. Some part of him found this news obscurely amusing. He didn't quite know why, but he couldn't help thinking that somehow it served Mike right. 'Well, well, well,' he chuckled. 'Dave Ross Junior.'

'Not Dave. Devlin. Devlin Lancaster.'

Richard's eyes widened, and he tried yet again to sit up, ignoring Paul's half-hearted efforts to stop him, and the fiercely painful complaints from the various battered parts of his body. 'Devlin Lancaster? Well-spoken guy, slim, just under six foot? Handsome? Very handsome? Very, very rich?'

Paul nodded, curious at this abrupt change in Richard's behaviour. 'That's the guy. Do you know him?'

Richard nodded. 'Oh, yes. We've . . . met.'

Paul noted the inflection, knew there was more here than Richard was letting on. 'Through Mike? I got the impression that Mike only met him very recently.'

'No. I met him through work. In fact, he's going to be my big break into the world of real writing. At least –' Richard grew thoughtful '– I thought he was.' He told Paul about his first and to date only meeting with Devlin Lancaster. He omitted the more colourful details of his time in Devlin's bed. He had the uncomfortable feeling, though, that Paul was growing more skilful all the time about reading between the lines in such matters. 'Quite a coincidence,' he concluded. He looked extremely doubtful.

'Do you really think that?'

Richard lay back on his pillow. His face was pale, his eyes beginning to droop again. 'I think that my head hurts, my body hurts and I don't know what to think any more. That's what I think. I do know Devlin's legit.'

'How do you know?'

'Looked him up on the Internet. I'm not completely stupid.' He winced as his bruised ribs reminded him of his recent abuse. 'Well, not all the time.'

'And you'd stand to make a lot of money from him. Enough to make you want to believe that his turning up in your life and Mike's at this time is just a coincidence.'

Richard gave a feeble chuckle. 'He really rubbed you up the wrong way, didn't he? OK, I stand to make a solid career jump because of him. I'd have thought that was something you could appreciate, Sergeant Ferris.'

Paul stood up abruptly. 'Maybe you're right,' he said. 'And maybe I should keep reminding myself that I'm not supposed to be officially involved in your case any more.'

Richard closed his eyes. 'Hey, hey – I'm sorry. I didn't mean to be so sharp. I usually think a bit more before I open my mouth. I'm not myself right now, you know?'

Paul thawed, unable to help himself. 'I know.' He sat down again, drawing the chair close to the bed. 'Look, Richard, I came here because of Mike. I think he's going to end up in much more trouble than he can handle if he doesn't pull out of this Fellowship shit now. But he won't listen to me. I thought he might listen to you. But now . . .' He trailed off.

'But now what?'

Paul struggled with the words, and with the feelings behind them. When they came, they were rushed, as if he were trying to force them all out at once before he could be tempted to hold

173

any of them back. 'Now, I think you'd be better off without him. Safer, I mean.'

'Safer with you, maybe?'

'He goes with other men, for Christ's sake.'

'And so do I, Paul. It doesn't matter.'

'I don't believe that.'

'You don't understand that. Yet. There's a difference.'

Paul pushed his chair back and stood again. 'I've got to go. I'm sorry.' He walked quickly to the door.

'Paul. Paul!'

Reluctantly Paul stopped, hand on the door handle. When he saw the pain Richard's effort had cost him, he returned to the bed. Richard licked his lips and waited for the room to stop spinning. 'There's nothing to be sorry about,' he said eventually. 'Nothing at all. We've some things to talk about, but we can't do that here or now. Can we wait? At least until I can breathe without hurting?' Paul nodded, throat tight with emotions he couldn't express. 'Good.' Richard sighed and closed his eyes. Once again he could feel the darkness of unconsciousness rising in him like a black tide. 'And about Mike,' he murmured. 'Promise me you'll look after him for me? He can be a pain at times,' his voice faded, 'but he is worth it.' He fought not to lose consciousness until he had seen Paul nod once, then with a sigh he slipped into sleep.

Paul waited until Richard's breathing was slow and regular before he left the room.

He barely noticed the trip back to the police station, his mind taken up with too many unpleasant thoughts. At the centre of them was one name: Devlin Lancaster. It wasn't that Paul didn't believe in coincidences, it was simply that he didn't like them. And he didn't like Devlin Lancaster either. Was that an instinctive reaction to something wrong or a more understandable resentment of the smooth contempt he had felt back at Mike's flat? Or was it jealousy because he suspected there had been much more to Richard's meeting with him than Richard had let on?

Turning a corner, he nearly bumped into PC Alex Summers, the latest recruit to the station. PC Summers had been in the force

174

less than two years, and already his computer skills had landed him a desk job he was unlikely to escape before retirement. In his swerve to avoid Paul, the young constable let fall the manila envelope he was carrying. 'Sorry, Sergeant,' he began.

Paul knelt to pick up the envelope. 'My fault,' he said, and went to give back the envelope until the writing on the front caught his eye. Among other details was his name. 'This for me?'

'Yes. Well, that is, no.' Alex looked confused, embarrassed and worried all at the same time. He reached out for the envelope. Paul held on to it.

'You're going to have to run that one by me again,' he said.

'They're contact sheets,' Summers said. 'We think we've got matches from that bashing you were witness to.' Paul inwardly flinched at the word 'bashing' but said nothing. 'I'm just taking them over to Jane, WPC Robins, to take over to the hospital to see if Mr Green gives us a positive.'

'I was there, too. I should be able to ID them.'

Alex held his hands behind his back to keep from nervously twisting his fingers in front of the superior officer. 'But we thought . . . that is, I . . . we were told that you weren't on the case.'

Told not to show me these pictures, more likely, Paul thought, and he had a pretty good idea by whom. He didn't let the anger he felt show. He smiled at the young man, and was pleased to see him visibly relax. PC Summers was quite cute, and Paul was surprised he hadn't noticed that before, but then he'd been going round for so long making himself not notice such things. Maybe it was time to stop acting like that. 'I was a witness,' he reminded Alex. 'Sooner or later they're bound to end up on my desk anyway. Let's have a look now, eh?' He opened the envelope and pulled out the sheets inside. Summers looked uncomfortable but could do nothing to stop him.

Paul inspected the three A4-sized black-and-white photographs. 'Could be,' he said. 'Could very well be. It was dark but I'd say these two were very likely the ones I saw, and this one definitely is. Names?'

'Len McCoy, Sam Jordan and Richard Riley,' Summers replied with commendable promptness. 'McCoy and Jordan have both got form for assault. Riley has done time for bike theft and GBH. Not a pretty bunch.'

'But no form for simple muggings?'

Alex hesitated, as if about to question the phrase 'simple muggings', before shaking his head.

Paul pondered that. Like so much else, recently, events here just didn't fit together properly. 'Who's bringing them in?'

'No one, sir.'

Paul noticed the return to formality and the unhappy expression on the face of the young policeman. 'Why not?'

'Well, not these two, anyway.' Alex tapped the pictures of Len and Rick. 'They're dead.'

'What?'

'Turned up last night in the river. Shot, both of them.' He held out his hand for the envelope. Not really seeing him, Paul handed it back. Alex pushed the photos back into it. 'I'd better get on.'

'Hm? Oh, yes, of course.' Paul stood, lost in thought for a moment but, as the young man turned to go, he called him back. 'Alex.'

PC Summers spun round. 'Yes, sir?' he said eagerly.

'Could you do me a favour?'

Alex smiled broadly. 'Yes, sir.' His boyish enthusiasm dimmed momentarily. 'Something to do with . . .?' He held up the envelope.

How to answer that one? Since that first meeting in Mike's flat, Paul had met people and become embroiled in events that had confused and unsettled him. Nothing any more seemed to make sense the way it had used to. Now, he wanted to reach out for something, anything that he could latch on to and make clear and logical. He could see only one possibility. 'Maybe,' he said. 'Can you do a computer search for me on this name?' He scribbled down Devlin Lancaster's name on a sheet of his notebook, tore it out and handed it to Alex. 'American nationality. Businessman. Into publishing among other things.'

'No problems, sir,' Alex said and started off immediately to his computer station, his errand to WPC Robins apparently forgotten for the moment.

'No, wait – there's a small . . . complication.' Alex returned and waited patiently. 'I don't want anyone to know. In particular, I don't want Inspector Taylor to know. Yet.' Paul waited, searching for the young constable's reactions in his eyes. Paul was asking Alex to break procedure and wasn't giving him any real reason for it.

Alex didn't blink, didn't hesitate. 'Name like this shouldn't have too many matches. I should have it ready for you in just over fifteen minutes, sir.'

'Thank you, Constable.' Young PC Summers certainly was cute. And very keen to please. Paul wondered whether that was just professional enthusiasm or something else. 'And, Alex?'

'Yes, sir.'

'There's a drink in this for you.'

'Thank you, sir!' The young PC dashed off, with a smile that left little to Paul's imagination. Well, well, well. Look and you shall find. Paul headed to his office, hoping that Alex would find the same to be true in his computer search.

They'd arranged to meet at Dave's gym at six that evening. Mike turned up at four. Recent events had really screwed his training regimen, and he wanted to get at least one good workout in that day. What he also wanted was the inner peace that a session of hard-core iron-pumping could bring. He was troubled – unhappy, even – and this was the best way he knew to deal with that feeling. Ironic, though, that he should end up doing it here, in Dave's gym, when that was one of the things that was troubling him the most.

Inheriting the gym to the exclusion of Roy had been upsetting enough. Now there was Devlin. OK, so Devlin was rich. He could probably buy out Dave's gym a hundred times and still have loose change in his pockets. But he was still Dave's flesh and blood. Didn't that mean that the gym should really go to him now? Surely that's what Dave would have wanted? Of course, there was the will, but then maybe Dave hadn't had time to change it. He hadn't been expecting to die. Or maybe Mike still had meant that much to him, more even than his own son, whom he had never really known after all.

Baffled and depressed by the uncertainties, Mike readied the equipment, loaded the weights and stripped. With no one else in the gym, he could train the way he really enjoyed. Within fifteen minutes, his heart was pounding, blood flowing and muscles warm and pumped. Life's troubles took backstage, at least for that moment, and Mike felt more centred than he had for days.

He was halfway through a set of bench presses when he felt he was not alone. He let the loaded bar come crashing down on to its rest and sprang from the bench. Devlin was standing there looking at him, a slight smile on his lips. Mike had forgotten about his key. He stood there, dressed surprisingly casually in jeans and a white T-shirt. 'I'm sorry. I didn't mean to startle you.'

' 'S all right. No problems.' Mike was casting about hurriedly for something to put on. Devlin, still smiling, picked up the towel Mike had left draped over the barbell and threw it to him. Mike wrapped it round his waist. It was little more than a hand towel and only just covered his modesty, but it would have to do. 'Thanks.'

'Very impressive,' said Devlin.

'Eh? Oh, right. Yeah, well, I normally do more, actually, but, not having anyone to spot for me, I had to keep the weights down a bit.'

'I wasn't talking about the weights, Michael.' While Mike took that on board, Devlin sat down on one of the benches, indicating that Mike should join him. Carefully holding on to his towel, Mike did so.

'The arrangements are all made. When the Fellowship of Iron next makes contact, I think you'll find that your bank balance is more than ready to strut its stuff and grab their attention. Always assuming,' he added, with a mischievous glint in his eye, 'that it's the size of your account they're interested in.'

Mike laughed, oxygen debt making the sound breathy. 'I'm not sure you should be doing this, Devlin.'

'Now you're beginning to sound like –' Devlin broke off.

'Like who?'

Devlin was staring into the middle distance, not really seeing the gym around them, replaying some inner memory. 'Like my father,' he said, the words more clipped than previously.

It took a moment for the penny to drop. 'It was you. You paid off Dave's gym debts.'

Devlin shrugged. 'It was only money.'

'It must have been a hell of a lot of money.'

'For my father, probably. Not for me.' He grinned sheepishly. 'Sorry, does that sound like boasting? I was his son. I wanted to help him. He was managing but I was able to make things easier for him.' As he spoke, he let his hand fall on Mike's leg, just as Dave used to – just as he himself had, earlier, only this time the leg was uncovered, Mike's skin still moist with sweat from his exercise. Only inches away from the hand, under the small, thin hand towel, Mike felt his cock stir at Devlin's touch. 'Money isn't anything, Mike. Deals aren't everything. They're just games. I like playing games. Money just means I can play longer and harder than most.' He moved his hand slightly, slid it an inch or two further up Mike's thigh. 'Do you like to play, Michael?'

Mike cleared his throat, suddenly and absurdly nervous as a teenage virgin. He gestured to the weights that surrounded them. 'This is the only game I've ever played.'

'And you play it extremely well.'

Mike looked more closely at the man by his side. Jeans and T-shirt, yes, but now he could make out the designer labels so discreetly sewn on. He could also get more of a sense of the body that lay beneath. 'You're not in such bad shape yourself. Games?'

Devlin demurred modestly. 'College wrestling.'

Mike whistled. 'What, you mean like two falls, two sub-missions, that kind of thing?'

Devlin shook his head. 'I'm afraid you're thinking of the professional game. Not that that doesn't have a certain charm. No, college wrestling is a rather more civilised affair. I liked its grace, its simplicity. Man against man. It was also a rather good way to thrash about on a mat with young men in leotards. Would you like to try?'

The question took Mike by surprise. 'Don't we need a ring?'

'Again, professional. All you need is some space –' he looked around '– a couple of gym mats like those over there, and two willing men. We have some time to kill. Come on, give it a go.'

He gave Mike's thigh a squeeze. 'Unless you think you're not . . . flexible enough.'

'Flexible?'

'Well, all that weight-lifting. You're bound to lose some flexibility. Some speed, too, I guess. I understand.'

Mike smiled. He could see through Devlin's transparent, good-humoured goading. He wasn't blind to the most likely motive behind his challenge. But in the end that's what it was, a challenge: and, as Devlin already knew by then, Mike just couldn't help responding to them. Five years ago, Dave Ross had challenged him in this room to overcome his self-made barriers. Now this man with Dave's eyes and Dave's smile was challenging him again. He'd come out of the first a better man. How could he resist the second? 'OK,' he said. 'If you think you can handle the difference,' and he stood, holding his arms out to remind this man of his size. The towel slipped from his waist.

'Oh, I think I can handle that,' Devlin said before Mike could replace his covering. He pulled his T-shirt over his head.

Mike ran a professional eye over the body: nice tan, very good muscle tone. You might have expected someone as wealthy as Devlin to have let himself run to fat at least a little, but there was not a scrap of it. 'So were you good at this wrestling, then?'

Devlin kicked off the Gucci loafers he'd been wearing, peeled off the socks and unselfconsciously began to unbutton the flies of his jeans. 'College champion three times,' he said, letting the jeans fall to the floor and stepping out of them. His boxers were black silk. 'Course, I did cheat.'

Mike ran his eyes up and down the legs: dark hair, good thighs. He tried to remember just which muscle groups were best exercised by wrestling. 'Yeah?' he said, only half listening.

'Yeah,' said Devlin, clasping his hands behind his back and leaning forwards. 'I only took on guys in the weight categories two classes above mine. Anything else just didn't seem sporting.'

Mike laughed. Cocky. He liked that. It gave the challenge more spice. He walked over to the pile of his discarded clothes and picked up the white cotton briefs he'd been wearing. They did little to hide his growing excitement. He didn't care.

Together, they dragged out a couple of gym mats and threw

them down into the centre of the room. Mike gave Devlin a few more minutes to limber up while he took the opportunity to watch. He found himself aching to get hold of that supple body, his erection building at the thought of wrapping his arms with their bowling-ball biceps around that waist in a bear hug, perhaps even rolling about on the mat and contriving to rub his briefs into Devlin's face. He decided he'd play along for a while, hold back so he didn't hurt his lighter opponent, maybe even let Devlin take a fall or two or whatever they called it. After that, when they were both nicely warmed up, well, who knew? 'Ready?' he said.

Devlin indicated Mike's briefs and his own satin boxers. 'Black and white.'

'Does that make you the bad guy and me the good guy?'

'Maybe.'

'Good guys always win.'

'Only on the television. Let's play.'

The two men circled each other. Mike grinned and feinted a forwards lunge. Devlin dodged back adroitly. Mike tried to see if Devlin's shorts were tenting with as much enthusiasm as his own briefs at this macho competitive display, but the cut of the boxers and play of light on the shot silk made it hard to see. He'd just have to get a closer look. Devlin's hands shot out and took hold, left hand on Mike's shoulder, right hand around his neck, a classic wrestler's hold. Mike tried to mirror him. Before he had time to take a proper grip, he was on his back, the wind knocked out of him, and looking up at Devlin, who was circling him, grinning down at his fallen opponent.

Mike climbed back to his feet, shaking his head and smiling ruefully. OK, the man was quick; he'd have to watch out for that. 'First fall to you.' Well, there was no harm in giving him a head start. It gave the fantasy an edge. Devlin said nothing, circled and closed in again.

Again, Mike just about managed to get both hands on Devlin in a rough approximation of the hold the other man was using. It did him no good. Devlin ducked, twisted, bent swiftly at the knees and Mike's centre of gravity was abruptly once again out of his control. He flew through the air, crashing once again in an undignified heap on the ground.

'Just as well this isn't television pro wrestling,' Devlin said. 'Those bouts were always best of three. And you'd have just lost.' He commenced his circling again. He wasn't even breathing hard. 'Would you like to "give"?'

Mike looked up at the slighter man. There was little doubt about it: he'd been suckered. Devlin hadn't been joking about those championships, possibly not even about the weight categories. The man was a master, and Mike saw that no matter how much of an advantage he had in weight, in muscle, there was very little chance of his getting the upper hand over this man in a fair fight. Logically he should give in there and then, accept Devlin's mocking offer and probably spare himself a lot of humiliation, possibly even injury.

He grinned fiercely and clambered to his feet. 'No way,' he spat in mock American, flexing his biceps one after the other before crouching low, arms outstretched, an exaggerated snarl across his lips. 'You are gonna pay, man. Let's play.'

'Your funeral.' Devlin's teeth flashed. He was obviously delighted that Mike had entered fully into the spirit of his fantasy. And, much to his own surprise, Mike had. There was something elemental in the struggle of one man against another, both barely dressed, with nothing but their own wits, speed and strength to help them. It was really turning him on. He'd expected to have to hold back, but for all his undoubted power it was he, Mike, who was the novice in this physical showdown, and he found he rather liked the new sensation. He glanced down at his briefs. The white cotton was already soaked with much more than just sweat.

Devlin closed in again.

Mike ducked, he dived, he gave it everything he had. It was all useless. Devlin feinted, twisted, turned and outmanoeuvred him completely. Mike soon realised that if he was standing it was only because Devlin was allowing it, and if Devlin wanted him on the mat then there was nothing he could do to stop it.

As the bout progressed, it grew rougher. To begin with, Devlin had thrown Mike to the mat and then allowed him time to climb to his feet. Now he followed Mike down, pinning his shoulders with apparent ease to the mat, twisting Mike's arms, legs, the trunk of his body to achieve his ends.

'OK, OK, I give,' Mike yelled out, as Devlin folded his body back on his own neck until Mike could stand the strain no longer. 'Thought you said there were no submissions in this kind of wrestling?' Mike groaned, rubbing the back of his neck.

'Sometimes you can't get what you want without a little pain,' Devlin admitted. 'That can be part of the fun.' And he lunged at Mike again, forcing the muscle man on to the defensive.

At last there came a point where Mike finally thought he had gained an advantage. Devlin had slipped behind him, lacing his legs round Mike's – preparation, Mike was sure, for some diabolical throw that would leave him flat out for the umpteenth time. Well, not this time. Mike gritted his teeth and hurled himself backwards. His full fifteen stone came crashing down on Devlin's body. It wasn't neat, it might not have been sporting, but by that time Mike was too exhausted and had been beaten too many times to care. It was in the end a victory. 'Got you!' he panted, lying back, confident that his foe was crushed and defeated underneath him.

'Oh, yes,' came a muffled voice, 'right where I want me.' Too late, Mike understood he'd been outmanoeuvred yet again, that Devlin had slipped to one side even as Mike had been falling backwards. Now, with a speed that left Mike helpless, Devlin's legs thrust themselves from under his body and round his waist, while before Mike could tense them to resist both his arms were pulled up and pinned into hammer locks behind his back.

Mike struggled, flexing his powerful muscles to bull his way out through sheer strength. A sharp push upwards on both arms and a squeeze of the legs round his waist very quickly made him think again.

'I give!' he gasped. 'I submit,' and he stopped struggling.

Devlin eased up on the painful pressure but he kept his legs twined around Mike's waist, kept both Mike's arms pinned up high between his shoulder blades.

Mike could hear Devlin's breathing from behind him. It was heavier now. Devlin's thighs tightened and Mike flinched, waiting for more pain, but his opponent didn't take it that far. Without speaking, Devlin loosened his scissor hold and edged his bare feet down Mike's body. They moved smoothly and easily over the sweat-slicked flesh until both heels were hooked into his victim's crotch, the soles of his feet pressing inwards, catching Mike's rigid cock in a firm vice.

Devlin squeezed and Mike gasped. He knew he'd been excited but, caught up in the struggle, with demands on every muscle in his body, he hadn't realised just how much his dick was crying out for relief. Still keeping Mike's arms up high behind his back, Devlin kneaded the stiff member, pressing and stretching it out, squeezing out the copious pre-come until the soaked white cotton of Mike's briefs was practically transparent, the hardened meat of his penis clearly visible.

'Let me!' he gasped, trying to work one arm free of Devlin's hold so he could grab his cock and wank it harder. He gasped again with mingled pain and pleasure as Devlin simultaneously compressed his cock and upped the pressure on his backhammers to prevent Mike's escaping.

'Not yet,' he whispered into Mike's ear before he pushed his tongue into it and nipped at the lobe with those bright, even teeth of his. Mike groaned and arched his body, thrusting his groin up to meet the pressure of Devlin's feet. Dimly, through the ecstasy, he became aware that Devlin was shifting his weight again. He was sitting up, forcing Mike to do the same. Mike opened his eyes. They were in front of one of the full-length gym mirrors. He could see his own glistening body helpless in Devlin's hold, the more skilful wrestler's legs twined around his body, his own arms caught up behind him, throwing out the heavy pec muscles of his chest, sweat beading on the nipples and dropping into his already soaked crotch. Behind him, over his shoulder, he could see Devlin's face, looking into his through the reflection of the mirror. The sight made his stiffened tool throb hard with remembered desire. The eyes were brighter, sharper perhaps, the smile more mocking, but those were Dave's eyes looking back at him through the glass, just as they had done years before: that was Dave's smile by his ear, smiling the way he always had as he'd brought his younger lover to the peak of his pleasure.

Devlin released one arm. If he hadn't, Mike truly believed he would have torn it free with brute strength, oblivious to the pain it would have caused him. He had to seize his cock. He had to release the orgasm that Devlin had brought to the point of explosion. As he pumped feverishly, Devlin let his free hand roam across the broad expanse of Mike's chest, toying with the nipples briefly before pinching each in turn hard.

Mike's come sprayed across the mirror in front of them, the thick white cream obliterating the image of the two men, sliding slowly down the cold glass to pool heavily on the floor at the bottom. 'Oh, God!' Mike gasped. 'Oh. My. God!'

He didn't know how long it was before he came back to himself. When he did, he found he was still lying on the gym floor, Devlin still underneath him. Devlin had let his heels slip to either side of Mike's thighs now, and had released his other arm from its backhammer hold. Both Devlin's arms were around Mike's neck. With just a bit more pressure, Mike thought drowsily, that would make a pretty inescapable stranglehold. Slowly he turned himself.

There was a moment's instinctive reaction from Devlin as the arms around his throat tensed, but then they relaxed and Mike was able to turn over completely so that he was face down on the man underneath him, supporting the weight of his muscular body with his own thick arms. Gently he pressed his groin into Devlin's. His own cock was still large. It always took him a long time to stand down after action. Devlin, he could feel through his boxers, was soft. He wondered just how long he had lain there on top of Devlin, exhausted and blissed out after one of the greatest climaxes he could remember. Still, he didn't think it would take long to bring Devlin back to the pitch where he could enjoy himself, too. If he was lucky, he'd enjoy it as much as Mike had. Slowly Mike relaxed his arms and let his body sink towards Devlin's. He lowered his face, prepared to kiss the other man on the lips. Devlin closed his eyes.

The sound of the mobile phone made them both jump. 'Leave it,' Mike said.

'This could be it, Mike.'

'If it is, they'll ring again. Leave it.'

With a laugh, Devlin pulled up one leg, placed the sole of his foot against one of Mike's knees and pushed. Suddenly unbalanced, Mike couldn't stop himself rolling to one side, and as he did Devlin sprang to his feet from under him and headed to the phone. 'You really do need a businessman on this team, Mike,' he said, keying the phone pad. 'You can't afford to let moments like this pass.' He handed the phone over to Mike.

Mike took the phone. 'It's them,' he said, covering the mouthpiece and speaking to Devlin. 'They want to meet. Tonight.'

'Good. I told you. That's the way business works.'

'They're talking about some club miles away.'

Devlin shook his head. 'No. There has to be some element of trade-off here, otherwise you're starting from a position of weakness. Tell them we'll meet at my hotel room. It's a neutral location, discreet. They can't argue with that.' Devlin gave Mike the address.

By the time Mike had finished on the phone, Devlin had dressed again and was waiting for his answer. 'OK,' Mike said. 'They'll be there in one hour.'

Devlin frowned. 'Pushing it. Fixing the time because you fixed the location. OK. We can do it.' He threw Mike a towel. 'You'd better shower.'

Mike hesitated, unsure just how to put what was uppermost in his mind at the moment. 'I thought you'd want . . . I mean that we could . . .' He gave up. 'It seems kind of unfair. You know what I mean?'

Devlin stepped up to him and kissed him lightly on the lips. 'There'll be plenty of time for all that, Mike. And more.' He stepped back. His eyes were blazing. 'But, right now, we've got a chance to do something about the guys who killed my father. We haven't got time to waste.'

Shamed, Mike nodded and headed for the showers. Devlin watched him until the door closed behind him then turned and faced the mirror that had just reflected their exertions. He stood looking into it until Mike came out again and they were ready to go.

Paul had barely had time to make himself a cup of coffee and sit at his desk with the mountain of paperwork Taylor had arranged to be waiting for him before there was a tap at his door and a breathless PC Summers came in, not having waited for a reply. He was brandishing a printed sheet. 'No problems, sir,' he said, waving the paper around. 'Got him first time. Devlin Lancaster. American and all the rest of it, just like you said.'

Paul ushered the young man in and shut the door before they went any further. So Richard's research had been right. He knew he was disappointed. But Alex still had access to records that Richard did not. 'No criminal records, then?' He was almost ashamed of his own eagerness that there should be. Was it because that would have given him something to work at, or was it simply because it would have been something to discredit the man in Richard's eyes?

He was surprised to hear Alex laugh. 'No, sir. Nor likely to get any now, I shouldn't think.'

Paul regarded the young man with a puzzled expression. 'Why not?'

Alex held out the printout for his inspection. 'Because Devlin Lancaster is nearly eighty years old!'

Ten

They came during one of his more lucid moments, just after the latest batch of pills had begun their work of dulling the pain but before they tipped him over the edge into sleep. There were three of them, all in suits: dark colours, nothing distinguishing in any way, very conservative cut. He was pretty sure he'd have identified them as policemen, even before they flashed their cards at him and ushered out the startled-looking nurse who had come to check his readings.

'Not again,' Richard groaned. He didn't have to fake the pained look on his face. 'I have been through all this with one lot already. I've given descriptions of the guys who beat me up. What do you want me to do? Paint their pictures for you?'

Two of the men stayed by the door; one, the oldest, stepped forwards. 'No, I do not think a painting would help us, Mr Green,' he said, 'but I do think you would be helping us, yourself and your friend if you told us everything about what happened to you.'

Richard blinked and pushed himself up as much as he could against his pillow. This wasn't like the previous police interview. This man was much more direct. No phoney friendliness here; this man was almost threatening, and there was something else . . . Fuddled by his recent pain and the drugs, it took Richard a while to work out what it was. His accent. It wasn't British.

French maybe? Not German. Perhaps Swiss, though he wasn't exactly sure what a Swiss accent sounded like. 'I have told you everything, Sergeant . . .? Inspector . . .?'

'Fernmann,' said the man, not indicating which, if either, of the ranks was correct. He sat uninvited on the edge of Richard's bed shaking his head. 'No, no, Mr Green, you have not. You have not, for instance, explained why you were where you were when you were attacked.'

'I told the last lot –'

Fernmann went on as if Richard hadn't spoken. 'And you have not mentioned the Fellowship of Iron.'

Ah. That was true. Although he was unhappy with Paul's inability or refusal to help him and Mike any more, Richard wasn't spiteful enough to wish him dropped in it with his superiors. It had therefore seemed prudent to say nothing that might have led back to Paul and a case he'd been ordered to abandon.

'And you also,' Fernmann added, 'have not yet spoken to us about Mr Devlin Lancaster.'

Richard struggled to take in this latest twist. 'Devlin?' Fernmann waited as patient and as stony-faced as a gargoyle on the side of his bed. Richard tried to swallow but the painkillers had dried his throat. The drugs were also making his head muzzy and he knew he was reacting more openly than he would have normally. He felt out of control of the situation – didn't like the feeling, but could do nothing about it. 'What is it with you people? One minute you don't want anything to do with this Fellowship of Iron business, the next you're spying on people and sounding like you know all about it.'

Fernmann sighed. 'We have always been interested in the Fellowship of Iron, Mr Green,' he said. 'Very interested. For a very long time. The Fellowship of Iron is a nasty business, but it is only one branch of a very large organisation. My colleagues and I, in this country and in Europe, have been spending long years investigating and infiltrating this organisation. At last we had come to the very brink of an operation that would in all probability have brought every part of it, including this Fellowship, the subject of your own personal crusade, crashing to the ground –'

189

and he smashed his hand down on to Richard's bed, the violence of the blow mirroring the growing vehemence of his words, his fist only just missing Richard's damaged leg '– and then you came along. Yourself and Mr Kilby. And Mr Devlin Lancaster.'

'I don't understand.'

'No, Mr Green,' Fernmann hissed, 'you do not. You have put this entire operation in jeopardy because you do not understand.' He leaned in closer. 'You have put your friends in danger. What you can now do, for us and for them, is tell us everything. Everything. And you can tell us now.'

Richard told, from that first meeting with Paul and his inspector to the attack two evenings ago. The man on his bed listened. Richard assumed the other two did as well, though he was no longer sure they were able to understand English. They gave no sign of comprehension, reacted in no way at all. Unlike any of the policemen Richard had seen since this whole affair had started, none of them took notes. As he spoke, Richard couldn't shake the feeling that Fernmann already knew almost all of what he was saying, that the man was waiting for something in particular, though what that was he had no idea.

'And Devlin Lancaster?'

Just how many details of his involvement with Devlin did he go into? The man on his bed sensed his hesitation. 'Mr Lancaster has involved himself in this affair. Understandably, it seems. A family connection we were not aware of. It therefore follows he is in as much danger as the rest of you.'

'You keep using that word.'

Fernmann gestured at Richard's bruises and bandages. 'You have been lucky, Mr Green. What I want now is to make sure you do not turn out to be the luckiest one of all. Where did you meet Mr Lancaster?'

Richard spoke of their meeting at the *Far Out!* office, about their meal afterwards and drinks at Devlin's hotel. He did not mention their sex session.

Fernmann stood up. 'Thank you, Mr Green. You have been most helpful. I wish you a full and speedy recovery.' He turned to go. One of his colleagues already had the door open.

'But wait! Hang on there!' Richard winced at the pain raising his own voice caused him but he had to call this man back. 'Is that it? What are you going to do?'

'What we have to do, Mr Green.'

'Can't you tell me anything else?'

'Always the journalist, Mr Green? Stick to that. Leave matters such as this to those whom it concerns.' He swept from the room, his silent colleagues closing the door to behind him. Richard was left feeling cold and very, very small.

He'd expected someone like Sam, suspected it might even be Sam. What they got was another Mr Ratherson.

Mike and Devlin had made it back to Devlin's hotel room with only minutes to spare before the call had come through that someone had arrived to see Mr Lancaster. Devlin had the man shown up and he and Mike just about had time to rearrange the room, according to what Devlin described as 'optimum negotiation settings', before there was a knock at the door and the representative from the Fellowship of Iron entered.

If this man had ever used drugs, Mike thought, they had certainly never been steroids. Something perhaps that could dry a man out, remove every last trace of humour, emotion or downright humanity, but nothing that had ever done anything for his body. In his black suit, black tie and white shirt, he made Mike think of someone who had turned up for a funeral and then been mildly disappointed to discover the deceased was in fact still alive and kicking.

He glanced dispassionately at Devlin. 'My name is Pace.' Devlin inclined his head in greeting and with precise courtesy indicated the chair he and Mike had so carefully placed for him. Mike offered him a drink as per Devlin's instructions.

It was all part of the psychology, Devlin had explained, to establish Mike as the host, the man in control. 'I won't even talk unless you ask me to,' he'd said.

Pace declined the drink.

Mike poured Devlin a whisky, himself a tonic water and then the two men sat down in the chairs facing Mr Pace, who ignored them while he opened his attaché case and removed various papers. The whole procedure reminded Mike irresistibly of Mr

Ratherson. At the end of that meeting, he had walked away the owner of a new gym. He wondered what his situation would be at the end of this meeting.

Pace wasted no time. 'Mr Kilby. You have opened negotiations with my clients operating under the name the Fellowship of Iron, hereafter to be referred to as the Fellowship. Is that correct?'

'Opened negotiations.' That was putting it rather strongly, wasn't it? He glanced at Devlin, who nodded slightly. 'That is correct,' he said, unconsciously adopting the formal speech patterns of this man he presumed was a lawyer.

'And you have a working understanding of the operational parameters and economic aims and objectives of said organisation?'

Mike ground his teeth silently. Yes, you bastard, he thought. It's to sell dangerous drugs to kids who don't know any better and who are prepared to put their lives on the line to get what they want. 'I am,' he said out loud.

Mr Pace nodded once. 'Good,' he said. 'Let us now discuss what you have to offer this organisation.'

Mike looked across to Devlin, who mouthed one word at him even while keeping his burning eyes fixed on Mr Pace. 'Money.'

Mike pulled out the paper Devlin had prepared for him on their way over to the hotel. It contained sums of money that made his head spin, arranged in order of increasing value. Devlin had said he was to start at the bottom and expect the negotiator to take him to the figure one from the top. He had also assured Mike that all of this money was available to him. Mr Pace pushed a legal notepad over to him and waited. Mike scribbled down the first of Devlin's figures on it and passed it back. 'I believe you will find this a sufficient sum.' He searched in vain for some flicker of reaction on the lawyer's face.

'May I suggest an amendment?'

It was, Mike realised, a game of sorts – dry and humourless, at least from his point of view, but a game nonetheless. He would scribble down a figure, pass it to Pace, who would mutter something vague that Mike didn't really follow, amend the figure and pass it back. As the minutes ticked by, Mike found himself climbing further and further up the list of figures that Devlin had prepared for him, and yet as far as he could tell there was no sense of the slightest readiness to accept on the part of Pace, who received each offer with equal impassivity before changing it and handing it back.

Mike could feel the pen in his hand slipping from nervous sweat and he glanced across to Devlin to see if he was the same. Devlin remained silent, sitting back in his chair, hands steepled, a picture of calm even as his eyes took in everything that was happening. Trust me, he seemed to be saying to Mike, this is just business. Mike raised the figure once again.

'I believe we may have an understanding, Mr Kilby.'

It took a few seconds for the words to have their full impact on Mike, so convinced had he been that nothing was working and the whole deal was going to fall through. Involuntarily, he looked across again at Devlin, who quickly gave a warning frown at the smile that was beginning to spread across Mike's face. Mike forced himself to be as inscrutable as the two practised negotiators with him. He was way out of his depth here and he knew it. Without Devlin, he could never have managed. He knew Pace would've eaten him whole and spat out the bones. But now they were almost there, within sight of crushing the Fellowship forever.

Pace had reshuffled his papers and was pushing several towards Mike with one hand while with the other he extended a gold-plated fountain pen. 'I believe if you would just sign and date the relevant sections, we can conclude this deal to the great satisfaction of all parties concerned.' Mike took the pen.

There was a sudden fusillade of blows to the hotel room door. His nerves wound up tight, Mike shot to his feet, the pen falling to the thickly carpeted floor in a shower of ink drops. Pace's face remained impenetrable but he snatched the papers back from the coffee table between them and stuffed them back into his case. Whatever his immediate reaction might have been, by the time Mike looked to Devlin again he was completely calm. He said nothing but with soothing gestures indicated that Mike should retake his seat and that they should wait. A second passed, another. Then there came another volley of blows on the door. 'Might I suggest,' said Mr Pace, licking his lips, 'that such an amount of noise in a hotel such as this could very well draw unwanted attention.'

Mike looked to Devlin. Devlin nodded, rose, walked carefully over to the door and opened it.

Sam flew into the room and stopped dead to take in the three men gathered there. He was panting heavily, sweating, his eyes rolling wildly around the room. Devlin closed the door and stepped round him. 'Len and Rick. They're dead!' Sam yelled. 'We are in deep shit! You have got to get us out of this now!'

Mike turned to Pace. How the hell was this desiccated legal type going to deal with this crazed leatherman? Pace wasn't even looking at Sam: his eyes were fixed on the ground. Mike got to his feet. OK. There was him and Devlin. With his weight and Devlin's wrestling skills they should be able to handle Sam between them, no matter how violent he got. And then he froze. Devlin was still calm, regarding Sam coolly. Maybe a skilled wrestler like him didn't need to worry, but that wasn't what stopped Mike in his tracks. It was the discovery that Sam wasn't, as he had thought, ranting at Pace. He was shouting at Devlin. 'You got us into this mess. Now fucking well get us out!'

'Richard! Wake up! Wake up!'

Slowly, like a deep sea diver rising from the darkness, Richard surfaced from the depths of a bleak dream where he and Mike were being chased round some huge, artificial globe by men in trenchcoats wielding knives. 'Wha . . .? I told you everything. I . . . Paul?'

Where the forbidding Mr Fernmann had sat, what seemed to Richard like only minutes previously, now sat Paul Ferris. From just behind him Richard caught a glimpse of his nurse. She was glaring daggers at Paul, the latest in a series of men to expel her from Richard's room. 'At last. Here.' He thrust a mobile phone in Richard's befuddled face. 'Call Mike now.'

For a second, Richard wondered if he was still dreaming. The man whose trousers he'd been so assiduously working to get into was telling him to call his boyfriend? There just had to be some deep and Freudian meaning behind that. He rubbed his eyes. Paul remained, and so did the cell phone.

'He's in trouble. The man you know as Devlin Lancaster is an impostor.'

Jolted into full consciousness, Richard accepted the phone and keyed in Mike's number before saying anything else. As they waited for an answer, Paul filled Richard in on what he had found out.

'No answer,' Richard said finally, letting the phone drop on to his bedspread.

'Damn! I knew he wouldn't listen to me but I thought maybe if it came from you we could get him away from Lancaster.'

'And now?'

Paul sat, hands clenched impotently, and Richard watched him. They both knew what Paul had to do. He had to go himself to find Mike. Or he had to make it official and go through the police. Either way he had to get involved himself. The seconds ticked by, and still Paul hung back.

'They already know, Paul,' Richard said finally. 'The police. Not your lot specifically, but a bunch from way up high.' He told Paul about the meeting with Fernmann. 'About the only thing they didn't seem to know was that Devlin wasn't who he said he was. Or if they did, they didn't let on to me.'

'Shit!' Paul covered his face. 'This is one hell of a bigger mess than I realised.'

'That,' said a voice from the door, 'is what I have been trying to make clear to you right from the start of this sorry affair.'

Into the room marched an angry Inspector Taylor, followed by two men. Richard just caught a glimpse of one very agitated-looking nurse before she was physically manhandled away from the room. Paul sprang to his feet, his face drained of blood.

The man behind Inspector Taylor pushed his way forwards and past Paul until he stood by Richard, thrusting a card with a photo on it into his face. 'Woodward. Chief Inspector Woodward.'

Richard put a hand to his aching head. 'Again?'

The new arrival looked at him sharply. 'What do you mean, "again"?'

'I mean, that I have not long ago spoken to you guys about everything: the Fellowship, Devlin Lancaster, the complete and utter balls-up Mike and I have made of your international operation. What more do you want?'

'What I want, Mr Green,' said Woodward, in a blunt northern

accent, 'is to know what you've said and to who. Because whoever you've spoken to, it wasn't the police.'

'What? Then who . . .?'

'Later, man, later. What did you tell them? What did they ask?'

'Everything.' Disoriented by the drugs, alarmed by events, Richard gabbled.

'Wait, wait.' Woodward gestured for him to stop. 'This is getting us nowhere. Think, man. What was the last thing you told them?'

Richard struggled to remember. It had been about Devlin, hadn't it? Their meeting at *Far Out!*? No, their time at his hotel.

'Which hotel?'

Richard told him.

Woodward turned to his companion. 'That could be it. Get on it. I want reinforcements ASAP.' He charged from the room, followed by the other man, who was already talking into his mobile.

'What the fuck is going on?' Richard gasped.

Inspector Taylor was following the others. He turned in the doorway. 'We are trying to get your "friend" out of the mess he has so determinedly, with the help of others –' and here he shot a furious glance at Paul '– got himself into. If we're lucky we'll find him before it's too late. You –' and he jabbed a finger at Paul '– stay here.'

Paul looked across at Richard. The appeal in Richard's eyes was as clear as the memory of his promise. 'No, sir,' he said to Taylor. 'I'm coming with you.'

'I think you'd better go.'

For one crazy minute, Mike thought Devlin's softly spoken words were addressed to him. The snap of Pace's attaché case locks as the lawyer rose to his feet made it clear to whom Devlin had really been speaking. 'We will be in touch, Mr Lancaster,' Pace said as he walked through the door that Devlin had again opened. He did not look at Devlin and Devlin did not reply as he closed the door behind him.

'Have you calmed down now?' This time Devlin was speaking to Sam. The leatherman nodded, though to Mike he looked every bit as agitated as when he had first burst through the door. 'Right. From the beginning, what has happened. And this had better be damn good.'

Mike stepped forwards. 'Devlin, I . . .'

'Shut up!'

Mike stepped back, an instinctive reaction to the unexpected and shocking violence of Devlin's words.

Sam looked nervously from one to the other of them. 'They're on to us, Mr Lancaster. They caught Len last night at The Buckle. They made him tell them where Rick was – me too, probably. I was just lucky. They both turned up in the river this morning.'

'You've no doubt it was them? You mix with shit, Sam. If you've wrecked this because of one of your other scams –'

'No, no, Mr Lancaster. I swear. It was them.'

Devlin nodded. Mike could sense the rage burning inside him, could see the effort he was making to control it in the tightness of his jaw, the narrowness of his eyes. Devlin was silent for a moment, deep in thought. 'Go get the car, Sam,' he said finally.

'But they're looking for me! If I'm seen –'

'So what are you going to do, man? Hide in this room for the rest of your life? Go and get the car.'

Trapped between his fear of the men outside the room and his fear of the man inside, Sam eventually nodded, reluctantly. 'Can I have a drink first?'

'No. I need you clear-headed. Go. And, Sam . . .?' He held out his hand.

Sam pulled something from within his jacket and passed it over. It was only when Devlin turned back to him after having closed the door that Mike could see what it was. A gun, and it was pointed unwaveringly at his chest. 'Did I tell you I was pistol champion at college too?' Devlin asked. Mike shook his head. 'Trust me,' said Devlin. He waved the gun towards the chair Mike had vacated. 'Sit down again. I think we have some waiting to do.'

Mike sat down slowly, on the very edge of the seat, some half-baked idea about jumping Devlin at the back of his mind. Devlin shook his head and gestured with the gun that Mike should sit well back. Mike did as he was told. 'What the fuck is going on, Devlin?'

'The game has just become a little more complicated than I anticipated, that's all.'

'You're part of the Fellowship, aren't you? You have been all along.'

'Yes.' Devlin gave that lop-sided smile. It was colder now than it had been before. 'And no. Yes I have been working for the Fellowship – or more accurately for the organisation behind the Fellowship – for some time now. I'm a head-hunter, if you like. I search out new markets, new lines of supply.' He waved the gun at Mike. 'New blood. And it has been very profitable. There's very little I do that isn't profitable. But there's been more than just money on my mind, this time. Much more.'

'What?'

'You. Well, my father first, and then you. Age before beauty.'

Mike felt his anger gathering like a cold fist over his heart. 'It was you after all, wasn't it? You killed Dave. You killed your own father.'

'No!' The response was swift, emphatic: a split-second glimpse into the emotional turmoil Mike had never guessed lay just below the surface of Devlin's steel self-control. 'That was an accident. It wasn't part of the plan.'

Mike nodded towards the door that Pace and Sam had just exited through in such a hurry. 'Your plans seem to have a habit of going wrong.'

Devlin shrugged. 'Risk is all part of the game. Ask any businessman. No risk, no fun.'

'You call killing your own father *fun*?'

'He wasn't a father to me!' It was there again, the seething raw emotion, held in check, but only barely. 'Was he a father to you, Mike?' Devlin moved in closer, the muzzle of the gun coming closer and closer to Mike's chest. 'Was that what you liked about him? Did you call him Daddy?'

'We were lovers.'

'Walks in the park, holding hands in the cinema, a fuck every night and always there when you needed him? Is that what you mean? Is it?' Devlin's voice rose, hints of the suppressed American accent coming to the surface. 'Well, he was never there for me, Mike. Never. What did he ever do for me, eh? Walked out and left me before he even knew me. My life was shit while he was back here making himself big, making his collection of tin trophies and screwing muscle-bound morons like you in this gym.'

'If you think the gym should have gone to you, I –'

Devlin's laughter was an ugly sound. 'You are so dumb! You haven't worked it out at all, yet, have you? I knew you'd get the gym. I wanted you to get the gym. Believe me, the day I want it I'll take it, and when I do I'll probably have it bulldozed into the ground. Or maybe I'll just give it away.'

'But you paid off Dave's loans, all his debts. You helped him.'

'No, Mike, I helped you. The debts were paid off *after* my dear father died. Mr Pace, Mr Ratherson and their firm may be a bunch of boring little pricks, but they can do an excellent job of massaging financial records. You can say thank you if you want.'

Mike shook his head. 'I don't understand!'

'Of course you don't,' Devlin sneered, his handsome face twisted into something ugly through his contempt, 'because you've spent all your life living in your muscles or your dick and not in your head. I wanted my loving father broken. Do you understand that? I wanted him to know something of what I'd known as I was growing up. The frustration. The misery. The hopelessness. I wanted him to have nothing, to have no one. That meant breaking him and everyone around him, especially you.'

'You wanted him hooked on Iron?'

'I wanted him bound to the Fellowship. Then I wanted you bound to the Fellowship. That's why I put money into the gym. That's why I've put the money into your account. It's all untraceable. It's all very incriminatory.'

Finally Mike began to see the shape of Devlin's plan. 'So eventually you could just pull the plug . . .?'

Devlin nodded slowly, unable to conceal his pleasure at finally being able to reveal the truth behind his actions. 'And walk away. Leaving you and my dearest father rotting in jail. Except it didn't quite work that way.' He sighed in mock resignation. 'Still, it's been a good game. A good series of games, you might say. It's fun to play with people's bodies, isn't it, Mike?'

Mike made no response. Devlin just laughed. 'But playing with people's heads is much more fun. And that's what I've been doing, starting with my father.' He crouched next to Mike, resting the gun barrel on Mike's chin. His voice was low, slightly breathless, a conspiratorial whisper. 'We're all so frightened of being alone, Mike. We say we like it, say it's part of our "lifestyle", build up our muscles and our bank balances so that no one can say we're weak, but underneath it all every one of us is terrified of growing old and being alone. Poor Daddy. Can you imagine the effect of being like that and then having a son turn up on your doorstep who's heading for thirty? It was easy to play with his head. It was easy to push him into going for competitions again, and I wanted him to. I wanted him to fail.

'It was me who introduced him to the Iron. He didn't want to use it, not at first. Gave me all the right reasons for not taking it. But there was no one else around except me, his loving son. Drip, drip, drip. Until in the end . . .' Devlin shrugged. 'Pity you weren't around. You could have put the other point of view. He'd have listened to you. He might still have been alive now. But, of course, you left him.'

'Don't try to blame me, you bastard!' Mike's hands were fists. His body trembled with the urge to fling himself at his tormentor and beat him senseless, anything to force Devlin to stop pouring his poison into his mind.

Devlin laughed softly and traced a line with the gun muzzle from Mike's chin, along his jaw to the fleshy point just beneath one ear. 'I don't need to, do I? Or myself, for that matter. Nobody could have known the effect it would have on him. Just one pill, the first and pffft!'

'Then all the other stuff they found in his flat?'

'Planted by me, yes. A little obvious, I grant you, but the boys in blue seemed to fall for it – largely because they wanted to, I think. They really don't seem to like us, do they? Except for Sergeant Paul, of course. He likes us. One of us, anyway.' He stood and stepped back. 'So there he was, gone before I'd had a chance to turn his use of Iron into a fully-fledged and illegal membership of the Fellowship. Where did that leave me?' He answered his own question. 'It left me with you. The game still wasn't played out.'

Mike surged to his feet. 'Fuck you, Devlin, this isn't a game!'

Devlin's other hand flew to the gun as he drew a bead between Mike's eyes. 'Of course it's a game, Mike. Everything is. If it wasn't nothing would make sense. You play to win and that's all there is to it. I'm a winner –' he cocked the trigger of the gun '– and you're just a loser. By the time this is all over I'll have screwed you every which way.'

Mike bared his own teeth in a vicious grin. 'Every way but the one which counts, eh, Devlin? One of life's losers in that department?'

The gun swung in a silvered arc and cracked against Mike's skull. When the blinding light in his eyes had faded and Mike had wiped the trickle of blood away Devlin was up close, the gun jabbing into his T-shirt. 'I haven't told you about Richard, yet, have I?' he spat. 'Or shall I just show you?'

There was a knock at the door. Without taking his eyes or the gun off Mike, Devlin called out, 'Who is it?'

'Sam.'

Devlin backed away from Mike, keeping him covered all the while. He reached behind himself and opened the door. For the second time that evening, Sam bowled in, slamming the door into Devlin as he did. Devlin swore as the hand with the gun was knocked to one side and for a brief moment Mike thought this might be the chance he needed. His hopes of escape evaporated almost immediately afterwards as he saw just why Sam had cannoned into the room.

Three men in dark suits were following right behind. With smooth ease the leading, younger man knocked the gun from Devlin's hand and sent a second fist smashing into his stomach. Devlin fell down to the carpet, gasping. The remaining two men entered the room and closed the door. One was holding a gun which was trained on Sam. The man who had punched Devlin reached into his dark suit and pulled out another which he trained on Devlin. The oldest man turned to Mike, whose last hopes faded at the coldness he saw in his eyes. This was no rescue operation.

Having silenced Mike, the apparent leader of the new arrivals looked down dispassionately at the grovelling Devlin. 'Mr Lancaster,' he said, with no more emotion than if he'd been starting a board meeting. 'My name is Fernmann. I bring a message from our mutual employers. They are very angry with you. Very angry indeed.'

Woodward hadn't been pleased when Paul had piled into his car, but the urgency of the situation left no time for argument. On the way he grudgingly filled Paul in. 'Devlin Lancaster, as you know him, works for the organisation we've been investigating. That much we've known for over a year now. What's come to light recently is that for the past three or four months he's been using part of that organisation in the pursuit of his own agenda.'

'The Fellowship of Iron?'

'Right. Financially, he's a genius. He's pretty much isolated the Fellowship from its parent group. It was only pure luck that we stumbled across what he was up to. We were fairly sure Lancaster's superiors didn't know anything about it. We had thought we might be able to exploit the situation for ourselves, use it as another way in. And then –'

'Dave Ross died.'

'Right again.' Woodward acknowledged reluctantly Paul's putting the pieces together.' Lancaster's bosses didn't like that. They like things kept low-profile, for obvious reasons, especially a new operation like the Fellowship. And now, there was Iron flashing up on computer screens in every police station in the country, linked to a death under suspicious circumstances. They sent out their own investigators, the charming Mr Fernmann and his associates, to find out what was going on. As soon as we realised what was happening, we tried to put a lid on things, pulled the local investigation to give things a chance to calm down again until we were ready to make our move.' He paused and looked significantly at Paul. 'Only that didn't work, did it? Despite repeated warnings, despite repeated orders from your superior officer, you, Sergeant Ferris, insisted on helping two civilians, one of them a reporter, to well and truly stir up the shit. Well, now it's hit the fan.'

Woodward stopped. Had he been Taylor following in the car

behind, he would have gone on, would have flayed Paul for his stupidity, his naïveté, his insubordination. But this man didn't need to. Paul saw the whole picture now, understood the misinterpretation of Taylor's motives that had been partly to blame for his insubordination, and if he could have crawled under a seat to escape the superior officer's accusatory gaze, he would have done.

'The one thing out of all this we don't understand,' Woodward concluded, 'is Devlin Lancaster's motives. We know that under all the charm and good looks he's a pretty nasty piece of work – unstable, even – but that doesn't explain what he's done. He's already got money. He didn't stand to make significantly more from messing around with the Fellowship in the way he has, so why did he take the risk he did of upsetting his bosses when he stood to gain so little in return?'

Paul was reluctant to speak, but suspected that here at least he held a piece of the puzzle that the big boys did not. 'Did you know,' he said tentatively, 'that Lancaster was Ross's son?'

It was obvious from Woodward's expression that he did not. 'Something to be gained from independent investigations after all,' he said quietly as he mused on what Paul had told him. He caught Paul's look of surprise. 'I didn't say we don't understand, Ferris. I'm saying that sometimes, in this line of work, we have to do things, follow orders, that we don't like. No matter who they come from. Do you hear what I'm saying, Sergeant?'

'Yes, sir.' The affirmation was completely sincere.

They pulled up outside Devlin's hotel. 'All right, so we know there's three of them,' Woodward said. 'Probably at least one more in a car nearby. We're outnumbered.' Taylor and Paul exchanged glances. In Woodward's eyes, when it came to an operation like this, they didn't count.

'We could have some of our men here in five minutes, sir,' Taylor said.

'Too late – and with all due respect, Inspector, we don't work with your men.' Woodward stood, irresolute, assessing the situation. 'But if we don't act fast,' he muttered, more to himself than to any of the others, 'we may lose this one.'

Alarmed by what he heard, Paul stepped forward. 'Then until your men get here, you'll have to make use of us, sir.'

Woodward looked at him and Taylor, weighed the odds then nodded grimly once. The small group of policemen moved into the hotel.

A flurry of police cards, a few whispered words with the receptionist and a startled manager secured the location of Devlin's suite and the start of a discreet but hasty evacuation of the lobby. The police made their way up to Devlin's floor.

As they stepped out of the lift, the door to Devlin's suite at the end of the corridor opened. Swiftly, they fell back round a corner.

'What now?' hissed Taylor.

Woodward hesitated. 'We can't take them on here. We'll have to let them go. Follow them, hope we can deal with them somewhere safer.'

'But if we lose them?' demanded Paul.

'We have little choice.'

Paul took a deep breath. 'Yeah, well, sometimes we have to do things we don't like, don't we, sir?' It wasn't false bravado. It was a moment of cold clarity, a moment in which he saw a way to pay for some of his mistakes, to perhaps make up for some of his stupidity. And behind it all, perhaps even more important than all the rest, was the memory of his promise to Richard. Mike was in real danger, maybe because of his ill-considered actions, maybe because of his later inaction. Either way, like Woodward had said, he really had no choice.

With no time for explanation, Paul pulled off his jacket. On a small table beside them was a vase of roses. Paul swept it to one side, grabbing the silver salver it had been standing on. He held it in front of him like a waiter. 'You in?' he said to Taylor.

Taylor nodded.

'Right.' Ignoring Woodward's hissed imprecations, Paul stepped out into the corridor.

Devlin and Mike were there, and another man in a leather jacket Paul recognised from Richard's mugging. Behind each of them walked a man in a dark suit. Each had his hand in his pocket. With a sickening lurch of his stomach, Paul understood why. He caught the widening of Mike's eyes as he approached but ignored it. He could think of nothing beyond his plan, which

accounted for all of the next five seconds. 'Gentlemen, gentlemen,' he squealed.

'Not now,' the lead suit said, Fernmann presumably, shoving
Devlin in the small of the back in an attempt to move past Paul.

'But your orders. I have come to take your orders for drinks.'
Paul pushed himself into the midst of the group.

'I said, not –'

Paul swung the salver round and into the teeth of the man
covering Mike with a startling crack. He fell to the ground but
even as he did he was pulling his gun out. Paul dived on top of
him, trusting to Mike now to play his part.

Mike wasn't slow in seeing his opportunity at last. With a roar
of pent-up frustration, anger and fear, Mike launched himself
forward and rugby-tackled the guy covering Sam. He toppled
forwards. There was a muffled report as the gun in his pocket
went off. Not sure even if it had been he who had been hit, Mike
punched the man in the face twice, not holding back any of the
weight or power of his muscle-laden body, before dragging the
man's arm out of his pocket. He'd intended to wrest the gun
from him, perhaps even use it himself, but there was no struggle
and no need. The gun's stray shot had smashed into its owner's
leg and he was in far too much pain to put up a fight. A wide-
eyed and liberated Sam spread himself, back to the wall, and
waited, petrified, for whatever turn events took.

With the tables so suddenly and shockingly turned against him
Fernmann pulled out his gun, heedless now of who might see it,
and jammed it up against Devlin's head. 'Move!' he barked.

Woodward and the others emerged from round the corridor
corner in front of him. 'Dieter Fernmann. I arrest you –'

With an inarticulate shout, Fernmann thrust Devlin forward
and into them, and ran off down the corridor in the confusion.
'Get him!' Woodward and his remaining support ran off after
Fernmann. Taylor and Devlin disentangled themselves and leaped
to their feet. Taylor stepped forward. 'Devlin Lancaster,' he began,
'I'm arresting you for –'

Devlin looked down the corridor, saw Paul slapping handcuffs
on his man, saw Mike easily pinning his. He turned back to
Taylor and grinned. 'Sorry, old man,' he said.

Eleven

I t could, Paul decided, all have been a lot worse.

Woodward and his men had caught Fernmann. Fernmann, for his part, had since proved more co-operative and a good deal more knowledgeable about the organisation he worked for than had been realised. The Fellowship of Iron debacle may have set Woodward's team back, but Fernmann's 'help' looked like it might more than compensate for the damage done. While not a candidate for imminent promotion, it at least looked now like Paul wouldn't be drummed out of the police force, either. Not that this had saved him from another severe bollocking from Inspector Taylor. But then Taylor had had reason to be foul-tempered. He had let Devlin Lancaster escape.

'One minute I was standing there, ready to slap on the handcuffs; the next I was flying over his shoulder,' he'd said, dazed.

'I know what you mean,' Mike had said with a slow smile. 'I'll tell you about it some time. Well, some of it.'

That, Paul suspected, was largely why he was where he was now, alone in Operations Room One with a mountain of paperwork and personal effects, the price of bureaucracy that had to be paid at the conclusion of any case. Somehow, this one seemed to have generated more than any other he had ever known. He suspected that was down to Taylor, too. 'Good experience for you,' the inspector had spat. Paul thought that army squaddies given mountains of potatoes to peel had probably been fed the same line.

Two things kept him cheered during the long hours of plodding through the duplicate, triplicate and quadruplicate forms. One was a visit from PC Alex Summers with a mug of coffee, a doughnut and a sympathetic smile. They'd fixed a date for their drink. The other was the memory of Mike's grateful smile, right at the end there, after their respective captives had been carted off, when they'd both been sitting on the plush hotel carpet, backs to the wall, panting. 'Thank you,' Mike had said simply, and he'd reached out and shaken Paul's hand. For a moment Paul had thought Mike was going to hug him, maybe even kiss him. At the time, he wouldn't have objected if Mike had.

It was late in the afternoon when he came across the video tape. It was unmarked, a conventional three-hour tape that had been found among Devlin's personal effects left behind in the hotel. Intriguingly, it was in an envelope with Mike Kilby's name and address on it. With only the briefest of hesitations, Paul slipped it in the Ops Room's VCR and sat back to watch. He watched as Devlin led Richard into the bedroom, tied him to the bedposts and left him so that he could attend to the camera manually, zooming in and out, moving the view frame up and down Richard's bound body. And he watched as Devlin returned and fucked Richard unmercifully with his sex toy. He had to hurriedly reduce the volume as Richard's shouts and cries filled the room.

By the time he'd finished watching the tape Paul was actually sweating, his heart racing and his dick like a gatepost in his trousers. His head was filled with the images of Richard and the sounds of Richard from the tape which, as he ran them over again and again in his mind, became overlaid with the smell and the feel of Richard, remembered from his own all too brief encounters with him.

He hadn't seen Richard since that last time in the hospital. He knew he'd have to again, knew that he wanted to, very much, but had put it off. In a way that he didn't want to admit to, he was afraid. Things had gone so far between them by now that their next meeting he knew would be a decisive one. One way or another. Coming across the tape now was like a sign. He knew that he couldn't delay matters any longer.

Paul rose, grabbed his coat and walked smartly from the room. He took with him the video tape, which he tapped thoughtfully against his chin as he headed for his car. Yes, a sign. And also perhaps the means to a very satisfactory end.

It was, Richard discovered, coming across a calendar under a pile of papers on his desk, an anniversary. It was two weeks ago exactly that he had been beaten up outside the old glove factory. Occasion for a celebration, he thought, if he hadn't been feeling so rotten.

It wasn't the aftermath of the attack that was making him feel so low. True, he still had some quite colourful bruising on parts of his body, but only the most incautious of movements brought on any twinges now, and even the bruises were long past their peak spectacle. He was whole, he was well, he was free of medication and almost all of his bandages.

And they had found out the truth behind Dave Ross's death. Even if the organisation that was behind it was still, for the moment, operating, the Fellowship of Iron was well and truly out of business, and that was surely cause for celebration.

But then there was Devlin. Not who he said he was, and not about to fulfil any of those glittering promises he had held out. Police investigations had uncovered some of the truth about him. For some years he had been the paid 'companion' of the real Devlin Lancaster, a man wealthy enough and grateful enough for the attentions of a much younger man to shower him with gifts and money, until the day he had disappeared, taking with him considerably more than his patron had intended. The police had found out one other thing as well: his real name. It had been Mike.

Curiously, that single fact had disturbed Richard more than almost any other. How must 'Devlin' have felt when he came back to this country and found that the father who had, in his eyes, abandoned him, had taken a lover younger even than him with his name? And had Dave known his child's name? If so, how had he felt when a handsome young bodybuilder had come into his gym and introduced himself with the name of his long-lost son? Had there been some truth after all in those taunts of Devlin's about Dave being a 'Daddy', a father figure? He didn't like to think about it.

Richard understood now, after hearing from Mike about that last meeting, that Devlin's playing with his life had all been a part of his playing with Mike's. The bastard! The memory of it, particularly of their sex session in Devlin's suite, made Richard feel gullible and stupid. He was heartily glad there was no evidence of what they had done together. It hardly seemed likely that Mike and Devlin were going to be holding many conversations in times to come and there was no way he was going to bring it up.

And then there was Mike. He'd been there every day Richard had been in hospital. They'd spent as much time as Richard's put-upon nurse would allow them, talking, chewing over what had happened, but always staying away from what was at the heart of it. Them. Their relationship. When the time had come for Richard finally to leave hospital, it had been Mike who had taken him home, made sure he was comfortable and had everything he needed. But then he had gone. Two days had passed and Richard hadn't seen or heard from him. He didn't expect to. He knew Mike. He knew Mike was waiting. The next move was up to him.

Because then there was Paul. Richard had been angered by Paul's reluctance to compromise his career, but was that fair? Paul had still done more for them, for him, than anyone else, and in the end, when push came to shove, he'd risked his own life for Mike. So where did that leave him? How did he feel about Paul? He couldn't deny one feeling: the thought of Paul physically was still very exciting. The memory of policeman Paul's active truncheon in his hand stimulated a powerful ache, a need all the more acute for the two weeks of compelled inactivity in a hospital bed with precious little opportunity for physical release of any kind. Was that all there was to it, though? And would he ever know, if not? Paul had not been in contact since that last meeting with Taylor and Woodward in the hospital. Was he also waiting for

Richard to make the first move? 'Who died and left me centre of the universe?' Richard sighed.

The doorbell rang. Richard raised his eyes to the ceiling. 'My mistake,' he said. 'Sorry.' He took a deep breath before going to answer the door. It was Mike or Paul, he just knew it, and whichever one it was this had to be more than simply a social call. He recognised that the time had come at last to make decisions, and if these two men, each in his own way strong, determined and confident, were unable to do it then he, Richard Green, would do it for them.

'You've tidied up,' said Paul after Richard had shown him in.

'Well, actually Mike did. Or rather he just gathered things together and put them in boxes somewhere out of sight. He said it would be better for me to come back to a place that was uncluttered. I'll be searching for things for months.'

'How are you?'

'Fine. Fine.'

'No grapes, I'm afraid.'

'Good!' Unfinished business hung heavy in the air between them. 'So don't I get a kiss?'

'Course.' Paul's arms slipped around him easily, his lips firm on Richard's mouth. He pulled Richard into him but then hesitated.

'It's all right, it's all right,' Richard said quickly.

'No, it's . . . I didn't know if you still hurt anywhere.'

'We'll just have to see, won't we?' Richard said softly, and he pulled Paul back into him, opened his mouth and took the policeman's tongue into it.

For long minutes they kissed, arms tight around each other. 'I'm not settling for a quick dive into your pants this time, Paul.'

Paul shook his head and pushed his mouth on to Richard's neck, his face, into his hair. Without further words and without breaking contact, Richard led them into the bedroom. They separated for as long as it took them to tear off their clothes and then they were wrapped in each other's arms again, Paul letting out a helpless cry as skin met skin and their erect cocks drove into each other. Richard laughed and thrust forwards again and again, Paul crying out helplessly each time. As one, they fell back on to the bed, still unmade from that morning.

In years, they were much the same age, but in terms of experience Richard might as well have been a decade older. Paul's lovemaking was as rough and uncontrolled as a teenager's. He pushed his hands up and down Richard's lithe body, sucked greedily on his neck, his chest, his arms, forcing himself back into Richard's mouth again and again like a diver desperate for life-giving air, while all the time his cock ground into Richard's. His breathing was hoarse, his exclamations of pleasure inarticulate.

Richard felt like a man riding a tornado, on fire to satisfy himself with Paul but determined not to lose this moment in a brief explosion of lust, no matter how intense. With a breathless laugh, he pushed himself back. 'Whoa, there.' Paul looked up at him from the bed, gasping like a man who'd run a four-minute mile, hot for more but suddenly anxious that he'd done something wrong. Richard reassured him. 'It doesn't have to happen all at once.'

'Show me.'

Richard felt his stomach tie itself in knots and his cock swell to almost painful hardness. A policeman, young, fit, handsome, and in his bed so inexperienced, so vulnerable. It was the contrast, the contradictions he found so arousing. 'It'll be my pleasure.'

He started at Paul's feet, licking his way up past ankle and calf to the exquisitely tender areas of the inner thigh, dragging his tongue along the thickening hair, lingering over the spots that made Paul gasp and convulsively beat the mattress with his arms. As he travelled up with his mouth, he worked his hands under Paul's buttocks and lifted, until by the time his face was buried in Paul's crotch, his tongue pushing into the throbbing softness between ball sac and hole, Paul's lower back was completely lifted from the mattress, his legs up on either side of Richard's head. Richard pressed his face down and in between Paul's cheeks, licking at his ring which quivered deliciously at this unknown and unexpected stimulation. He thrust deep, lost in the warm darkness, the male musk.

When he pulled back to see how Paul had taken this, the look of incredulous pleasure on the man's face set his heart racing and his head plunging back between Paul's legs for more. When he finally resurfaced, he judged the time right to move on a stage.

With a gleam in his eyes, Richard sucked on his index finger then slipped it, without warning, into Paul's arse and through his ring. Teased by Richard's tongue, Paul's sphincter took the finger automatically even as his eyes snapped open with shocked surprise at this first penetration. 'It's OK. Relax,' Richard crooned, gently working the finger in and out, easing it in further each time, reaching for the prostate and the pressure he knew would bring such pleasure.

'What are you . . .? Oh. Oh!'

Richard grinned. 'You mean you've had this all your life and never known what it's for?'

'Fuck, no!'

'Fuck, yes.'

Richard worked Paul with his fingers, stretching and pressing. It was intoxicating, seeing the play of new sensations across Paul's handsome, flushed face. He knew that he couldn't hold himself back now for very much longer. 'Turn over.'

Slowly, Paul obeyed. Richard straddled him, knees either side of Paul's hips. He ran his hands up the smooth back, kneading the muscles at the top of the shoulders. They were knotted, tense. Richard brought his hands back down Paul's sides, down to the firm roundness of his buttocks. Paul's arse was under his erect cock. He'd be the first. The first man to push his dick between those gorgeous cheeks. The first man to make Paul cry out as he pumped his come into his sweating body. The first man to show him the pleasure that had been waiting for him all this time, if only he'd known how to reach out and take it.

Richard lowered himself gently, resting the length of his hardened meat on the crack of Paul's arse. He moved it slowly, lightly in the warm groove, hot pre-come spilling from him, making his own lube. 'Yes,' he muttered. 'Oh yes!'

'No.'

'It's all right,' Richard soothed. 'It's all right. I'll use a condom. I wouldn't do it without a condom.' He reached across to the bedside cabinet and its store of rubbers.

'No.' Paul twisted and pushed himself up off the mattress until Richard had to pull back and off him. Paul turned himself over until he was lying on his back, Richard kneeling to one side. 'I'm not ready,' he said. There was pain and confusion on his face but also determination.

Slowly, Richard nodded. It took more self-control than he suspected Paul would ever know, but he did it. Paul was right. He wasn't ready. 'That's OK,' he said. 'I am.' To banish any uncertainty, he took Paul's heavy member in one hand and slowly pushed down it, forcing the foreskin back from the engorged purple cock head. Paul arched, moaned and threw his arms back. When he opened his eyes again Richard was holding the condom he'd been reaching for and was freeing it from its foil wrapping. Now, though, it was Paul who was to be the wearer. Feeling absurdly like a child having its coat buttoned or its shoelaces tied, Paul watched as Richard brought the latex to the slickened head of his dick and carefully rolled it down the length of his stiff tool. As Richard lubed himself up, Paul touched himself very gently. He had never been so hard, so sensitive. He felt on the brink of some incredible explosion, literally and emotionally, his heart hammering, his breathing heavy, and yet at the same time he felt an uncanny calmness and clarity. He was in the eye of the tornado. His life had finally brought him to this moment, and it was right.

Richard straddled him again, sitting on his stomach, smiling down as he reached behind himself for Paul's dick, guiding it up, guiding it into him. He sat back and Paul cried out, reaching with both hands to grasp the young man as Richard let his weight bear down and he impaled himself on Paul's thick cock. With the ease of much good experience, Richard relaxed completely and let Paul slide deep, deep into him. For long moments they both stayed where they were, afraid almost to breathe too deeply, both of them glorying in this ultimate intimacy before Richard raised himself slightly on his haunches and fell back, rose again a little further this time, and fell back, again and again.

Paul lasted nearly a minute under Richard's quickening rhythm before surging up and forwards with a wordless cry, forcing Richard backwards so that it was now him lying with his legs in the air and Paul thrusting furiously into his arse. 'That's it. Do it! Oh, God, yes!' He'd led Paul by the hand up to this point but now Richard let go, abandoning himself to the frenetic ramming of Paul's magnificent cock into his prostate, filling him, driving him helplessly to climax. 'Yes, do it, do it to me!'

At the last moment, Paul opened his eyes and looked down at Richard. The man beneath him had his head thrown back, mouth open in an endless, soundless cry of pleasure. It was the face from the video, but this time it wasn't some plastic love toy stretching Richard's arse. This time it was him. This time it was him fucking another man. At last. At last! His come shot into the condom with a power he'd never known before in his life. For one terrible, confused moment, he even thought he'd split the latex with the force of his orgasm as he felt a shower of warm liquid across his stomach, chest and face until he looked again and realised that Richard had reached his own climax and was vigorously and uncontrollably spraying them both with the bounty of his ball sac. Paul basked in the blood-warm shower as if it were summer rain, and pumped every last drop of his come into Richard's sweating, gasping body.

'You don't have to,' he said afterwards, as Richard brought in a large woollen towel and began to tenderly wipe him down.

'I know,' said Richard, leaning over to lick Paul's stomach before continuing his ministrations. 'I like to.'

Paul smiled dreamily, lay back and let him, then watched as Richard did the same for himself. When Richard slipped back into bed, he snuggled close to Paul.

Automatically Paul put his arms round him. 'This is afterglow, isn't it?' he murmured.

'Mmm,' said Richard. 'Good, isn't it?'

'Fucking fantastic.'

They drifted off to sleep in each other's arms.

When Paul awoke, he was on his own. He was immoderately proud of himself to find that he was already aroused at the thought of making love to Richard yet again. He couldn't help some disappointment therefore when Richard entered the bedroom vigorously towelling his hair after a shower, redressed in jeans and T-shirt.

Grinning, Richard threw a towel at Paul. 'Through there. Watch out for the hot tap; it can get stuck.'

Paul took the towel and the hint and headed for the shower. By the time he'd cleaned up and dressed, Richard had made them both coffee. They sat and drank. Paul had absolutely no idea what to say.

Richard saw it and sighed inwardly. It was going to have to be down to him, just like he'd known it would be. 'I'm going to see Mike later,' he said.

Paul studied his coffee mug. Here it was. The crunch. The reason he'd come, though now it was here he wished he could put it off. He'd thought that if they ever did what they had in fact just done then this moment would be easier, that everything would be clearer, for Richard and for him. Now he was surprised to find it was not. 'Something to tell him?'

Richard looked up at Paul. 'Only that I love him.'

'Ah.' They drank some more of their coffee. 'It's because I wouldn't let you fuck me, isn't it?' Paul's voice was calm, caught somewhere between bitterness and resignation.

'Not really. Let's just say certain things clicked into place at that point.'

'Such as?'

Richard sighed. 'Would you take me to the Policeman's Annual Ball, Paul?'

'What?'

'Would you?'

Paul frowned, confused by the apparently nonsensical question. 'There's no such thing.'

'OK. So would you take me to your station's Christmas do? I assume you have those. Or a birthday bash for one of the other officers? Or just down to your local for a drink with some of the lads after work?'

'You know I couldn't.'

Richard nodded with a small, sad smile. 'Right. And what happens now if your mobile rings?'

'I'd answer it.'

'And Inspector Taylor says, "I need you. Come running."?'

'It's my job.'

'But it's not mine. And it's not my life, either.'

215

'You still love Mike, don't you?' It was more of a statement than a question.

Richard's reply was calm and steady, belying his very careful choice of words. 'I always have loved Mike, even when I've been angry with him. I loved him when you and I were first . . . getting to know each other.' He paused very slightly then pressed on. 'I loved him when I went out into the park afterwards for a bit of trade and quick relief. I love him now. It's who I am.'

Paul couldn't meet his level gaze. 'So you and me, what we've just done: it was nothing to you? Just another bit of "quick relief?"'

Richard wanted badly to reach out and touch Paul, take away some of the hurt he knew his words were causing, but he knew that would be wrong. It might hurt, but there was a truth that Paul needed to see and, until he did, Richard couldn't risk anything that might be misinterpreted. 'No,' he said simply. 'It was good and it was right, for both of us. It was something that we had to do. And –' he couldn't help a small smile '– I'd like to do it again some day. When you're ready.' He sat back and waited, hoping that Paul understood he was referring to so much more than just his being able to accept him as an active sexual partner as well as a passive one.

Paul sat tight-lipped, clutching the now cold cup of coffee. He wanted to be hurt and angry. He wanted to tell Richard he was being a patronising little sod and was totally wrong. But Richard wasn't, and Paul couldn't. Richard's calm, carefully-delivered words had cut straight through the uncertainty he'd felt on waking up. Oh, yes, he still desired Richard's body. He knew he had much more still to learn about sex between men. And he would have enjoyed learning it at Richard's hands. This man had opened his eyes to a whole new vital range of experience, and he'd always be important to Paul, special, for that reason. But Richard was right. Paul couldn't love him. Not as he was. Not as they both were. Not in the foreseeable future, anyway. Without thinking, Paul downed the cold dregs of his coffee. The truth stung, and it made something in him that he liked to think was his heart ache, but it was still the truth.

He would have left with a simple goodbye. Richard pulled him in close, and hugged him. When they separated, Richard kissed him once on the lips. 'Don't be a stranger,' he called out in bad imitation of a Californian fast food waitress. Paul went to reply, but in the end said nothing.

Back in his car, he sat. Where to now? On the seat was the envelope with the video. Send the video to Mike, maybe even drop it off himself, then sit back and watch the sparks fly? That had been his plan, even if he hadn't fully admitted it to himself. Mike would have thrown Richard over and he could have moved in to fill the space left. Mike couldn't have carried on with Richard after having seen for himself what he'd got up to with Devlin. Paul couldn't have, if he'd been Richard's boyfriend. But then Paul wasn't Mike. And that was rather the point, wasn't it?

Resignedly, Paul started the engine and turned his car towards home. He'd wipe the tape. Well, maybe he'd look at it again first and then wipe it. And there was always that drink with Alex in a couple of days' time. Yeah.

Mike lay naked in bed on top of the sheets. By his side lay an open muscle magazine. He'd spent the last half hour thumbing through the glossy colour photos of bodybuilders in briefs and thongs, flexing and smiling against a variety of backgrounds, imagining in detail what he'd like to do with each one of them. There was the blond Californian in the lime green briefs whose scarcely covered tackle Mike would lovingly have taken into his mouth and sucked to delight. There was the dark Spaniard in red briefs, spread-eagled across rocks by a beach. He could have done wonders for Mike's rocks. And then there had been the black muscle god, his gleaming, oiled skin a startling contrast to the white thong he was wearing. Mike focused on the thought of melting his look of macho defiance at the camera, bringing the stud to the point where he was begging for Mike to thrust his dick between his beefy buttocks and roger his brains out.

It was all no use. He'd fully intended to wank himself senseless over the magazine and blow his come from one end of the bed to the other. But he couldn't. Other faces kept intruding on the fantasies, superimposing themselves over the faces of the men in the photos. Real faces.

There was Dave. He'd been wrong about Dave after all. Dave had taken the steroid. But he'd been right, too. Dave hadn't wanted to, but in the end he'd been beaten by pressures and fears Mike just couldn't imagine yet. And by Devlin. Devlin had said Mike might have saved Dave if he'd stayed around, and at first Mike had believed that. He didn't now. Devlin had deceived them all; he was a master at it, and he would have deceived them then, even if Mike had been there. They had beaten him, though, and broken the Fellowship of Iron. He knew Dave would be pleased with that. It had to be enough, for now.

Devlin. How did he feel about him? For a brief period it had been like having Dave back, a second chance to say sorry, a chance to say goodbye. It had been a cruel illusion, but discovering that had been strangely healing. Devlin had been the last real link to Dave. Casting him off had allowed Mike to finally let Dave go. He'd loved Dave, he always would, but now it was time to move on. To Richard.

Except, of course, there was Paul, the man who had saved his life and who was also trying to take his boyfriend. How did you thank a guy for something like that and also tell him you wanted to break his legs? Richard would know. He was the one with a way with words. In the end it all came down to Richard, didn't it?

Mike knew you couldn't hold on to someone if he'd decided he needed to be with someone else. For the first time since he and Richard had become a couple, he contemplated the idea that his boyfriend might actually leave him. Why not? Paul was attractive, smart and successful in a real career. Mike was a performer, possibly even a freak in the eyes of some – loads of potential but, as Dave had told him, needing a damn sight more get up and go if he was ever to really make anything of himself in this crazy life he'd chosen. What could an intelligent, rising star like Richard possibly see in a man like him?

One hand curled into a fist and impotently punched into the mattress. It mashed the muscle mag lying there. Damn it. He loved Richard so much! Out of all the faces he'd been seeing, the ones in the photos, the ones in his fantasies, the ones from his memories, Richard's stood out the clearest. Richard's was the one that *mattered*.

Mike cupped his balls the way Richard liked to, held his cock in the palm of the other and closed his eyes to more clearly picture his boyfriend. After much fruitless fantasy labour, his dick began to stir and grow at the thought of Richard. He thought of how they liked to undress each other, starting with shoes and socks, trousers then shirt, until each was just in boxers or briefs, teasing the moments out with explorations of the flesh revealed. Mike had never had as imaginative and sensitive a lover as Richard, fearless and fierce, yet capable of such sweet tenderness. He'd knead the muscular mounds of Mike's pecs, slap at the hard glutes of his arse and suck greedily at Mike's cock, an impudent lion cub taking on the king of the pride, before kissing him softly on lips and eyelids, whispering his love for him and holding him through the night.

Uninhibited, unintimidated and supremely sure of himself, Richard had never made the assumptions about Mike that so many other men had made. Others saw a giant of a man, a hugely muscular stud who could shift weights that would leave other men literally throwing up and fainting, and they assumed he wanted only one thing in a partner, a passive fuck. More than any other of Mike's lovers, Richard knew how wrong that was. He knew how much Mike revelled in being fucked himself, that he adored taking another man inside himself, surrendering himself to the hardness of another man, and he was only too ready and willing to take Mike up against walls, bent over the ends of beds or chairs, face up or face down. Richard might be no match for Mike, pound for pound, but in the strength and vitality of his cock he was second to no one. Mike moaned in his imaginings, thrusting his crotch up into his hand, reaching round his own backside to probe his arse with his fingers.

'You'll go blind.'

Mike shot up, grabbed for a sheet then grabbed for his suddenly exposed dick, standing so eagerly and obviously to attention.

Richard stood in the doorway and smiled. He pointed to the crumpled magazine. 'I mean reading in bed without a proper light. Terrible for the eyes.'

Mike did his best to collect himself. Talk about dreams come true. 'Nothing else to do,' he said.

'Poor thing,' said Richard with mock sympathy. He came in and sat down on the edge of the bed.

Mike used his free hand to pull the sheet up over his legs and groin. His erection, hard enough before, was raging now at the sight of his lover so close to him again. The thin cotton sheet settled on it and did little to disguise its shape and size. A small damp spot appeared on the material at its tip and grew. Mike rested his hand over it. Was this it? Had Richard come to say goodbye?

'I've just seen Paul.'

'Is he all right?' Mike could hardly hear his own forced question for the pounding of his heart in his ears.

Richard nodded. 'Yeah. He's back at work now. Busy boy. Probably go far.'

'He saved my life.'

'And I've said thank you.' He looked Mike straight in the eyes. Mike met his gaze with understanding. 'I mean,' Richard went on, 'where would I have been at this year's office Christmas do without you?'

'The Christmas do?'

'Just something that's been on my mind recently.' Richard shifted on the bed, moved his hand under the sheet. 'Doing anything this evening, then?'

Mike watched Richard's hand, fascinated, unable to tear his eyes away from it as it made its way under the sheet and up towards him. 'No plans,' he said. His throat was dry. Involuntarily he gasped as the tips of Richard's fingers reached his thigh.

'No pumping to do, then, with your friends?' Richard indicated the magazine as his hand, apparently of its own volition, moved up Mike's quads, into the dark warmth between his legs.

Mike shook his head fiercely and pushed the magazine off the bed without a second look. 'I thought I'd spend some time on my own.'

'Oh.' Richard's hand, which was cradling Mike's balls by now, gently stroking the wiry hairs, stopped. 'Then I'll leave you alone.' He made one small movement, as if to get up off the bed.

'No way!' With a roar Mike flung the sheet back and pulled Richard down and on top of his naked body. He wrapped both thick arms around Richard's chest, both tree trunk-like legs around his hips and kissed him hard. When he finally pulled back, Richard was red in the face from the hug and the kiss. He was also laughing. Mike didn't let up on his crushing hold one bit. 'Yeah?' he said.

Richard gasped for breath. 'Oh, yeah!'

IDOL NEW BOOKS

STREET LIFE
Published in March Rupert Thomas

Ben is eighteen and tired of living in the suburbs. As there's little sexual adventure to be found there, he decides to run away from both A-levels and his comfortable home – to a new life in London. There, he's befriended by Lee, a homeless Scottish lad who offers him a friendly ear and the comfort of his sleeping bag.

£7.99/$10.95   ISBN 0 352 33374 X

MAESTRO
Published in May Peter Slater

A young Spanish cello player, Ramon, journeys to the castle of master cellist Ernesto Cavallo in the hope of masterclasses from the great musician. Ramon's own music is technically perfect, but his playing lacks a certain essence – and so, Maestro Cavallo arranges for Ramon to undergo a number of sexual trials in this darkly erotic, extremely well-written novel.

£8.99/$10.95   ISBN 0 352 33511 4

FELLOWSHIP OF IRON
Published in July Jack Stevens

Mike is a gym owner and a successful competitive bodybuilder. He lives the life of the body beautiful and everything seems to be going swimmingly. So when his mentor and former boyfriend Dave dies after using illegal steroids, Mike is determined to find out who supplied his ex with drugs.

£8.99/$10.95   ISBN 0 352 33512 2

Also published:

CHAINS OF DECEIT
Paul C. Alexander

Journalist Nathan Dexter's life is turned around when he meets a young student called Scott – someone who offers him the relationship for which he's been searching. Then Nathan's best friend goes missing, and Nathan uncovers evidence that he has become the victim of a slavery ring which is rumoured to be operating out of London's leather scene.

£6.99/$9.95   ISBN 0 352 33206 9

SLAVES OF TARNE
Gordon Neale
Pascal willingly follows the mysterious and alluring Casper to Tarne, a community of men enslaved to men. Tarne is everything that Pascal has ever fantasised about, but he begins to sense a sinister aspect to Casper's magnetism. Pascal has to choose between the pleasures of submission and acting to save the people he loves.
£6.99/$9.95

ISBN 0 352 33273 5

ROUGH WITH THE SMOOTH
Dominic Arrow
Amid the crime, violence and unemployment of North London, the young men who attend Jonathan Carey's drop-in centre have few choices. One of the young men, Stewart, finds himself torn between the increasingly intimate horseplay of his fellows and the perverse allure of the criminal underworld. Can Jonathan save Stewart from the bullies on the streets and behind bars?
£6.99/$9.95

ISBN 0 352 33292 1

CONVICT CHAINS
Philip Markham
Peter Warren, printer's apprentice in the London of the 1830s, discovers his sexuality and taste for submission at the hands of Richard Barkworth. Thus begins a downward spiral of degradation, of which transportation to the Australian colonies is only the beginning.
£6.99/$9.95

ISBN 0 352 33300 6

SHAME
Raydon Pelham
On holiday in West Hollywood, Briton Martyn Townsend meets and falls in love with the daredevil Scott. When Scott is murdered, Martyn's hunt for the truth and for the mysterious Peter, Scott's ex-lover, leads him to the clubs of London and Ibiza.
£6.99/$9.95

ISBN 0 352 33302 2

HMS SUBMISSION
Jack Gordon
Under the command of Josiah Rock, a man of cruel passions, HMS *Impregnable* sails to the colonies. Christopher, Viscount Fitzgibbons, is a reluctant officer; Mick Savage part of the wretched cargo. They are on a voyage to a shared destiny.
£6.99/$9.95

ISBN 0 352 33301 4

THE FINAL RESTRAINT
Paul C. Alexander
The trilogy that began with *Chains of Deceit* and continued in *Code of Submission* concludes in this powerfully erotic novel. From the dungeons and saunas of London to the deepest jungles of South America, Nathan Dexter is forced to play the ultimate chess game with evil Adrian Delancey – with people as sexual pawns.
£6.99/$9.95

ISBN 0 352 33303 0

HARD TIME
Robert Black
HMP Cairncrow prison is a corrupt and cruel institution, but also a sexual minefield. Three new inmates must find their niche in this brutish environment – as sexual victims or lovers, predators or protectors. This is the story of how they find love, sex and redemption behind prison walls.
£6.99/$9.95   ISBN 0 352 33304 9

ROMAN GAMES
Tasker Dean
When Sam visits the island of Skate, he is taught how to submit to other men, acting out an elaborate fantasy in which young men become wrestling slaves – just as in ancient Rome. Indeed, if he is to have his beautiful prize – the wrestler, Robert – he must learn how the Romans played their games.
£6.99/$9.95   ISBN 0 352 33322 7

VENETIAN TRADE
Richard Davis
From the deck of the ship that carries him into Venice, Rob Weaver catches his first glimpse of a beautiful but corrupt city where the dark alleys and misty canals hide debauchery and decadence. Here, he must learn to survive among men who would make him a plaything and a slave.
£6.99/$9.95   ISBN 0 352 33323 5

THE LOVE OF OLD EGYPT
Philip Markham
It's 1925 and the deluxe cruiser carrying the young gigolo Jeremy Hessling has docked at Luxor. Jeremy dreams of being dominated by the Pharaohs of old, but quickly becomes involved with someone more accessible – Khalid, a young man of exceptional beauty.
£6.99/$9.95   ISBN 0 352 33354 5

THE BLACK CHAMBER
Jack Gordon
Educated at the court of George II, Calum Monroe finds his native Scotland a dull, damp place. He relieves his boredom by donning a mask and holding up coaches in the guise of the Fox – a dashing highwayman. Chance throws him and neighbouring farmer Fergie McGregor together with Calum's sinister, perverse guardian, James Black.
£6.99/$9.95   ISBN 0 352 33373 1

THE GREEK WAY
Edward Ellis
Ancient Greece, the end of the fifth century BC – at the height of the Peloponnesian War. Young Orestes is a citizen of Athens, sent to Sparta as a spy. There he encounters a society of athletic, promiscuous soldiers – including the beautiful Spartan Hector.
£7.99/$10.95   ISBN 0 352 33427 4

BOOTY BOYS
Jay Russell

Hard-bodied black British detective Alton Davies can't believe his eyes or his luck when he finds muscular African-American gangsta rapper Banji-B lounging in his office early one morning. Alton's disbelief – and his excitement – mounts as Banji-B asks him to track down a stolen videotape of a post-gig orgy.

£7.99/$10.95

ISBN 0 352 33446 0

EASY MONEY
Bob Condron

One day an ad appears in the popular music press. Its aim: to enlist members for a new boyband. Young, working-class Mitch starts out as a raw recruit, but soon he becomes embroiled in the sexual tension that threatens to engulf the entire group. As the band soars meteorically to pop success, the atmosphere is quickly reaching fever pitch.

£7.99/$10.95

ISBN 0 352 33442 8

SUREFORCE
Phil Votel

Not knowing what to do with his life once he's been thrown out of the army, Matt takes a job with the security firm Sureforce. Little does he know that the job is the ultimate mix of business and pleasure, and it's not long before Matt's hanging with the beefiest, meanest, hardest lads in town.

£7.99/$10.95

ISBN 0 352 33444 4

THE FAIR COP
Philip Markham

The second world war is over and America is getting back to business as usual. In 1950s New York, that means dirty business. Hanson's a detective who's been dealt a lousy hand, but the Sullivan case is his big chance. How many junior detectives get handed blackmail, murder and perverted sex all in one day?

£7.99/$10.95

ISBN 0 352 33445 2

HOT ON THE TRAIL
Lukas Scott

The Midwest, 1849. *Hot on the Trail* is the story of the original American dream, where freedom is driven by wild passion. And when farmboy Brett skips town and encounters dangerous outlaw Luke Mitchell, sparks are bound to fly in this raunchy tale of hard cowboys, butch outlaws, dirty adventure and true grit.

£7.99/$10.95

ISBN 0 352 33461 4

---------------✂------------------------------

Please send me the books I have ticked above.

Name   ....

Address   ....

             ....

             ....

             .... Post Code ....

Send to: **Cash Sales, Idol Books, Thames Wharf Studios, Rainville Road, London W6 9HA.**

US customers: for prices and details of how to order books for delivery by mail, call 1-800-805-1083.

Please enclose a cheque or postal order, made payable to **Virgin Publishing Ltd**, to the value of the books you have ordered plus postage and packing costs as follows:

UK and BFPO – £1.00 for the first book, 50p for each subsequent book.

Overseas (including Republic of Ireland) – £2.00 for the first book, £1.00 for each subsequent book.

We accept all major credit cards, including VISA, ACCESS/MASTER-CARD, DINERS CLUB, AMEX and SWITCH.

Please write your card number and expiry date here:

....

Please allow up to 28 days for delivery.

Signature ....

---------------✂------------------------------

WE NEED YOUR HELP . . .
to plan the future of Idol books –

Yours are the only opinions that matter. Idol is a new and exciting venture: the first British series of books devoted to homoerotic fiction for men.

We're going to do our best to provide the sexiest, best-written books you can buy. And we'd like you to help in these early stages. Tell us what you want to read.

THE IDOL QUESTIONNAIRE

SECTION ONE: ABOUT YOU

1.1 Sex (*we presume you are male, but just in case*)
Are you?
Male ☐
Female ☐

1.2 Age
under 21 ☐ 21–30 ☐
31–40 ☐ 41–50 ☐
51–60 ☐ over 60 ☐

1.3 At what age did you leave full-time education?
still in education ☐ 16 or younger ☐
17–19 ☐ 20 or older ☐

1.4 Occupation _____

1.5 Annual household income _____

1.6   We are perfectly happy for you to remain anonymous; but if you would like us to send you a free booklist of Idol books, please insert your name and address

_____

_____

_____

_____

SECTION TWO: ABOUT BUYING IDOL BOOKS

2.1   Where did you get this copy of *Fellowship of Iron*?
      Bought at chain book shop   ☐
      Bought at independent book shop   ☐
      Bought at supermarket   ☐
      Bought at book exchange or used book shop   ☐
      I borrowed it/found it   ☐
      My partner bought it   ☐

2.2   How did you find out about Idol books?
      I saw them in a shop   ☐
      I saw them advertised in a magazine   ☐
      I read about them in _____
      Other _____

2.3   Please tick the following statements you agree with:
      I would be less embarrassed about buying Idol
      books if the cover pictures were less explicit   ☐
      I think that in general the pictures on Idol
      books are about right   ☐
      I think Idol cover pictures should be as
      explicit as possible   ☐

2.4   Would you read an Idol book in a public place – on a train for instance?
      Yes   ☐   No   ☐

SECTION THREE: ABOUT THIS IDOL BOOK

3.1   Do you think the sex content in this book is:
      Too much   ☐   About right   ☐
      Not enough   ☐

3.2 Do you think the writing style in this book is:
      Too unreal/escapist   ☐   About right   ☐
      Too down to earth   ☐

3.3 Do you think the story in this book is:
      Too complicated   ☐   About right   ☐
      Too boring/simple   ☐

3.4 Do you think the cover of this book is:
      Too explicit   ☐   About right   ☐
      Not explicit enough   ☐

Here's a space for any other comments:

SECTION FOUR: ABOUT OTHER IDOL BOOKS

4.1 How many Idol books have you read?

4.2 If more than one, which one did you prefer?

4.3 Why?

SECTION FIVE: ABOUT YOUR IDEAL EROTIC NOVEL

We want to publish the books you want to read – so this is your chance to tell us exactly what your ideal erotic novel would be like.

5.1 Using a scale of 1 to 5 (1 = no interest at all, 5 = your ideal), please rate the following possible settings for an erotic novel:

      Roman / Ancient World   ☐
      Medieval / barbarian / sword 'n' sorcery   ☐
      Renaissance / Elizabethan / Restoration   ☐
      Victorian / Edwardian   ☐
      1920s & 1930s   ☐
      Present day   ☐
      Future / Science Fiction   ☐

5.2 Using the same scale of 1 to 5, please rate the following themes you may find in an erotic novel:

Bondage / fetishism ☐
Romantic love ☐
SM / corporal punishment ☐
Bisexuality ☐
Group sex ☐
Watersports ☐
Rent / sex for money ☐

5.3 Using the same scale of 1 to 5, please rate the following styles in which an erotic novel could be written:

Gritty realism, down to earth ☐
Set in real life but ignoring its more unpleasant aspects ☐
Escapist fantasy, but just about believable ☐
Complete escapism, totally unrealistic ☐

5.4 In a book that features power differentials or sexual initiation, would you prefer the writing to be from the viewpoint of the dominant / experienced or submissive / inexperienced characters?

Dominant / Experienced ☐
Submissive / Inexperienced ☐
Both ☐

5.5 We'd like to include characters close to your ideal lover. What characteristics would your ideal lover have? Tick as many as you want:

Dominant	☐	Caring	☐
Slim	☐	Rugged	☐
Extroverted	☐	Romantic	☐
Bisexual	☐	Old	☐
Working Class	☐	Intellectual	☐
Introverted	☐	Professional	☐
Submissive	☐	Pervy	☐
Cruel	☐	Ordinary	☐
Young	☐	Muscular	☐
Naïve	☐		

Anything else? _____

5.6 Is there one particular setting or subject matter that your ideal erotic novel would contain?

_____

5.7 As you'll have seen, we include safe-sex guidelines in every book. However, while our policy is always to show safe sex in stories with contemporary settings, we don't insist on safe-sex practices in stories with historical settings because it would be anachronistic. What, if anything, would you change about this policy?

_____

_____

SECTION SIX: LAST WORDS

6.1 What do you like best about Idol books?

_____

6.2 What do you most dislike about Idol books?

_____

6.3 In what way, if any, would you like to change Idol covers?

_____

6.4 Here's a space for any other comments:

_____

_____

_____

_____

Thanks for completing this questionnaire. Now either tear it out, or photocopy it, then put it in an envelope and send it to:

Idol Books/Virgin Publishing
Thames Wharf Studios
Rainville Road
London
W6 9HA